The World Doesn't Work That Way, but It Could

# The World Doesn't Work That Way, but It Could

★ ★ ★

STORIES

YXTA MAYA MURRAY

**UNIVERSITY OF NEVADA PRESS** | *Reno & Las Vegas*

University of Nevada Press | Reno, Nevada 89557 USA
www.unpress.nevada.edu

LIBRARY OF CONGRESS CATALOGING-IN-PUBLICATION DATA

Names: Murray, Yxta Maya, author.
Title: The world doesn't work that way, but it could : stories /
    Yxta Maya Murray.
Description: Reno ; Las Vegas : University of Nevada Press, [2020] |
    Includes bibliographical references. | Summary: "Fueled by the ardor of
    the 21st century's political movement and from a writer's point of view,
    The World Doesn't Work that Way, but It Could is a work of short fiction
    that speaks about the struggles of many Americans in the fractured
    United States"—Provided by publisher.
Identifiers: LCCN 2020017104 (print) | LCCN 2020017105
    (ebook) | ISBN 9781948908696 (hardcover) | ISBN 9781948908719 (ebook)
Subjects: LCGFT: Short stories.
Classification: LCC PS3563.U832 A6 2020  (print) | LCC PS3563.U832 (ebook) |
    DDC 813/.54—dc23
LC record available at https://lccn.loc.gov/2020017104
LC ebook record available at https://lccn.loc.gov/2020017105

The paper used in this book meets the requirements of American National Standard for
Information Sciences—Permanence of Paper for Printed Library Materials, ANSI/NISO
Z39.48-1992 (R2002).

FIRST PRINTING

Manufactured in the United States of America

24  23  22  21  20     5  4  3  2  1

*To Andrew Brown*

# Contents

Miss USA 2015 . . . . . . . . . . . . . . . . . . . . . . . . . . . . . . . . . . . . . . . 3

The Prisoner's Dilemma . . . . . . . . . . . . . . . . . . . . . . . . . . . . . 29

After Maria . . . . . . . . . . . . . . . . . . . . . . . . . . . . . . . . . . . . . . . . . . 37

Acid Reign . . . . . . . . . . . . . . . . . . . . . . . . . . . . . . . . . . . . . . . . . . 55

Draft of a Letter of Recommendation to the
Honorable Alex Kozinski, Which I Guess I'm
Not Going to Send Now . . . . . . . . . . . . . . . . . . . . . . . . . . . . . 75

Paradise . . . . . . . . . . . . . . . . . . . . . . . . . . . . . . . . . . . . . . . . . . . 89

Abundance . . . . . . . . . . . . . . . . . . . . . . . . . . . . . . . . . . . . . . . . 109

The Perfect Palomino . . . . . . . . . . . . . . . . . . . . . . . . . . . . . . 125

Option 3 . . . . . . . . . . . . . . . . . . . . . . . . . . . . . . . . . . . . . . . . . . 145

Zero Tolerance . . . . . . . . . . . . . . . . . . . . . . . . . . . . . . . . . . . . 167

The Hierarchy . . . . . . . . . . . . . . . . . . . . . . . . . . . . . . . . . . . . . 181

Walmart . . . . . . . . . . . . . . . . . . . . . . . . . . . . . . . . . . . . . . . . . . 195

The Overton Window . . . . . . . . . . . . . . . . . . . . . . . . . . . . . . 207

The World Doesn't Work That Way, but It Could . . . . . . . . 241

Additional Sources . . . . . . . . . . . . . . . . . . . . . . . . . . . . . . . . . 249

Acknowledgments . . . . . . . . . . . . . . . . . . . . . . . . . . . . . . . . . 261

About the Author . . . . . . . . . . . . . . . . . . . . . . . . . . . . . . . . . . 263

The World Doesn't Work That Way, but It Could

Most of his wrath was directed at Mexico, which he accused of "bringing their worst people" to America, including criminals and "rapists."

RUPERT NEATE, "Donald Trump Announces US Presidential Run with Eccentric Speech," *The Guardian*, June 16, 2015

Univision Communications Inc. canceled its telecast of the Miss USA pageant next month, after [Miss USA co-owner] Donald Trump derided Mexican immigrants during his speech announcing his presidential campaign.

PATRICIA LAYA, "Univision Cancels Miss USA after Donald Trump Calls Mexicans 'Rapists,'" *Bloomberg*, June 25, 2015

# Miss USA 2015

THE PROBLEM WE HAD was with the two walks, bathing suit and gown. The body, it was workable. Good breasts, tight stomach, okay height. But the legs, no. The legs had issues also. A saddlebag issue, just a hint of it, but by competition we had her on nothing but water and lemon and squats, and you can't ask for more. And she was too old. Twenty-four. I don't know how she won her state except that she did a great interview. She came to me in January, and so we only had six months. It was insane. By February we had already lightened her, and Dennis got her new teeth and Botox and fillers. We ripped the accent and the trailer park from her personality with elocution and poise training. And she was smart. That's what she had going for her. Just a natural smart and reading newspapers all the time for the political questions. And she was black *and* Latina, which the judges find confusing. So we just said black. But of course we did the hair.

No, the problem was the walk. I could see it right away. She stomped into my office in Florida, bumping her buns through my door with a big smile like she had no idea how wrong she is. She wore this yellow dress with a big frill on it that made her look like a one-winged chicken. Her mother had come along, a beautiful Tapatía maybe forty-three years old, with fantastic legs and a tiny waist and dragging in two other kids. They'd driven sixteen hours in their Plymouth for the meeting. There was the big brother, about twelve years old, and the littler brother, about two years old. The older one was dark and the younger one came out lighter, but they both had the same round, grumbly faces. The mother looked exhausted, and no wonder, with the two sons and then this one with the attitude. The family sat quietly on my sofa, staring at the photographs I have on my wall. Me, I had my silver hair clipped into a very chic drop-fade crew cut. I also wore black bespoke Dege & Skinner trousers in a light vicuña, a purple smoking jacket, bespoke cotton Charvet shirting accented by a silk purple Charvet foulard, and Church's slippers. For a second I could see the mother looking at me and not understanding what she's seeing.

Who cared, though, because the girl, she stood in the middle of my suite like she's Pat Cleveland or Beverly Simpson or the great oh my God Donyale Luna. She didn't look at the pictures of the other girls or the framed key to the city. She stuck her boobs out and swayed the back, so you could see she knew nothing. But she stared at me like she's an empress and I'm her slave. So I liked that.

"I want you to make me Miss USA," she said.

"I don't know," I said, looking at the legs.

"You are going to make me Miss USA," she went on like she didn't hear me. She walked over to her mother. The mother opened her purse and took out some cash and gave it to her. The girl held the money like it's a billion dollars and then walked back over to me and gently put it in my hand. "You have twenty-seven weeks."

"Sssssssssss," I said, shaking my head, because I'd been watching her walk, of course.

"'15 is mine, and you're going to help me," she said. Her eyes shot fireballs and lightning storms all over the room so that I wanted to drop to the floor and kiss her feet.

I gave her the money back. "Go back to——" you know, the

place she came from, is what I said. I can't tell you which one I'm talking about. It was Miss USA, 2015. We sign an NDA, and they sign one too. I wouldn't tell you anyway. In any case, I already had my hands full with another USA contestant who was at the top level, and plus the franchises. By franchises I mean the life coaching and model schools, the ones I advertise in *Glamour* and on YouTube. I don't make money from stars or would-be stars like you; the winners are my branding. I earn from the hundreds and thousands of chubs who have the fantasy that they are going to be like Ali Landry or Gretchen Carlson, but really, they're just going to learn how to stop chewing with their mouths open and attract a man. So I was busy already, and this girl who came to see me was very pretty, but she had a five-buck strut. So I told her to go back home and make do with the broke-ass coaches she already fired.

"You big, huge, bald, old vaca," she said, getting all heated up.

She started yelling at me in Spanish that I was the brokest of all broke asses and she wouldn't let me coach her now if I crawled on my stomach and pleaded like a dog. The boys started crying. I cursed back at her in German and French, which are the scariest-sounding languages I know. The mother's crying. The girl's crying. Now even I'm wiping my eyes because I could see they're poor as pigeons and all surviving on whatever dimes and nickels her sponsor gave her after she won her ribbon.

"Walk over here," I said.

She walked, so bad.

"You are the worst walker I've ever seen in my life," I said. "It's like you got six feet."

"You'll teach me," she said.

"Walk over there," I said.

She walked.

"Even worse," I said. I began sashaying. "Walk like this."

She started waddling all over the place with a fat walk.

"Oh my Jesus," I said.

She's walking around my office like a panda and the mother's still crying and the boys too.

And then the girl strikes a pose, a profile, and I almost fainted again.

"No misdemeanors or felonies?" I said. Because there are rules. You know that, right? Qualifications. "And you have no man in your life?"

"That's Miss America," she said. "I can date."

"Not if you want to win," I said. Which is true. "Also, no disease? No children? No divorce? No annulment? Not pregnant? You have to do your own makeup and hair, so that it is perfect. You can be eighteen to twenty-eight only. They like it if you have a HSE or diploma."

"Yes, yes, yes," the girl said.

"High school diploma?" I asked.

"HSE," she said. "And remember, I won state already. I'm checked out."

"Your state is the dumps," I said. "Plus, I heard every story before. I trust nobody and nothing."

"I got the papers in the car. Health too."

"Okay," I said.

"Okay?"

"I don't know," I said. "Walk over there again."

She thumped around this way and that but all the time smiling at me like she could eat me down to the bones and still want more.

"Hm," I said.

As I mentioned already, I had another contestant in that year. The lady was a much better shot, from a bigger state. She was a beautiful white woman, or white enough when you dyed her. The package. She'd turned twenty-one the month previous and ticked the other boxes with height and *perfect* turns. She could talk great and projected just fabulous, with that kind of fantasy Park Avenue class but very sexual, which can sell depending on whether that year the judges want erotic versus more innocent. Plus the blonde had grown up low income and abused, but she'd still got a computer science degree from an Ivy. And she advocated for the disabled, so she had that too.

I took this new one on anyway, because of the way she made fires and flames with her eyes. I started calling her *my girl* right away as a kind of joke because she was just so, so wrong that it was like a pet project. She didn't have the ultimate body or any of the walk or the school or the politics in the right way. And what she projected could be scary as fuck for these judges because it was that deadly star quality that is really fear. It's beyond innocence or erotic and moving into goddess, if you train it right. It's what Dolores del Rio and Lee Meriwether and Iman took to the bank. I told Dennis and Sarah to see if they could get her to control it in the time we had left. And I sent Laila to her too, to perfect the diction and fill her with some current events. I wasn't going to burn a lot of minutes on teaching her, I said. I said I had to spend all of my time with the blonde because, with the disabled and her very large breasts and the Ivy, I knew she had an excellent chance to place.

I snuck out sometimes and would train my girl, though. She was secretly my favorite.

* * *

I started out in Jalisco, which is why I could spot that the mother was a Tapatía and I can see that you have a foot in Colima maybe, right? Were you born there? They don't like that. And you have your papers? Okay, good.

My sister Otila entered the Señorita Mezquite competition in 1986, when I was seventeen years old and she was eighteen. I was already becoming who I am, and I was beautiful. My hermanita knew that I could help her because I always had the eye. I had studied every move of the great Felicia Mercado, who won Señorita Mexico '77 in a skin-tight gold gown and Farrah hair and a beautiful application of frosted eyeshadow, very pale blue. And I studied Alba Margarita Cervera Lavat, who won Mexico in '78 and then was top twelve at Universe that year. Lavat made herself more of a virgin with short dark hair and a good girl walk, but with star factor. So I learned fast that there was some bullshit operating in the pageants, because there were generally only two ways to do it: more slutty and more innocent. That is, there are the two ways unless you're a divinity like del Rio or say Dietrich and everything mixes together into gold. My sister, God rest her soul, was more slutty so we did that.

For Señorita Mezquite, I made Otila a hot-pink chiffon gown with rosettes at the right shoulder and at the waist, with a long train detailed with fake pearls and tiny silver sequins that took a month to sew on. I would put on the gown and show her how to do the walk. You have to be able to move your charisma down the cat. Just smooth and then with the stance and the flirt. Bounce a little. But graceful. Elegance. And always, sex. Don't give your neck away. Don't look down.

I was born with it, but I am a king and so being a pretty beauty like that is not my personal taste. I only demand it of my clients and my wives. In my own way, I am one of the divinities, like my girl was and Dietrich and del Rio and Iman. I am actually more like Dietrich because I am both a particular kind of woman with that special seductiveness and also a particular kind of man, aloof and untouchable like a Roman soldier. Not that I have anything against friendly, silly girls because little Otila was a monster of sex. And that's why I know intimately that bad girls aren't really bad; they just screw around to survive, and on the inside they can keep their souls very pure.

Okay, everything's getting jumbled up and talking to you about this is making me feel weepy, so let's just get back to the details.

I showed Otila how to walk and how to smile. She won Señorita Mezquite. The next year, though, it was all over. She tried to walk out pregnant in Señorita Amacueca, and I swear to Christ one of the directors took her out into the street and I thought he would kill her. My sister took her beating and rose up very dignified and said to the director, and I will never forget this, "I am not one of your whores."

So that was my beginning. After that I did beauty queens in Acapulco and D.F. Next, I made my way to Connecticut and then here, Florida. It's been forty-three years of this for me. And I am the best, one of the best. I won five USAs and three Universes and two Worlds and six Miss Americas. I've been profiled in *People* and *Business Insider*, though wearing a hairpiece and my Jil Sander and Valentino dresses, and so looking like a lady they can handle. I bought myself two houses, and I've had many lovers and three marriages, and I speak Spanish, English, French, and German. The franchise operates out of four different cities and is growing. From all of this experience I know who will win. I know also when a girl is not quite right.

When my girl came to my office, I could tell there was something. A dilemma she didn't talk about. I made some calls to my contacts in her state, and they all said she was legit, the only problem being she'd fired three coaches and was a diva. And now also the sponsor, an oil man, was maybe not paying the bills anymore. In the end, I didn't care because she reminded me of my sister Otila in how she bossed me around. And also I thought, deep down, that if we could fix the walking and teach her how to master her persona, she could take the crown.

\* \* \*

"Don't cry," I said. We were in the studio. It was five thirty in the morning. We'd already been at it for an hour. If I was training her, I liked to do it myself, without Dennis blabbing on about silent third-person self-talk for emotion control and Sarah going on about swan movement. So they weren't there. The mother had come, though, with the older brother and the younger brother, the toddler. They sat on some pillows on the ground and ate the cottage cheese and apples that I'd bought them.

"I'm not crying," my girl said.

"Do you want to win?"

"I am going to win," she said.

"Do you want to be a winner?"

She put her shoulders back. "I am a winner already."

"That's right, baby," I said. "So walk."

She tried the walk again. There's the bathing suit and the gown, like I was saying. We were doing bathing suit. There's small and important differences. The gown hangs low, and you have to negotiate it with your heels. So there's less freedom and more danger. The bathing suit also has more danger because you have more freedom and could get carried away and fall. With Miss USA it's worse because it's sexier than America; the slut factor is most years pretty high, but of course we don't say that. If you think about it, it's no surprise, because Trump owned USA in those years. I would rather do Miss America than Miss USA 100 percent of the time even though *those* bitches are just cruel. There was the Donald on the one hand and then the bitches on the other. So I don't know. In the end, it's not like we have choices in this life.

My girl was neither erotic nor innocent. Instead she was everything, smart, beautiful, cranky, angry, on fire, scary, relatable, like—like a whole person, like a—I don't know. Something different. Still, because of the USA brand I told her to be friendly. And that means you're doing more of the bounce, which can get tricky.

It's bang bang bang. Like that, see? No, like this. Leg out, opposite arm cocked at the natural waist, not lower. Leg elongated always. We're doing the turn. Leg out but not too much. Then twist sideways. To the profile. Step back. The last thing to leave is the face. Also the face should be moving, not frozen. Big smile with teeth and then maybe no teeth and then when you're turning there's the flirt. Hell-o. Behind the eyes there has to be something. Leave them on the floor. And then you go back home. Bang bang *bang*. That's good.

She walked her normal fat walk down the cat and then put her leg out too far. She forgot to stop on the profile stance and put her head down so it killed the neck.

"How's that?" she asked, smiling at me.

"Just the worst," I snapped.

She started crying again. She walked over to the mom and the brothers and sat on the ground next to them. She wiggled her fingers at the little two-year-old brother and sang to him a little bit. The whole time I was yelling at her to get her ass up. I wanted her to repeat the half turn at least twenty more times in a row so that the muscle memory began to kick in.

"La la la," she sang to the kid and then grabbed him and held him. She tucked her face into his belly and cried into it. Her mother sighed and stretched her back.

"If you want a vacation, go back to your sponsor and tell him to take you to Hawaii," I yelled.

"His wife found out so he doesn't talk to me anymore," she said, hugging the baby.

I stared for a second while she squeezed her brother. "I told you there can't be any men and not any anything," I said very loud.

"I have no men and no anything," she said. "I have nothing but my family and Miss USA and you, Tito."

When she looked at me from under her hair, her eyes were angry and strong like a panther's.

We didn't give up. And she got the walk pretty okay finally, and just in time, about three months later.

\* \* \*

The reason why I'm telling you all this is because I can see that you're a long shot and not likely to make it. And Montana has not placed since the 1950s. But I'm also explaining the world to you to see how you take it and if you have anything to say. Then we can go from there.

\* \* \*

So then my other contestant dropped out, the mostly white, blond, tall one with the STEM degree from Brown and the disabled advocating. She said she quit because she had morals or something.

"I cannot have anything to do with this pageant as long as that man owns it," she said.

"Are you kidding?" I said. "What the fuck are you talking about?"

The blond lady had by this time paid me thirty thousand dollars. Laila and I had trained her exquisite on the four faces and verve. Also, her answers to the test questions were now brilliant, not only because she was smart as a professor but because we had taught her not to look like a slapped rabbit from the deep thinking when the question was presented to her.

The problem from her perspective was that in June, that guy, the pageant's owner, this maniac, he had said that shit about Mexicans being rapists and he wants a wall. And now he wants to be president. And Univision was dropping the show and who knew with NBC.

"Why aren't you boycotting it, Tito?" the blonde said. "He's bad on race, and he's going to be bad on transgender."

"Baby," I said. "Come on. What I haven't been through already."

"That's not exactly the answer that I'd hoped for," she said.

"It's not what?"

"I have to confess, I'm just very disappointed in you," she said. "I expected more from a person with your . . . difficult experiences."

"Yes, okay," I said, and now of course I was getting angry, but I am a professional and know how to not show it. "I respect your decision, and I wish you the very, very best."

"We should protest," she started gabbling. "We have the platform."

"It has been such an incredible honor working with you, and I hope you have a great day," I said, as I muscled her out the door.

Then I got on the phone and I called my girl.

"Do you know about what Trump said on TV?" I asked her.

"Oh, yeah, I know," she said. "It's all over the news. He wants his whites to kill us or something."

"My other one dropped out because of the morals," I said. "Do you want to too?"

"Huh?" she asked.

"Do you want to drop out because he's co-owner of Miss USA?"

"Oh—Jajajajaja!" she laughed, so loud, and dropped the phone. I could hear her mother yelling and the kids crying. She picked the phone back up. "Jajajajaja!"

"So no?"

"Do you know what I've been through?" she said. "This is nothing."

"That's what I said," I said.

"People like us don't quit, Tito," she said. "You been busting my ass, and now I have the questions down. I have the verve down. I have my faces down. I got the dancing and sincerity down. I got my third-person silent talk down. All I have to work on is my pivot." She starts yelling about how nobody will ever stop her from this and that and she's going to rule Miss USA and then the world.

"Okay," I said. "I'll see you tomorrow morning at four thirty."

\* \* \*

In the end, NBC pulled out and so did Univision. Zuleyka Rivera, who you know was Universe 2006 from PR, dropped out as judge. J Balvin was going to sing his super hit "6 a.m." as the major performance, but he bounced because he's from Colombia. Roselyn Sánchez and Cristián de la Fuente were going to be the hosts, but they quit too. To replace my blond-lady contestant from the Ivy League, Miss USA wound up getting her state's runner up, a very skinny Asian American twenty-four-year-old lawyer. The blonde herself wound up making a long speech about human rights that got on Vox and Canal 5.

"I don't care," my girl said. "That's my crown."

* * *

The show was in Baton Rouge, and we brought the whole team—Dennis, Sarah, Laila. And the family came out too, the mother and the boys. We all stayed at the Hilton, which is four stars. I splashed out for three rooms because we were there for two weeks and I wanted my girl to feel good. In Baton Rouge, she had to learn the choreography for the prelims and then the moves for the final pageant. And the director drags the girls around the host city so that the film crew can shoot them in groups with activities and also do the solos for the montages where the contestants talk about their passions. The contestants have to have a change of sportswear for every day's event. They have different evenings for the dinners and unique bikinis and one-pieces for all the water sports they schedule. It was a fortune. I kept the receipts for when my girl became a brand ambassador for Cover Girl or MAC and paid my ass back. The girls did a swamp tour where they rode around in a big boat. They also visited an alligator farm, where they touched the alligators and screamed, and a pet sanctuary with the dying dogs. They met the governor. They went dancing and tried to dance attractively at night clubs so that the hair doesn't get messed up and no obvious hairline or tit sweating, which is difficult. Mucho, mucho lemon water and cayenne and enemas. I had to keep my girl hydrated.

But the Trump thing was a shitstorm. That Mexican rape business and the president stuff was on the news every day. We didn't know if they were going to cancel or what. In almost every meeting, the director and the sponsors and the head of Visit the Bayou said, "This is about supporting the girls, not about politics." And "we are here to lift the self-esteem of women, and we are going to hold our heads high and concentrate on women power and girls loving themselves." And apparently the whole time in the dressing rooms the women are jumpy because Trump likes to come in when they're naked. But he was too busy with building the wall because he didn't make much of a showing that year.

At one of the nightclubs, during the second week, a news reporter from KNXX5 came up to a group of about thirteen girls and stuck a mic into their faces. All the contestants start punching each other to talk. My girl wasn't the tallest. There was a big fucking redhead with crazy white teeth and a white ash-blonde with robot-blue eyes. Both of them started elbowing forward. I'd put my girl in a white shantung Carolina Herrera off-the-shoulder bow-embellished mini loaner and gold-strap four-inch heels. I'd straightened her hair for the night and added two pieces in the front. I also did a very light dusting of tawny rose on the cheeks and a cat for the eye. She looked incredible, just miraculous.

"Ladies," the reporter said—she was a white woman with long brown hair and wearing a hot-pink dress and sneakers. "What do you all think about the co-owner of the pageant running for president when he has such harsh things to say about the Mexican people and also Black Lives Matter?"

My girl nudged the big ones under the armpits so that they fell away. She gave the camera a light series-two smile with no teeth and just enough smolder. We had eliminated every piece of the Spanish accent in her elocution, and so at least she didn't have to worry about that. "I think that America is the land of free speech," she said, in the voice I'd trained her on, like Claudette Colbert with just a touch of southern friendliness. "And the First Amendment, thank the good Lord, lets every man say his own opinion."

"Well, beauty and brains, there you have it, Louisiana!" the reporter said.

When we got back to the Hilton, her mom and brothers were watching *Game of Thrones* on TV. My girl didn't take off the Carolina Herrera, which is four thousand retail, and she didn't wipe off the makeup or remove the expensive hairpieces. Instead, she went straight to the bed and lay down crumply. She put her arms around her little brother and cried into his belly from I thought exhaustion and being so hungry. The mom curled around her too and said "shhh," and then the other brother started crying and piled on top. I sat on the bed and petted my girl's hair. I never showed this, because she was much too young for me, but whenever I got near her, my heart would smash up into pieces. I only touched her very light, patting, like an uncle.

"It's okay, baby," I said.

"It'll all be okay if I win, Tito," she said.

"You'll win," I said.

She nodded into her little brother's belly. "I'll win."

I felt glad that the blonde with the human rights problem had quit. My girl worked hard and now was the best of them all. Everyone could see it. From her walk to her verve and her focus. She practiced the pivot, over and over. She did the silent third-person self-coaching. Rehearsing in her mind, all the time, and she never lost that beautiful hunger and anxiety. That's why I think the other girls all looked at her sideways. Even when they're screaming at the alligators and petting the dead dogs and running around the swamp or scratching each other to be on TV, they could all tell that she would destroy them.

Already, I made plans for her. I decided that she and I would have everything. After USA, Universe. After Universe, cosmetics and hygiene contracts. Maybe a children's cancer charity and starring in an *E!* original series or doing guest-hosting on *RuPaul's Drag Race*. From there, a movie. A fashion line. A makeup line. Housewares.

* * *

Except, her problem did come up again at the preliminaries.

As you better know, there are basically two competitions for USA. First, you do the whole thing at the prelims, where they do the first set of cuts. And then you do it all over again, like ten days later, at the televised final show. The prelims were July 8, at the Baton Rouge Raising Cane's River Center.

Well, three days previous, my girl kept getting these phone calls, and they made her secretly upset. Her phone would ring. She ran out of the room to take it. She came back with a huge smile, but her panther eyes would look scared, in a naked and unpowerful way. I knew it was bad.

"What, what?"

"It's nothing," she said.

Her Mom looked at her and shook her head, then went to take care of the boys.

"YOU ARE GOING TO TELL ME RIGHT NOW," I said. I shouted about how I'd spent this much on Carolina Herrera and that much on Zac Posen and this on Jimmy Choo and that on Registration. I yelled about how I was the number-three pageant coach in the nation. I begged her, if there was a problem, I had to know because I could not let anything go wrong now.

"My ex-boyfriend's wife is giving me problems," she finally said.

"I told you, NO MEN," I said.

"There's no men," she said, her eyes glimmering and starving. "There's nobody but you, Tito."

Her eyes hurt me. I know that I should not be telling you this, but I fell in love with her at that moment. It was bad for business, but what could I do? Eventually, I just let my stomach get ulcers. I spray-lightened her and I plucked her hairs. I gave her manicures. I fed her lemon water and I ran her through the mantras. I gave the family money to go away and eat at restaurants while we did breathing. Every free moment, we went over the intro dance steps and the stance and the pivot and the half turn and the full turn.

But apparently that didn't work, because she tripped.

It happened during swimsuit. The judges were Darius Baptist, Jennifer Palpallatoc, Lori Lung. I didn't know all of them. I knew Darius. I have my own personal rules, so I didn't try to seduce them with little presents like some other people I know. But even if I had, you can't gift bag your way out of a runway fall. It's very terrible. It's not *death*, though, not necessarily. Crystle Stewart fell at '08 Universe and Rachel Smith did too, in '07. Crystle Stewart wound up placing in the top ten and afterward worked with Tyler Perry. And Rachel Smith placed in the top five and then got on *Good Morning America* and *Nightline*. But that's not the way to bet. The way to bet is, if you fall, you're dead.

When they called her state, my girl came out in a gray and white bikini with white rosettes at the hip bones and nude four-inch platforms. I'd put a full hairpiece on her, which had long, long waves. She stood at the top of the three-stair rise just amazing, her left leg fully extended. She held the pose like Betty Grable. She looked out at the judges with her eyes like hypnosis. It was everything. It was my God. Down she came the stairs, perfect. Down she walked to the center of the stage, perfect. Even the saddlebags you couldn't see. Breasts up and down and stomach shining, with just a little muscle, not too much. Hair moving this way, that way. Smile, not too white teeth. Not stiff. Fluid and the face moving, holding my number-two smile for a beat beat beat, and after that the closed smile, the wide smile, the flirt. She did a full turn and then fell on her ass.

Along with the mother, the brothers, Dennis, Laila, and Sarah, I sat on the far-left-hand side of the lower floor. The mother starts tearing her hair and biting her hands. The brothers are both asleep; they don't know. My team all cover their mouths and begin sobbing. I did not yell out or act dramatic. I am a professional. But I die inside. I die. I sat there staring straight at her with a supportive and positive smile on my face just in case she sees me through the lights. I wanted it so that she would know I was there for her and that I love her even though she can't walk any better than a one-legged flamingo.

But she didn't need me, the beauty. The thing that saved her was how she laughed. I knew she didn't want to laugh because she probably wants to drown herself right now. But she dropped straight down on the ass bones and didn't show any pain, no anger. She threw her head back and laughed so everything becomes funny, joyful, light. It made everybody like her, maybe better than if she did it flawless.

So then she did become like Crystle Stewart and Rachel Smith, because she placed. She made the top fifteen.

* * *

We prepared her for the questions, hard. Since Trump was screaming about us Mexicans and Univision and NBC got pissed, we knew there would be nothing about immigration. But maybe something about police brutality or college rape or economic inequality. Laila is our person for these things because she has a master's in sociology from CUNY and a PhD from Georgetown. Yes, impressive. But more impressive was my girl. She got everything right away. It was all of her reading. She wanted to go to law school and become a big bastard who tells everybody else what to do. And she had the smarts for it too.

"The police need the freedom to do their work if we are going to have safe streets," my girl said, smiling.

And: "We must protect women against sexual assault, because it is our responsibility that our women and girls live without fear. But at the same time we must not overreact. The men who are accused must be given due process."

And: "America is the greatest nation in the world, and if you work hard, I truly do believe that you can achieve anything here."

Two nights before the pageant, I did ask her. She was so convincing. I don't usually care, but, you know, I loved her. I was obsessed with her, in a way.

"Baby, do you really buy all that crap?" I touched her very light and fatherly on the hand. "You're not letting all of this garbage get into your mind, right?"

She looked at me and laughed, but softer, not like she laughed when she fell on her butt.

"Come on, Tito. What am I going to say, 'All these rich fuckers should go to jail?' Am I going to tell them, 'Mr. Trump, sir, vete a la mierda?'"

"Yeah, but just between you and me," I said. For a second, I thought I would tell her the story about my sister, but then I knew she wouldn't be interested.

"Between you and me, I think we're going to win, Tito," she said, jumping up and running around the room like a crazy thing.

* * *

The day comes for the final competition, and I'm sick, and she's sick too. All that calmness from before is just gone. What if she falls again? What if she sounds stupid during the question? It's easy to fail, so easy. That's why everybody does it.

Here we go, back at the River Center, in downtown Baton Rouge. Now the judges are serious and know the business. Kimberly Pressler, Miss USA '99. Leila Lopes, Universe '11. Rima Fakih, USA '10. And on and on. None of them dropped out even with the Trump crap because they owed. But they knew what to look for. I relaxed my rules a little and tried to gift bag them, but they had so many body guards I couldn't get through even to the assistants. The director got *Family Game Night* show MC Todd Newton and Miss Wisconsin '09 Alex Wehrley to host after the others bowed out.

The bathing suits were solid red, white, and blue. My girl got assigned white. I'd made it for her, custom. Tiny, tiny sequins over two layers of white cotton. Tiny briefs, with side ties, so the straight men and lesbians and bisexuals and pansexuals in the audience can think about pulling them and undoing them, which leads to more clapping and higher points.

My girl comes out, walks down the three steps, and *floats* to the center of the stage. She does the full turn like a ballerina. Smiling with that god smile, eyes on the judges all the time. It was just the end. It was just gorgeous. She was one of the greats.

Like an old-school Aphrodite, on the level with Vanessa Williams and Janelle Commissiong and Norma Beatriz Nolan.

Like in the prelims, I'm sitting next to the mother, the brothers, Dennis, Sarah, and Laila on the left-hand side of the floor. We're all of us rolling around in our seats and screaming. Everybody was shouting at her. I saw men and women get on their feet clapping. The mother of course is crying again, and so am I. The brothers are yelling because everybody else is. Sarah's getting everything on social media, and Dennis and Laila are filming it with the Nikon. I'm so happy I'm like dead.

Off she goes, triumphant. You only get twenty-four or so seconds. The rest of the girls make their entrances, the big redhead smiling with the bad dentures, the ash-blonde with the blue robot eyes sent from the future to kill you, the actually not bad Asian-American who took the place of the blond one that I'd been representing but who quit to make the speech on Vox and Canal 5. Who cares about any of them? Me and the mother are still crying. The mom looks over at me and says, "Maybe my bitch of a daughter will now give me some rest."

"Jajajajajaja!" I'm laughing. "Don't bet on it!"

What happens of course after swimsuit is that it's time for the next cuts, down to ten. So we had to wait. The hosts came on and said a bunch of nothing, and then we had to get through an intermission with a song by Travis Garland, "Want to Want Me." The mom and I yelled along to the lyrics. We hollered so loud people are saying to shut up.

And then I got the call from my girl's cell.

"Tito," she said. "Come back to the dressing room now, please, and bring my family."

"We're not allowed back there," I said. "Calm down! You did great! Focus on the next cuts!"

"I already know I made the cut."

"Wait, they told you? You made the next phase?" Sometimes,

with some pageants, they do tell you beforehand about the results. I'm not saying Miss USA, but it's not unknown.

"Yeah, but that's not why I'm calling," she said. I didn't like her voice. "Just come." She hung up.

I told my team members to wait. I grabbed the mother and the boys. We ran to the dressing room. I thought she maybe had a fever or was throwing up. But when we got there, we saw like four producers, a body guard, and some assistants. And it's not good.

My girl didn't look at me. She didn't even look at her mother. She looked at her little brother, the two-year-old one. She bent over and picked him up. She started kissing him all over the face.

"Hey, baby," she said. "Hey, my baby."

"What's going on?" I said, to her and to the producers.

"She has a child," a producer said. The producer was a new white woman I didn't know. She wore a gray suit and had a Bluetooth in her ear and held three phones in her armpits. This producer woman had a look on her face like she'd been murdered from the inside already and this wasn't the worst of it. "She's disqualified."

Now the mom went quiet and very still and looked at her feet. The older brother started playing with some of the makeup and talking to the other contestants, who had bright, shiny faces like they just won Christmas, which they did.

"We got a call from——" the producer said. The producer named the wife of my girl's sponsor, the oil guy, worth billions. "Mrs. So-and-So emailed us the papers proving paternity, and then the girl confessed."

"Yeah," my girl said, still kissing the boy on his fat cheek so his grumbly face softened.

"Your client hid her child from the director at the state level, and so now we have to clean it up," the producer's droning on. "Which is just great."

"Okay," the mom said, behind me. "Oh, well. You did good, honey, very beautiful."

I just stood there sweating buckets and didn't say anything.

"Let's pack up and get out of here," the mom said, starting to bustle around. "But Tito spent a lot of money on this stuff, and we need to get it to the car safe, so she gets her money back."

"My money back," I repeated, and I felt so much fire in my head. I started thinking about the cash I laid out for the Botox and filler and lightening, the airplane tickets, the Hilton, and the loaner fees on the Herrera and Posen. I thought of my precious track record. I thought about my franchises. I thought about how she's not going to be a brand ambassador and there will be no housewares. I think about how I crawled my way from Jalisco to Florida to become the number one or maybe three coach in the nation, and now my reputation is ruined. And how she lied to me. And how this and how that. "I ain't never going to get my money back," I said.

"You're not leaving," the producer said, to my girl. "We've had enough scandal. We're going to replace you in the cuts, but you're going to walk the evening and the finale. You're finishing out the show."

"Tito," she said to me.

I had very strong anger about the money and my brand. Why didn't I think about my sister, who did like the same thing? Stupid. The money made me say these evil, wicked things to my girl.

"You are a goddam user and you are a nobody," I yelled. "You are from the sticks and you belong there. I don't know what I ever saw in you. You are a thief. You don't have the character or the elegance to be Miss USA. You are trash." On and on, I go. I don't know what I was doing.

"Get out," the producer said to me.

"Tito," my girl says. "I'm sorry." She started crying.

"Never talk to me after this day," I said. "You betrayed me."

"Tito," my girl cries.

"Madam, get the fuck out," the producer said, to me.

I got out.

* * *

I flew back to Florida. I ate myself up with bad feelings for two days, and then got over the "catastrophe." After that, I missed her like crazy and knew I had done something terrible to her. Yes, she had a kid. Women have children. My poor sister had my nephew Fernando. It's natural, it's good. Why do they penalize? My girl only did what girls do. I didn't care about the lies or the pageant.

In the middle of the night, she and her mother left all my stuff on the front stoop of my office, all wrapped up in butcher paper and plastic in case any rains came. Not a speck on it, not a stain. But my girl didn't leave a note. And she never answered any of my texts or my calls. I don't know where she lives, if you can believe it. I don't have her physical address. Sarah found one mention of maybe her on a city college website, out of West Texas, but when I contacted the school, they said they couldn't help me except to forward the message. And then, nothing.

I saw her do the last evening-gown walk on the Reelz streaming, about a month later. I watched it in my bedroom, drinking. I was still bananas to find her then. We'd put her in a gold Zac Posen with a sequined train and a slit on the right leg and just a tiny bit of frill on the bodice. She wore five-inch gold platforms with crystals glued on the sides, and she had a matching crystal pedicure that I'd given her myself the day before. They didn't shoot her face when the cuts were made, and then in the finale she was just a blur.

I already knew something was up, so why did I say all of those evil things? I knew already—I thought maybe she's pregnant, she's got a man, she's got a felony. Maybe the brother. Yeah, I smelled it. But when the success came—after she placed in the top fifteen and then did the second swimsuit immaculate—I lost my mind. I just started thinking about the damn franchises and skin-care lines. I don't know why. I can't say why, when I already knew she'd screwed it up.

And that's the thing that I want you to know if you want to train with me and my team, is that it's easy to get confused. There's so much nastiness. What you tell yourself is that evil in this business all belongs to other people but that doesn't make you one of their whores. You play ball and survive, but you can keep your soul pure. Except that maybe the blond contestant with the fake Park Avenue la-di-da who made the speech on Vox and Canal 5 was right all along. I don't know, I think actually she just wanted to get famous in a different way. But maybe she figured out what I know now, which is that you shouldn't let wickedness touch you because it gets inside. I'd thought, well, my life has been hard and there's been suffering for me, and so I do what I have to do. And I did. I won five USAs and three Universes and two Worlds and six Miss Americas. I've been profiled in *People* and *Business Insider*. I have two houses and a corporation that takes me all over the planet. And I'm an old queer who has been hated by cruel people every day of his life. So I thought that I knew what is evil and what is good and how to scoot around the bad to get to the other side.

But it turns out that I didn't know anything at all. And so I lost her. *

The latest flashpoint is PSSST, a 5,000-square-foot nonprofit arts space located in the predominantly Latino neighborhood of Boyle Heights. . . . Despite its seemingly progressive mission, PSSST has recently received strong opposition from activists both within and outside the Boyle Heights community, some calling for increased dialogue with community groups, while others simply want the space gone.

MATT STROMBERG, "In LA, Fear of Gentrification Greets New Nonprofit Art Space," *Hyperallergic*, June 3, 2016

The *Boyle Heights Alliance Against Artwashing and Displacement* is a coalition born from the complex specificities of Los Angeles. We are new and old friends who find ourselves at the intersection of multiple overlapping struggles. We have come together to confront the current crisis of evictions and abusive real estate practices in L.A., to question the role of culture in gentrification and the narrative of "inevitability," and to push to stop displacement in its tracks.

Boyle Heights Alliance Against Artwashing and Displacement, http://alianzacontraartwashing.org/en/bhaaad/

The ongoing controversy surrounding art and gentrification in Boyle Heights caused PSSST to become so contested that we are unable to ethically and financially proceed with our mission. Our young nonprofit struggled to survive through constant attacks. Our staff and artists were routinely trolled online and harassed in-person. This persistent targeting, which was often highly personal in nature, was made all the more intolerable because the artists we engaged are queer, women, and/or people of color. We could no longer continue to put already vulnerable communities at further risk.

BARNETT COHEN, Pilar Gallego, and Jules Gimbrone, "Dear Friends," posted on Defend Boyle Heights Facebook page on February 21, 2017, https://www.facebook.com/defendboyleheights/posts/one-of-the-new -galleries-here-in-boyle-heights-just-announced-they-are-closing-t /1200300376753621/

But voters who agreed with the statement "people like me don't have any say about what the government does" were 86.5 percent more likely to prefer Trump.

DEREK THOMPSON, "Who Are Donald Trump's Supporters," *The Atlantic*, March 1, 2016

# The Prisoner's Dilemma

Zillow listing of 1329 East Third Street, Los Angeles, CA 90033

**Heavy Industrial Property 4,716 sqft**

**For Sale** $800,000, was $1,160,000

**Zestimate®**: $836,850

**Est. Mortgage** $2,169/mo. Get pre-approved. Listed by: Remax.

**Facts:**

1329 East Third Street is a heavy industrial property in Boyle Heights, Los Angeles. It has an estimated value of $836,850, which is 94 percent higher than the $432,354 average for similar parcels in the 90033 zip code. However, the owners have reduced the price to only $800,000. They want out of Boyle Heights as soon as possible and so this is a perfect opportunity for a buyer with ready cash and an unapologetic disposition.

This property was purchased in 2014 for $975,000 by Investors Who Would Like to Remain Anonymous and who used it to host the incipiently defunct PSSST Art Gallery. These Anonymous Investors first sank money into Boyle Heights in 2009, which is when the city's Metro Rail System built its light rail Gold Line subway station at First Street and Boyle Avenue and initiated the still-advancing Boyle Heights Boom. It's too bad that the Anonymous Investors don't have the stomach to wait out the current political controversy, because since they bought in, intrepid developers have brought many exciting projects to the neighborhood. These include a growing number of art galleries, which, unlike the minority- and queer-friendly PSSST, enjoy expanding revenue and so qualify as harbingers of the gentrification that makes Boyle Heights so attractive to pioneer stakeholders.

It cannot be said that PSSST failed as an art gallery per se because of its location. It just ran into some bad locational luck that will evaporate when the full and terrible force of the invisible hand soon arrives in Boyle Heights to bat it away. In the meantime, 1329 East Third Street's values are depressed, and for reasons that we here at Zillow have never witnessed before. Since the dawn of creative capital, art galleries have been viewed by local communities and media outlets alike as the veritable Mother Teresas of the real estate world. Look at what happened in Soho, New York. Soho was a ditch full of minorities and sweatshops called "Hell's Hundred Acres," and then in the 1970s came along gallery owners like Paula Cooper. Now the *New York Observer* hails Cooper as a Lower Manhattan visionary and a two-bedroom on Prince Street costs a baffling $13 million. And take a look at Wynwood, Miami: in 1990, the *New York Times* reported on the Puerto Rican neighborhood's problems with extreme poverty, drug dealing, and riots. Then in 1998, the "bleeding edge" Locust Projects Art Gallery exsanguinated all over NW Twenty-Third Street. And today, an old factory on N. Miami Drive is on sale for $6.9 million.

The same thing will surely happen in Boyle Heights. East LA gentrification is as inevitable as the seasons and as death. The only reason why Boyle Heights presents such delicious low-hanging fruit for people richer than on-sufferance Zillow copywriters who earn $27,432 a year and cannot afford even its depressed rentals is because of certain disruptive elements in the neighborhood. These elements are known by the amazing alias of Boyle Heights Alliance Against Artwashing and Displacement (BHAAAD). These anti-real-estate rabble-rousers want to expunge all art galleries from Boyle Heights, because they fear that these galleries' presence foretells the priapic escalation of Boyle Heights real estate prices that is probably at this point unstoppable. BHAAAD are poor minority people who for obvious reasons do not want to see rising real estate and thus rental values. BHAAAD people, in fact, want (according to their website) "all new art galleries [to] immediately leave Boyle Heights." Some of these BHAAAD no-art people also go so far as to quote Mao Zedong for ideological support, which is incredible. They have additionally run around the new local galleries threatening the art people with maybe violence. This forms another reason why the real estate values in Boyle Heights are temporarily underperforming but will skyrocket as soon as this nonsense is dealt with by local police.

Mao Zedong! He was a really good urban planner. We here at Zillow are joking when we say that. What we are actually insinuating is that BHAAAD people do not understand the market. The market is an implacable force for Progress, we at Zillow still pretty much think even after working in the web real estate business for two years since graduating from Connecticut College with $180,000 of debt.

The market is a form of Free Choice, unrestricted by governmental controls. People vote with their dollars and create the world that they desire through market elections as opposed to governmental interventions, which restrain liberty. We here at Zillow learned of the market's awesomeness in high school, way before we hit undergrad and got an expensive East Coast business degree. When we were at also-expensive Choate and still believed that the world was our own personal steaming hot bowl of delicious clam chowder, we read Adam Smith's *The Wealth of Nations*. Adam Smith taught us the basic lesson that the market allows for conscious evolution, a crowd-sourced path to progress. Which is to say, the social advancement created by the market is a good thing, or usually a good thing. It is typically a really good thing for people who got into Brown and who are not now collapsing beneath the Northwest's gig economy but are rich. Such rich people who will be able to give you an even better pep talk about capitalism would be our Seattle-based Zillow founders, such as former Microsoft exec Rich Barton, who is worth $400 million.

Not that we here at Zillow are about to quote Mao Zedong! Zillow does not hire fanatics, even at the lowly copywriter levels. Zillow believes in algorithms, accurate Zestimates, cobranding, and company cohesion. But the BHAAAD people do not believe in these forms of rationality. For example, BHAAAD looks like it is made up of mostly Hispanics, who might actually prefer to be called "Latino," though we're not sure. Yet note that some of the art people whom the BHAAAD people are attacking are also minorities. It is true that the two art directors of PSSST, Barnett Cohen and Jules Gimbrone, are either white or mixed Asian and white and went to Vassar and Smith, respectively. But Cohen designed PSSST as a "queer space," and Gimbrone is transgender. Gay and trans people are still, as far as we here at Zillow can tell, minorities.

The BHAAAD people do not care about this and say that their lives are being destroyed by art-gallery-driven gentrification that is really a brand of propaganda known as Artwashing and Pinkwashing. Artwashing means sweetening the bitter gruel of gentrification with sparkly frosting made of art galleries and ceramics studios. Sprinkling studios and galleries among rapidly transforming warehouses/lofts and panicked scattering homeless people makes ubercapitalist urban upcycling look attractively progressive because artists are usually talented, socially conscious, and starving. Pinkwashing designates official supports of gay-friendly spectacles in order to divert public attention from authoritarian acts like dropping bombs on stateless people or cleansing cities of undesirables via urban renewal.

Working at Zillow is interesting. In the two years that we here at Zillow have been writing real estate ad copy, we have had occasion to draw on the theories expounded on by our unaffordable college teachers. In our junior year's Organizational Behavior class, we learned about the Prisoner's Dilemma. The Prisoner's Dilemma describes how competitors who want limited resources (the chance at escaping prison, say) have a choice of either working together or defecting from their cooperative agreements in order to obtain such goods. In an imperfect world, full of misery, poverty, paranoia, distrust, and misinformation, prisoners usually fall into the false-consciousness trap of zero-sum-gamism. As a result, they "defect," that is, betray one another in order to grab hold of the tasty crumbs that might fall from whatever mighty hand is controlling them. This usually results in their greater degradation and ultimate doom.

Our two years at Zillow and our expensive educational degrees make us wonder if perhaps the situation in Boyle Heights is not, indeed, a zero-sum game and if the scary situation currently forming between BHAAAD and PSSST could be replaced with cooperative behaviors. Boyle Heights does not have to go the way of Soho or of Wynwood, does it? A variety of progressive economic experiments spring to mind: PSSST could allocate a certain percentage of its gross to a fund that would help pay for residential rent and food, for example; or PSSST could let Boyle Heights homeless people sleep at the gallery at night.

But even as we at Zillow begin to imagine such utopian urban possibilities, we grow shocked at ourselves. We wonder if we have somehow been lobotomized by the Bernie Sanders cult or castrated by the unstoppable Clinton brigade, despite the fact that we still plan on hopelessly voting for Donald Trump, who is the only jackass around who seems to even minimally care about the kinds of marginal males who spend their time quietly sobbing into their keyboards while they should be writing zingy copy for Zillow.

All of this is to say that the valiant investor who wants to take over the property from The Investors Who Would Like To Remain Anonymous should roll around the floor giggling with excitement at all of the Pinkwashing and Artwashing that is going on in Boyle Heights. The fruit is hanging so low that it has already been plucked and scrubbed and is waiting on a golden platter for your fangs. In no time at all, the PSSST gallery will be outpriced from 1329 East Third Street, and its queer and Latino artists will be staggering around Riverside stapling their art to utility poles. Intelligentsia Coffee, Anthropologie, and Medispas will occupy the ever-increasing rents, and condos will rise like ginormous Godzillas where creaky, single-story, circa-1960s bungalows now squat. And you, our dear, faithful Zillow reader, will be driving your convertible Merc down East Third Street with the top down and a twinkle in your eyes, eyes that will be looking beyond the Boyle Heights horizon toward the dingy but promising shires that are LA's high-crime but still fiscally underrated Compton, Leimert Park, and Chesterfield Square.

Features

- Fireplace
- Parking
- View: City
- Neighborhood: Desperate *

"They want everything to be done for them when it should be a community effort," he continued. "10,000 Federal workers now on Island doing a fantastic job."

BRANDON CARTER, "Trump Slams Puerto Rico: 'They Want Everything to Be Done for Them,'" *The Hill,* September 30, 2017

In our survey, interruption of medical care was the primary cause of sustained high mortality rates in the months after the hurricane, a finding consistent with the widely reported disruption of health systems.

NISHANT KISHORE, DOMINGO MARQUÉS, AYESHA MAHMUD, MATHEW V. KIANG, IRMARY RODRIGUEZ, ARLAN FULLER, PEGGY EBNER, CECILIA SORENSEN, FABIO RACY, JAY LEMERY, LESLIE MAAS, JENNIFER LEANING, "Mortality in Puerto Rico after Hurricane Maria," *New England Journal of Medicine,* May 29, 2018

# After Maria

I was excited to help. The response here, officially, was bad. A lot of us knew we needed to react to that somehow. We wanted the victims to know that not everybody here felt like he did. But also, yeah, that's the word for it, exciting.

I applied to go through my union. I'm a nurse in San Bernardino Memorial's critical care unit. My union had asked for names of people who were willing to go there and do first aid, public health, whatever was needed. Our representative didn't say anything outright political, but a lot of us didn't like the president's tone. He'd said, "They want everything done for them." We knew that you can't talk like that about patients, victims. I signed up right away.

My husband looked bashful with pride when he saw me packing my bags. He told everybody at his work that I had been chosen to do triage in a crisis zone. He said he'd get his mom to help with our daughter and that everybody at home would be okay without me for a little while.

"You're an amazing woman," he said. That made me feel good. Two days later I left.

* * *

We landed in Luis Muñoz Airport in San Juan. A bunch of girls and guys from all over California, not just San Bernardino, were on the flight. We were very geared up on the trip over. Nobody drank anything, and we discussed how serious the situation was.

But there was also a lightness about it, people glowing and speaking loudly and quickly, like they were on a date.

* * *

At the airport, you could see the beginnings of the real damage. The lights were out. Hundreds of people lived in the hangars. Families sleeping there, eating there. We did first aid on many children. It was not clean. It was wet, there was a smell. We hiked up our bags onto our shoulders and ran out into the crowds. One mother cried as I cleaned up her daughter's foot, which had been cut by falling branches. Another old woman came up to me and asked in English for penicillin. I had a few small bottles on me, and I gave her two, which I later knew had been a stupid mistake. At the airport, it was a populated area, and those people had some care: there were doctors and nurses. The older woman was really grateful, though, you know. I told people at home about it later. I said her reaction was the real story of the people there and gave a picture that folks in the States, I mean, in our parts of the US, weren't getting over the news. Anyway, she was thankful. She kissed my hand.

* * *

The government sent us cars to take us to the city, the capital. It's a little over seven miles to get there on the 26 Expressway from the airport. The sky by that time had turned blue again, but power lines and tree branches still scattered on the freeways. We weaved back and forth on the road. Our driver had seen some bad things already. He was tall and nervous, sort of zany. He acted serious when the advisers assigned him to our group and told him where to take us. But once he got on the road, he zipped back and forth through the power lines, smiling at us through the rearview so that we could see his spaced-apart teeth.

"The fast and furious!" he yelled, I guess like the movie. He kept laughing.

We'd been in good moods on the plane, but we smiled at him

with closed lips like we were being empathetic but didn't think it was funny.

* * *

San Juan. At first I thought, *Oh my God, this is terrible.* Some of the buildings were crushed, and people milled around, asking for food and supplies. That's when I first saw the huge lines. FEMA set up shop in the middle of the city, and victims lined up to get applications for hurricane relief, if that's what you call it.

The nurses gathered into groups of ten or so. The FEMA officer in charge of our quadrant assigned my group an attaché, Brian, from Kansas City. I'd peg him at forty years old, and he wore a Bluetooth that he talked on constantly. He wore glasses, and he had to clean them with his shirt every five minutes because of the humidity. He wore the blue FEMA slicker. He gave us rubber pants and boots and our own FEMA ponchos for the rain, even though we weren't government employees. He was getting pulled in every direction but would click his Bluetooth off to listen to our questions.

"Where's the deepest impact?" one of our group asked.

"Have you segmented by pathology?" another inquired.

"Is there a geriatric unit around here?" is what I wanted to know, as I'd had some experience with the elderly.

"Well, we'll see what kinds of trouble we can get into," Brian joshed. He brought us to the Coliseum. There, we did a little triage again like before at the airport. The hundreds of victims made the space dirty, hot, and steamy, but guards and nurses and doctors had stationed there. From what I could tell, the Coliseum wasn't like the Superdome in Katrina, where people did die.

After a couple of days, Brian took us to the historical district, with the romantic pink and blue colonial buildings. We saw more flooding. Trees and a couple of cats floated in one of the streets. The police kept people clear. We passed by the Capitol, a white building with marble or concrete steps that had been covered in sludge. Three men washed the steps clean with huge hoses. Brian then brought us to a clinic at the San Jorge Women and Children's Hospital, where we showed a mother how to breastfeed and treated four children for dehydration. The power had all switched over to auxiliary. We walked around the plaza and saw other groups from our union walking around too and waved at them. We saw Mayor Yulín Cruz running across Avenida Juan Ponce de León. She had this blue sweater on her shoulders that dropped on the street, and she just left it there, racing to wherever. She had this totally fierce look on her face, just furious.

The people had no power, no reliable power. The grid had gone out the first day the storm hit, on September 20. In the capital, people used generators. You had to come to the main city, mostly, to get help. FEMA didn't really go to you. A lot of people had traveled. I don't know how the folks from the mountain towns got to San Juan without any juice up there. Maybe the Army? And they'd traveled all that way just to stand in line. They stood in long rows, and I saw a lot of people falling asleep, just like that, on their feet.

The most FEMA investigators I saw were in the capital. I didn't see them anywhere else. In San Juan, they sat at tables and gave out the applications in one section and the water and beef jerky and cookies in another. Everybody spoke English. FEMA made their announcements on Twitter, though bilingually. At first I didn't question it, because I use social media constantly. But then, later, I wondered.

"What the hell are we doing?" Craig asked after a week of this. He was one of the nurses in our group, a big, tall guy with a red beard from Chicago. He'd just put a Band-Aid on a man with no mobility issues.

"Yeah," I said. "Let's get out of here."

"I'm in," Latisha said. She's a girl we met from Oklahoma, an emergency RN.

Another girl, Ranee, wanted to tag along too. She came from New York.

"I didn't come here to be a tourist," Ranee said.

So we looked around and scrounged for the food, medicine, water, batteries, and a satphone that we thought we'd need. Finally, we also got a hold of a Rambler. We split.

\* \* \*

We went to the mountain areas. We had the rubber gear, rubber boots and pants and gloves, and our FEMA slickers. We ate power bars. We cursed and swore when we looked out the Rambler's windows and saw the smushed cars and ripped trees. Meanwhile, we also talked some about the political scene, but then Ranee wound up saying she liked the president fine, and so I kind of kept all that to myself.

The thing is, these people are Americans. They are United States citizens. That's what a lot of people didn't understand back home at the time.

\* \* \*

I felt better once we left. I had that feeling again on the road, that this was new and I was doing something important and big. Like it was war. I mean, it looked like warfare out there, past the city. The roads were just destroyed, often unpassable on account of live electrical cables, cracked surfaces, and huge palms that had been pulled from their roots. Boulders toppled from cliffs or mudslides and landed in the highways. Utility poles had tipped over. The mud ran thick and filled with rocks, and our car skidded out of control over the slick parts. Trash spread out everywhere in huge piles—plastic, torn furniture, hazardous materials like asbestos and electronics, chemicals, batteries, televisions. Aluminum hung on the standing utility poles and dragged down the cables, which shot sparks. About ten miles out we had to physically pick up the cables to make the car squeeze in beside the piles of trash, a big mound made up of what looked like a broken sofa and plastic bags and gas cans that spilled everywhere.

The worst part was the flooding. We saw dead animals, dogs and cows. The water stood sometimes two feet up on the road, three feet, as we splashed through.

About twenty or thirty miles out of town we saw a man walking through a passable part of the current with his little girl on his back. We stopped and yelled at him to get out of the water. When we got them into the car, we freaked because he had a cut on his arm and the girl had one on her stomach. We stuffed them with Cipro and cleaned the wounds as best we could and then drove them to shelter in higher ground.

"Don't walk in the water," I told him, in English. I swear to Christ none of us spoke Spanish. It was stupid. A lot of nurses have some medical Spanish, but none of us did. We'd tried to get a hold of a translator in San Juan, but they were all doing administrative tasks and didn't want to go to the mountains. I told the man, "There's sewage, chemicals, viruses, mold. Don't touch the water. Don't let your daughter touch the water. If you need to drink water, clean what you get from a tap with bleach or chlorine tablets. Don't get near it otherwise."

"Thank you," he said. He had streaked dirt all over his face from where he'd rubbed it with a cloth.

"Do you understand what I'm telling you?"

"Thank you, thank you," he said.

"Thank you," his daughter said. She was like six, with light-brown hair and wrapped up in my sweatshirt. My daughter at home is four years old, so it was like, you know.

"Yeah, you're welcome," I said.

But at least we saved them.

After we dropped them off, we zoomed through the flooding, and the water splashed into the Rambler from a crack I'd idiotically left open in a back window.

\* \* \*

What was he doing at this point? This was, like, October 3. I think he was throwing paper towels to rich people in Guaynabo. But the people in the mountains didn't know about that. They didn't know where anybody was or what was happening.

I don't know why the people in the mountains stayed so long. I'm talking about the ones that the Army for some reason didn't get out. Mostly, it might have been because they just couldn't walk or drive out on their own steam. But I think other people got confused by how smooth things went down in Houston, earlier—when, oh, Hurricane Harvey happened those last weeks of August 2017.

I think the people in the mountains thought that if they stayed put, they'd get the same kind of help that folks in Texas got.

\* \* \*

We saw a woman standing on top of her house in Camarillo. She was a large, heavy lady, really broad, wearing a mud-covered dress and waving her hands. She was crying. The flooding had come up halfway to her house, and when she saw us, she started screaming about her dogs. Latisha in our group knew the word for dogs, *perro*, and when I thought about it, I knew the word too.

"Here we go," Craig said.

"She's in trouble," I said.

We ran out to save her. We pulled on our rubber pants and wandered through the water, trying to figure out how to get her down. Latisha found a ladder sticking through a smashed window, and we pulled that up and propped it up to the roof of her house. I climbed up first.

The woman's eyes looked strange, but I'm a nurse and so I'd seen that before. A real spaced-out look, like an animal. Maybe I shouldn't say that. It's just a human thing, though. You get animal when you get that scared. We all do.

She fucking grips onto my legs yelling about her dogs, and I thought she was going to pull me down.

"Wait, wait!" I yelled at her. Craig came climbing up, and he's got a way with the ladies, I guess. He knew how to use his voice to calm her. She clambered up on his back and kept slipping down, so I held her up by her bottom, like to support her. We lugged her down the ladder somehow. Then we carried her over the water, the whole team did. She kept crying. She yelled at us about her dogs. We finally hauled her to higher ground, and she sat down in the mud, exhausted and talking excitedly in Spanish.

I ran back to the house. Climbed up through the smashed window where Latisha found the ladder. The house smelled awful. Black mold. Gets in the lungs. The woman had been stranded for a week maybe, but I think more. The ceiling curdled or buckled or something. The walls had cracked with water damage. I tried not to breathe. I went wading through the kitchen, the water up to my stomach, pushing past floating plastic forks and spoons and cups, until I got to the bedroom.

Two of those little itty-bitty types of dogs looked straight at me. Soaked and trembling. They stood up on a bureau, just above high water. Those pop-eyed dogs. Chihuahuas. They started howling with their poor little mouths. I chugged through the water and grabbed them and hauled ass out of there before the ceiling came crashing down.

I don't know how I got through the window with a dog under each armpit. One of them started biting me. I was, like, laughing, I guess from fear. I gave the dogs to Ranee, and she ran over to the woman and gave them to her.

The woman stuck her face into the dogs and just cried and cried. We all started crying.

We looked at her feet and asked her, "Are you diabetic?" The word, thank God, is almost the same in Spanish. She said yes. She didn't have her medicine. Later I learned that a lot of people didn't know that it could go unrefrigerated, and they threw it away.

We cleaned her wounds and bandaged them. We gave her insulin and Cipro and water and some food. We treated the dogs too, even the bitey one. They had sores.

After a while some girls from higher ground showed up, and all of them starting talking really fast in Spanish. The girls spoke

English and said that the woman was very thankful. The girls said that they knew the lady, and she could come stay with them because their house was undamaged.

We dropped everybody at the girls' house. The parents came out and wrapped up the woman in a blanket.

I felt like a hero.

\* \* \*

Toa Baja sits on the northern coast, about twenty-five kilometers from San Juan. It's a smallish city, maybe eighty thousand people. It looked deserted. It got really ripped up. A lot of the little houses there didn't have roofs. It's a tourist place because it's by the water, which wasn't perfect when the storm came. Later I learned that the Army had come and evacuated a lot of people. But they didn't get everybody.

We found a man on the outskirts of town. He waved at us from the top of a small apartment complex, trying to yell, but his voice didn't work anymore. He looked to be about eighty years old. I couldn't see that then, exactly how old he was, but I've learned the general look of geriatrics. We stopped on the side of the road and yelled back up at him that it was okay and we were going to get him.

His apartment complex had been crushed on the side and was not stable. It was only two stories. The ceilings had come crashing down on the interior and blocked the staircase. I don't know how it was still standing. We couldn't get up through inside of the building itself.

I could hear him trying to yell at us for help. "Heeeeehhh Heeeeehhhh." His voice had just been completely thrashed.

"Call San Juan," Ranee said.

Craig called on the satphone. He got through to Brian, but Brian said there was nothing he could do right now. I said to Craig, "Call Brian's boss at FEMA." I said, "Call the Army." We didn't know who the hell to call. We just dialed Brian again, and nobody answered.

"What are we going to do?" Latisha said. She looked really tired and wiped her eyes with her hands, until she remembered about infection.

I looked over at the much taller, four-story stucco building next to the one where the guy was. It was crushed too. But it had some black metal balconies sticking out from the side. These balconies were so close to the old guy's apartment complex that they were in an almost jumpable distance. I thought that maybe I could climb up those balconies and then somehow scramble to the other building's roof. It was only two or three stories to reach level with it. It'd be like Spiderman. Like parkour. You had to be creative out there.

"No," Craig said, when I told him my plan. You know, a man. But the victim was still trying to scream at us, and I said fuck it.

I ran over to the side of the building with the balconies and started to climb up, from floor to floor, from the outside. I'm in good shape, thankfully. I lift weights, and I do trail running. I do yoga. Not that it helped me much.

I climbed up to one of the first-floor balconies. It was wrought metal, black, and very slick from the water. I clambered up and jumped down into it. It was fine. And then it turned out that there was a little fire exit extending from the second floor's balcony to the first, and so I climbed up that, even though it had been broken in the storm. I grappled onto the little steps, but the fire exit swayed almost all the way out, and I thought I'd come crashing down.

The nurses below were all yelling at me, and I thought, *Yeah, maybe not a great idea.*

But I hooked my foot onto the second balcony railing and swung the fire exit back. I hopped into the little balcony. It didn't feel very stable. It creaked. But from there I had a good view of the roof of the two-story building where the old man was stranded. I could see that he needed immediate crisis care. He had this old shriveled face. His hair came down over his eyes. He was hurt.

His whole left side was just red. I couldn't tell exactly what was going on. But from the position of the leg I could see it had broken. And he had some serious hematoma and lacerations. Exterior wounds of that size mean a good chance of internal bleeding too. He must have fallen or had something topple on top of him. I don't know how he made it to the roof. He had crawled over it to scream at us from the edge.

I could see him, pretty close. I could see his eyes. He didn't have animal eyes like the lady. He had the kind of eyes that terminal patients get when it sinks in and they know they have to get ready. The light goes out of them.

I yelled when I saw that. I said, "Hey! Hey! Hey! Hey!"

He nodded and laid his head down on the ground.

"Hey! Hey! Hey! Hey!" I'm yelling. "I'm coming to get you!"

I couldn't hop to the roof from the second balcony. From that height, there was a good chance I'd just hit the wall and have to grab the edges with my fingers. The third balcony up rose higher than the top of his building. I could do a long jump down from there maybe. But when I grabbed up at the third balcony's ironworks, it shook loose from the stucco. Then it just collapsed. It popped out from the top, swung all the way down, and then hung toward the ground from one rivet. I had to duck because it almost knocked my head off. I started trembling then. I knew I was a complete tool with no idea what I was doing.

"Sindy!" they're all yelling down there.

"It's fine!" I yelled back. It wasn't fine. I couldn't jump from building to building. I'm not Spiderman and I don't do parkour. Also the balcony I stood in was creaking and shaking.

I looked across at the other building, at the man, who still lay down on the roof by the edge, trying to raise his hand at me. I looked at his eyes, at the red on his skin and clothes all down the left side. On the part of his rooftop I could see, there was a red stain around his body. I didn't know how long he had been there, but the bone can set wrong, and there is a serious problem with bacterial infection, septicemia, in those conditions.

He looked at me again and shook his head. I could see him really well. That's how close I was. But not close enough to get to him. We looked at each other for a long time.

Then he started shuffling. He tried to scream I guess from the pain but couldn't. He was rummaging through his pocket with his good hand. He took something out of his pocket and dropped it from the roof into the shallow water below. I heard it plop.

"He dropped something!" I yelled.

"I got it," I heard Ranee say.

"I have to get down," I said to man.

He didn't say anything to me. He laid completely flat on the roof, and then I couldn't see him as well.

"Just wait here," I said. "We'll send someone for you."

He still just didn't say anything.

"We'll send somebody," I said.

I climbed down.

We got back in the Rambler and drove away. Craig drove, and Latisha sat in the front. Ranee put a blanket over me.

"What did he throw down?" I said.

Ranee had put it inside her rubber pants and fished it out. It was a small, soaked square object. She handed it to me.

It was his wallet. I opened up and saw his identification cards. He was smart. It had his address, his location.

His name was Antonio Hernandez.

* * *

As soon as we got to San Juan, I tracked down Brian, and I was like, "This guy needs our help. He lives here." I showed Brian the address. "We need to call the Army," I said. "We need FEMA. We have to get the police."

Brian took the wallet that I handed him. He said he'd write the guy's name down. "I'll let our team know," he said.

"No, you don't understand that we need to get him now," I said. I explained about the hematomas and the balconies.

Brian took off his glasses and cleaned them with his shirt, from under his FEMA slicker. He tilted his head at a line of people who were waiting for I don't know what. The line was so long I couldn't see where it ended.

"We'll do what we can do," he said. "But we have our hands full."

"You need to listen to me! This is an emergency!"

Brian walked away.

\* \* \*

Later, that night, in our hotel, I got so mad. I realized that if I could just somehow get a hold of rescue equipment or some people myself, I could go save Mr. Hernandez before he died. I could get a ladder, like the one I'd used to help the woman and the dogs.

I just lay there all night thinking of his whole left side that had been turned red from the hematoma and the cuts. I thought of his eyes. Thought how stupid I'd been to just give his information to Brian and then expect a miracle. I had to do it myself.

Thing was, I couldn't remember exactly how to get back to the apartment in Toa Baja. I tried to track it in my mind but couldn't. I called Craig about it, in the middle of the night. He said that he didn't know how exactly to track back either, because we'd been going all over the place without a plan. So I called Latisha and Ranee, but they didn't know either.

"Didn't Brian say they'd get him?" Ranee said into the phone, sleepy.

What I needed was that wallet. With the wallet and the ID card, I'd plug in the address using GPS.

I got up the next morning, and it was raining. I prepared by putting on my rubber pants and my slicker, so when I got Mr. Hernandez's information, I could just get a car and go. After that, I started running everywhere looking for Brian. The mother and child clinic, the Coliseum, the historical district. When I found him, around three o'clock in the afternoon in the cantina, I started hollering at him that I needed the wallet. He was like, "What are you talking about?" Then he remembered. He said, "I gave that to So-and-So." A supervisor. He said, "They'll take care of it when they can."

I said, "Just give it back to me, and I'll get a car and a ladder. I'll get supplies. I'll go up there myself."

Brian looked at me sort of sympathetically. "I can see this is getting to you," he said.

"Just give me the wallet back," I said.

He put his arm around me and gave a little tug on the FEMA slicker I wore. "You've done really great work here. You've been such an incredible part of the team."

We stood by a pile of sandwiches wrapped up in plastic, but in my mind I saw the long lines with the people sleeping standing up and the FEMA guys handing out applications. I said, "No, I'm doing something different. We went up to the mountains."

"Every little bit helps," Brian said.

"I'm not part of *this*," I said. "We went up to Toa Baja, and I have to get back."

Brian looked at me and said, "Sorry, I'm coming. I'll be right there."

"What?" I said.

"I have a meeting," he said, getting suddenly busy. He'd been talking to his Bluetooth.

"His name's Antonio Hernandez," I said.

"I know, thank you, good," Brian said. He took off again.

He never got back to me about the wallet. I must have called him six or seven more times, but he didn't answer.

Two days later it was time for us to leave.

* * *

I heard that the president said that the death toll was sixteen. He was like, this is a really impressive number.

Later, there were some studies, by Harvard and George Washington Universities.

Those estimates said that eight hundred to eight thousand people died in Puerto Rico, mostly from "interruptions in medical care." That just means that they didn't get seen by surgeons or doctors or nurses. Fewer people died from drowning, or direct impacts.

* * *

So I went home. I came home to my husband and my daughter.

They looked so crazily happy to see me that at first it was okay. At the airport, my daughter crawled all over me and got too excited, so I had to sing to her so she'd stop screaming. My husband wrapped me up in his arms and then drove us all back to the house. I slept in the car, and when I woke up, we were there.

Our place looked like a palace, I swear.

I slept in our bed. It was good to be back. Like the other wasn't real almost. My husband cooked me eggs and pizza. I was just so grateful to have my family. My daughter showed me some pictures she'd taken while I was away. They were of flowers and grass.

I told my family about the woman with the little dogs and how I'd held her by the butt and saved her Chihuahuas by basically swimming through the house. My daughter liked that. I told my husband, later, at night, about the man and his daughter in the floodwater and how we'd treated their wounds and given them Cipro. I talked about how FEMA stayed in San Juan while we went to the mountains in that Rambler and how we'd had to pick up the fallen cables with the electric sparks. I drank a lot of wine and went on and on about it. How the old woman at the airport had kissed my hand and blah blah. I told my husband all of the stories except for the one about the man on the roof. And he, my husband, was really, really proud of me.

The problem was that after a few days I started to feel like just lying down on the floor and not getting back up. I got this idea that Brian had been right, when he'd said that I was "part of the team." He'd hinted to me that I didn't count as some special superhero. I hadn't wanted to hear that at the time, when I was yelling at him about Toa Baja. But after a few days of telling my stories and eating my husband's cooking, I saw that he had a point.

Because I didn't speak Spanish. I let myself feel all puffed up when that old lady kissed my hand just because I gave her a couple little bottles of penicillin. Me thinking that I'm righting some wrong, sort of resisting the political crap. But the truth is I never even thought about Puerto Rico until the union emailed us about the opportunity. I'll just say it, too, that I didn't realize they were citizens until the rep explained it all to us. And then, even though I knew he was still out there, might be dead already, I'd just gone home when the time for our trip was over.

I tried to call Brian again, but I just got dumped into voicemail.

The way he'd dropped the wallet into the water, hoping. Just hoping to live.

About a month later I was crying into the sink in our kitchen, and my husband found me.

"Honey, baby." He hugged me and kissed me and rocked me back and forth. "What's wrong?"★

Mr. Pruitt in his resignation letter cited "unrelenting attacks on me personally" as one of the reasons for his departure. Mr. Pruitt had been hailed by conservatives for his zealous deregulation, but he could not overcome a spate of questions about his alleged spending abuses, first-class travel and cozy relationships with lobbyists.... Seeing those deliberations being aired publicly, amid a string of other damaging reports, focused Mr. Trump's attention, a person close to the president said.

CORAL DAVENPORT, LISA FRIEDMAN, and MAGGIE HABERMAN, "E.P.A. Chief Scott Pruitt Resigns under a Cloud of Ethics Scandals," *New York Times,* July 5, 2018

# Acid Reign

O N FEBRUARY 17, 2017, the United States Senate confirmed the
Administrator as the new warlord of the Environmental
Protection Agency. The Administrator is a white Christian man.
He loves Jesus, but his Savior is corporate and horrible, not the
vegan version with the sandals.

After graduating from college, the Administrator went to law
school, because, like the rest of us, he leads a fear-based life. After
law school, the Administrator worked at a Christian law firm,
where he defended Christians. The Administrator next prayed his
way into a midwestern state senate and office of Attorney General, where he tried to give men property rights over fetuses and
ban transgender children from going to the bathroom. Building
on these victories, he scratched up to the heights of the presidential Cabinet and began to threaten the whole world.

The Administrator wore a dark-blue suit and a burgundy tie
during his confirmation hearings. He waved his small, pale hands
as he pontificated. Some Democrats observed scathingly that the
Administrator had, while an AG, signed his name to an EPA protest letter written by Devon Energy, which objected to proposed
limits on methane gas that leaks from oil operations; the Administrator shruggingly explained that he had only been serving the
interest of his state. Other liberals complained that he'd once sued
the EPA when it strengthened the National Ambient Air Quality
Standards in order to give relief to the seven million American

children with asthma. The Administrator smiled and said he'd sued on the reasonable grounds that the heightened Air Quality Standards were unattainable.

The Administrator was thereafter rescued by Senator Joni Ernst (R-Iowa), who softballed him an interminable and confusing anti-Obama question. When she finally finished speaking, the Administrator nodded earnestly, and said, "This paradigm that we live within today, that if you're pro-energy, you're anti-environment, if you're pro-environment, you're anti-energy, is something that I think is just a false narrative."

Then the Senate confirmed him.

\* \* \*

Ten days after the Senate confirmed the Administrator, I received the following email:

> From: Mike B. Kendall
> [mailto: Kendall.Mike@epa.gov]
> Sent: February 27, 2017 4:56 P.M.
> To: Marta Mendoza
> [mailto:Mendoza.Marta@epa.gov]
> Subject: Denial of 2007 Petition to Revoke
> Tolerance for Pesticide Chlorpyrifos under
> 21 U.S.C. § 346a(d)
> Marta please draft an order denying the NRDC's and PANNA's 2007 Petition for a Chlorpyrifos tolerance revocation as per the Administrator's oral briefing 2/26/17 that I asked you to memorize as note-taking has been banned temporarily as per oral order issued 2/20/17. Pls submit draft by 0900 3/3/17. The file is on my desk so you'll have to come and get it ASAP.
> Thank you Marta.
> MBK
> Mike B. Kendall
> Principal Deputy General Counsel & Designated Agency
>     Ethics Official
> Office of General Counsel
> US Environmental Protection Agency
> Main Office Line: 202-564-8064

\* \* \*

"It's a simple assignment: just deny the petition," my new boss, Mike, said about an hour after sending me the February 27 email. As he talked at me, he stared into his computer and, as usual, never once looked my way, as I am a forty-five-year-old nonwhite female with zany black hair, dark skin, and a penchant for plastic glasses. "Say that there's good evidence that it's potentially harmless and we're still researching the matter." Mike is forty-eight, Anglo, Baptist, divorced, and sports a salt-and-pepper brush cut. I'd been at USEPA since '08. He arrived in winter '17 after a decade running dark ops for the Independent Petroleum Association of America and then doing something scary for Exxon.

"But we already know that it's dangerous, which is why we were going to ban it," I said, standing in his doorway on the third floor of South Building and holding the thick chlorpyrifos file that he'd just handed me.

"Well, the opposite of what you just said is the position we're taking now," Mike rapped out, still glaring at his screen. "So go write that up."

"Yes, of course, excellent idea," I said, dazed. "What a stroke of genius." Mike waved me away. I remained in the doorway for a few seconds longer, waiting for that old bat Hillary Clinton to come streaking around a corner yelling, "Ha ha ha gotcha!" When that didn't happen, I fled through the EPA HQ's beige corridors (in the WJC building off Twelfth), which crawled with construction workers carrying in black snaky cables and puffy soundproofing material. I skittered by the Administrator's guarded and locked suite (from which an ominous construction noise could be heard rattling away) and kept going until I reached the North Building's fourth floor. From there, I made my way to my co-office.

"Oh my God," Khaled Aziz wheezed as I entered.

Khaled occupied the desk tucked into the left southwest corner of the room. He sat hunched over and squinted at his IBM while ignoring a huge accordion file that he'd thrown onto the floor. I'd decorated my side of the space with a silver-framed photo of my parents and paper clips. I dropped into my mesh ergonomic chair while clutching the chlorpyrifos file to my chest.

"How is this our job now?" I asked.

"What, poisoning people?" Khaled said, gaping at a blindingly illustrated website titled "Household Toxins and Your Child."

I crunched the file in my hands. "What's so great about being rich if everyone is dead?"

"Fucking Comey," Khaled gasped.

Khaled's a thirty-eight-year-old expert in the Toxic Substances Control Act, 15 U.S.C. §2601 et seq. (1976), as well as a Yale PhD in American Studies. Back in 2009, after his boyfriend, Charles, died from a leukemia possibly contracted from benzene exposure, Khaled wrote his Am Stud dissertation on the queer ecology of Rachel Carson, which earned him zero job offers from the three universities with open positions in his field. He rallied by teaching poetry, composition, flute, history, soccer, and geography at Philips Andover, becoming addicted to Ambien, and then drying out at Harvard Law. He came here in '14 from Beveridge & Diamond after weeping during a Superfund status conference. Khaled's soft, lima-bean belly spreads out luxuriously from beneath his cashmere V-necks. He has grief and anxiety problems, thick silvery-black hair, and huge hazel eyes that seemed to be constantly widening in shock ever since the inauguration.

Khaled kicked a leg toward the file he'd thrown onto the ground. Papers spilled out of it. "I just got the house-paint case, with the low-income infants and the lead. And I'm not doing it."

"I have chlorpyrifos," I said.

"The PANNA petition?" Khaled shook his head. "What are you going to do?"

I raked my hands through my hair. "Slow-roll it?"

"There's no slow-rolling that. *He's* turned this place into a pit."

"What's he building in his office?" I hissed.

"They say it's a soundproof phone booth," Khaled said.

"A what?"

"That's not the worst of it. I've heard this weird stuff about his housing and that he's going to Morocco for a vacation-slash-working trip with energy consultants, I think?"

"This is a nightmare," I jabbered. "We just have to wait it out until the impeachment, and then things will be more normal around here."

"You don't seem to understand that we lost." Khaled slowly and gently lowered his head onto his desk. "What we have to do is *quit.*"

I flapped my file at him. "Somebody's got to care about these farmworkers and indigent fetuses."

Khaled muttered into his keyboard, "They're not news, Marta."

"Right," I said.

I swiveled in my seat toward my computer. I was supposed to write an administrative order explaining that, despite objections from the Natural Resources Defense Council and the Pesticide Action Network North America, the EPA would continue to permit, that is, in legalese, "tolerate," the agricultural use of a pesticidal neurotoxin. I did not do that, though. Instead, I logged onto Westlaw. I typed in the search, "pesticide! w/2 chlorpyrifos w/5 how awful is it really."

Then I started to cry.

* * *

My parents were Graciela and Felipe Mendoza. They each stood around five feet tall and possessed the same white, square, strong teeth that I inherited, though they gritted theirs through the excitements of life with far more aplomb than I have ever been able to manage. My mother had beautiful hazel ox-eyes and liked to sing opera in an untrained voice. My father possessed a slightly built and superbly delicate bearing, which he accessorized with courtly gestures, like the tender way he would touch my mother on her lower back as he'd guide her protectively on her way to the hairdresser's.

Professionally, both of my parents could claim an expertise in table- and wine-grape harvest and management, forged after decades of episodic employment in the lucrative California vineyards. Their métier was pest control. The government had already helpfully approved the use of organophosphates in the grape war against the destructive mealybug in '65, and so they would venture out among the vines, applying the spray during the dormant season, that is, the vulnerable period just before bud break. I accompanied them in their labors during my early years. When I was an infant, they would bring me into the fields tied to one of their chests in a cotton sling. Later on, I used our backpack sprayer myself.

I was only exposed directly until the age of sixteen. In junior high and the first two years of high school, I spent every summer and many after-class hours making a 0.5 percent spray by pouring in two and two-thirds fluid ounces Chlorpyrifos EZ to each gallon of water. With my parents doing likewise, I'd stand in the tangy barn of whatever winery we were working for and busily mix the solution into big, white plastic buckets while wearing a cotton mask. The pesticide splashed about when I'd agitate the containers. It inevitably covered my arms and sometimes my face and thighs. I'd then pour the solution into the black plastic body of the sprayer and screw on the lid. Afterward, I dashed about the vineyards, feeling the sun warm my forehead and listening to the few remaining birds cheeping and tweeting. I remember that I was happy. The chlorpyrifos would gush out of my pump and rainbow the vines while interfering with mealybug neural systems and brain function. I was good at my work. I used a coarse droplet nozzle, which is a good choice for insecticides because it allows for deeper penetration into ground soil. It seems that this choice of technology also proved excellent for saturating the entirety of the human respiratory system.

When I reached eleventh grade, my parents wanted me to stop spraying because I developed a nasty cough, which the Valley Urgent Care nurses treated with Robitussin Extra Strength Cough Syrup that I didn't take upon escaping from the clinic because it made me sleep all day. Instead of working in agriculture, Mom and Dad suggested, I should rest and focus on my studies. And so I quit the fields and matriculated eventually to California State, Bakersfield.

I loved school. This was in 1989. In my freshman year at CSB, I would clench over my books in the library, flipping pages, writing wordy poems, and discreetly divesting myself of unmentionables into handkerchiefs. I submitted lengthy papers to my exhausted TAs, who would look at me dead-eyed over their spectacles and nod at my flaming love for learning with mournful recognition. I thought I might be a writer. I plotted out an excitement-packed future where I'd compose novels laced with lacerating leftist subtext inspired by George Orwell and Herman Melville. I would Jean-Paul Sartreishly work for radical newspapers, reporting on atrocities in exciting far-flung nations. I'd pen poems and stories that would change the world, like Langston Hughes and James Baldwin.

But, in fact, I would not do any of that. Because I coughed, I continued coughing. I coughed some more. I could not stop coughing.

In the middle of my first semester of my second year, my parents whisked me out of class and took me to a proper doctor. From there, I was made hackingly to endure a battery of x-rays, blood tests, and other Frankensteinian ordeals. The proper doctor, I recall, began to sob when trying to explain certain difficult facts. But my memory grows fuzzy after this point. I found myself splayed in a gurney at Bakersfield Mercy Hospital's pulmonary ward. Lung cancer. But I didn't smoke. "Could it be the pesticide?" my father asked, his right arm trembling. The goop that I bathed in every summer since the age of zero? The proper doctor was now gone and had been replaced by a team of harried oncologists. These experts looked at my parents and me with the same enervated expression as my CSB TAs. They checked their files and admitted that they could not determine the answer to my father's question either way. The studies—the tests—the etiology—the causation— they nodded at us sagely, explaining that all of the hypotheses and conclusions concerning pesticide toxicity remained complicated and confusing, and no, they couldn't say.

And my prognosis? Good, they said. Bad, they said. You're dead, others said. You'll live, one said.

Meanwhile, my parents began to wither away. One moment they were there, wiping my face with cool towelettes and making incredible grieving sounds, and the next minute, they seemed to simply vanish from the hospital's bleach-scented halls. It seemed that during my medical sojourn my mom and dad had experi- enced some unpleasant symptoms, gotten checkups, and received bad news from the family neurologist.

Within two years they were dead.

* * *

It turned out that enduring mind-blasting grief is not in my wheelhouse. Losing my parents in this way was so painful that I thought it was more likely to stop my heart than the broncho- genic carcinoma was. That's why, for a long time, I worked hard to bury the hardest memories from this chapter of my life by culti- vating my interests and following my passions and forgiving myself. In so doing, I exhibited the same kind of dimwittery as people who say that you should live in the present or think that you can safely dispose of nuclear waste and recyclable plastics.

Still, after running gently amok for a few years, I will say that the details did begin to blur a bit. I grew super busy, beating cancer and finishing college in the early aughts. I thereafter applied to law school with a vague idea of making the world a less unbelievably ghastly place. Meanwhile, the dominoes that began tipping at my birth continued clicking and crashing until I found myself lawyering at the EPA and stumbled onto my current career as an enforcer for the Dow Chemical Company.

At the EPA, we housed activist environmental widowers, like Khaled, who obsessively attacked every toxin as if it were a mass murderer and seemed to believe that bullet-point memos contained actual ammunition. But after an initially energetic phase waging war on any and all environmental mutagens in the loving memory of my parents, I abandoned that path because it just made me so . . . exhausted. After nine years at the Agency, I'd satisfied myself with being a good team player who worked on changing the system through maybe slow-moving but still positive gains. My modest but well-regarded output included writing a third of the first version of the Clean Power Plan (leashing the carbon output of power plants) and editing the sixth draft of Obama's new standards on methane emissions (which would shrink CH4 output to 33M tons of carbon pollution a year). The rest of the time I pursued what some people called a balanced life but what I now understand is a form of socially sanctioned amnesia, which I cultivated by reading, dabbling in pottery, maybe drinking *just* a little, occasionally dating—the basics.

But my perfect and stupid life was soon to be upended in February '17, when the Administrator and Mike showed up and started breaking shit within the first hour. "Breaking shit" is administrative law patois for neoconservative Earth-wide destruction via regulatory rollback. As of late March of that year, about half of our lifers had already contracted a psychic virus that left them resting their hands lifelessly on their computer keyboards while their polar-bear posters slowly peeled off the walls. We'd learned in the first exciting phase of the Administrator's arrival that he wouldn't let us take written notes in meetings and had also asked for a bulletproof desk because he feared that Code Pinkers would break down his door to assail him with Venezuelan guns donated by George Soros. In my nightmares at the time, the bullets ricocheted off the bulletproof desk and splattered my

IBM with my own personal brains, which I actually deserved. During the past weeks Mike had shoutingly optimized workplace productivity so that I had already helped the Administrator sign off on Enbridge's expansion of the Alberta Clipper Pipeline. I'd also obeyed directives to scrub the words "climate change" from EPA webpages directing state, local, and tribal governments to alternative energy resources.

And now Mike had tasked me with writing the order denying the petition to revoke the EPA's chlorpyrifos permission. The Natural Resources Defense Council and the Pesticide Action Network North America had petitioned us back in '07 to revoke the tolerance that the EPA had issued in the '60s for the pesticide's use on food and feed crops, such as apples, cherries, nectarines, bananas, strawberries, and—yes—grapes. In 2015 and also 2016, the EPA had proposed pulling the allowance based on a reported possibly heightened neurological risk in recently exposed children and exacerbated hazards for farmworkers who *mix, load, and apply chlorpyrifos pesticide products*. The EPA then subjected the tolerance revocation to the necessary "notice and comment" period. This is the administrative interlude when the public may and does copiously comment on proposed rules and the Agency responds. Except for certain furious addendums offered by stalwart advocates of the chemical industry, the commentary looked supportive of the change in policy, and, bolstered by a court order, during the last golden days of the Obama administration, we idiotically set it for a final decision on March 31, 2017.

After this, a short and explosive chain of calamities ensued, and Mike had called me up to his office with the instructions to reverse our position. I was now saddled with the mission of ensuring that farmworkers could still spread the pesticide as if it were the Good News and chemical company COOs could keep sleeping in hyperbaric chambers made of gold bullion.

\* \* \*

Five days later, I sat at my office desk, which remained cluttered with my computer, the silver-framed photo of my parents, and the bulging, brown chlorpyrifos folder. Khaled grumbled next to me as he plucked out papers from his massive lead-paint file and tore them into neat little strips and threw them in the air like streamers.

"Don't do it," he said.

"If we get fired, then we lose any influence." I looked at my blank screen. "I still have a chance to work from the inside, here. I still have a shot at fighting this."

"What you have is Stockholm syndrome."

"When are you leaving the Agency?"

"I talked to Charles's mother yesterday and told her the week after next." Charles, again, was Khaled's lover who had died after benzene exposure and the maybe resulting leukemia.

My hands loitered on my keyboard. I waited for something to save me. I looked at my parents' shiny smiling faces. I looked at the file.

I began to type.

> In this Order, EPA denies a petition requesting that EPA revoke all tolerances for the pesticide chlorpyrifos under section 408(d) of the Federal Food, Drug, and Cosmetic Act. . . . EPA has concluded that, despite several years of study, the science addressing neurodevelopmental effects remains unresolved and that further evaluation of the science during the remaining time for completion of registration review is warranted to achieve greater certainty as to whether the potential exists for adverse neurodevelopmental effects to occur from current human exposures to chlorpyrifos.

★ ★ ★

"Did you get my pens?" I overheard the Administrator ask Mike and Clarissa Bender, our new third in command, a week after I wrote the order denying the chlorpyrifos petition. The entirety of the Office of General Counsel's legal staff was assembling in the maple-paneled Polaris conference room, on the Concourse level in the Ronald Reagan Building. Housekeeping had prepared the space with multiple rows of burgundy-upholstered chairs, enough to hold the 230 lawyers who worked for the Agency at the time.

A wooden lectern presided at the front of the room. Behind it stood the Administrator, sweating lightly. He's about five foot eight and has a big balding head frosted with steel-gray fluff. He wore a soft blue suit of a beautiful cut and a red tie with little white polka dots. The buzz-haired Security Chief flanked him, along with twenty or so gun-bulging special agents, some wearing blue jackets and others police clothes and sheriffy badges. One of the Administrator's assistants, a champagne-haired youngster called Tracey, hovered at his far right side, jangling her earrings and clutching a phone. To the Administrator's direct left sat a panel table. This hosted our newly manufactured subclass supervisor, Clarissa, a pretty redhead who wore a blue bodycon frock that seemed to be an exact replica of Ivanka Trump's style. Mike sat next to her, wearing gray and reading a file of notes with insane-looking concentration. I had a good view of the circus as Khaled and I had arrived late and the only remaining seats were in the front row.

Mike and Clarissa looked up at the Administrator, confused.

"The pens?" Clarissa asked.

"Do you need a pen?" Mike asked.

"I thought we weren't supposed to bring pens, sir," Clarissa said.

Tracey with the earrings darted forward. "I have twelve silver fountains customized with your signature and the Agency seal."

"All right," the Administrator said.

"Do you want more?" Tracey asked.

"Umgh." The Administrator began frantically searching his pockets for his phone. When he discovered that it was strapped to his belt, he said, "Let's get started."

Next to me, Khaled bent forward and held his head in his hands.

*Beep beep beep*, we all suddenly heard. *Beep beep beep.*

Everyone checked their pockets—but along with writing implements and paper, we hadn't been allowed to bring our phones either. The Administrator glared at us for a moment before he realized that the noise was his own. He grabbed his phone from his belt and looked at it. Then he walked swiftly out of the room, followed by a spasm of guards.

"Okay!" Clarissa said in a leadership voice after a half-second delay.

"Okay!" Mike said at the same time in a louder voice.

Clarissa stood up and smoothed her skirt. But Mike was quicker. He moved silkily toward the podium and began booming at us while Clarissa sat awkwardly back down.

"The Administrator will be right back, and until then, welcome! Let's get started here. I really want to thank everybody for coming today and for all the amazing work you've been doing. We've been able to dial back on the overreach from the prior administration, and now environmentalism can truly partner with industry and growth and regain the faith and confidence of the private—"

Sitting directly behind me, a forty-something white woman from the Air and Radiation Law Office named Lisa Beasley began hiccupping loudly and violently.

Mike continued talking. "And what we're excited to tee up this year is a full coordination of the lead, emissions, and particularly pesticides strategies so that this office remains on message at all times about the synergy between clean water, clean air, and the New Federalism."

Lisa's hiccups were loud. She'd whipped up her wispy brown hair into an untidy bun, and it shook like an abused puppet on the top of her head.

Mike ceased talking and smiled at her.

"Sorry, I've just been having a little anxiety," she said.

"Well, just stop," Mike said.

"Okay," Lisa said, jerking.

The Administrator and his killers now came striding back into the room.

"All right," the Administrator said, beaming genially while coursing with sweat.

"I was telling them about all the success that we're having with the chlorpyrifos case," Mike explained, drifting an inch away from the podium.

"I have to get out of here," Khaled murmured, while still fetally curling in his seat.

"Who's running point on that?" Clarissa practically yelled out.

"On—what?" Mike asked, as he'd been squinting at Khaled.

"Chlorpyrifos," Clarissa said.

"Marta," Mike said.

I began to lightly touch my eyes as if fending off a small horde of wasps while Khaled looked at me sideways.

"Uh," the Administrator said.

"Wait, what's happening with chlorpyrifos?" asked Brenda Ortiz, a forty-odd-year-old black female water-law expert and breast-cancer survivor sitting four rows back on the far left side. She wore a pussy-bow blouse, recently had adopted the constantly outraged expression of a high school algebra teacher, and two years previous had nearly put me in a headlock while trying unsuccessfully to bond with me over our similar medical problems. "Are you talking about the PANNA petition? I thought we were yanking that crap."

"We're pivoting," Mike said.

"We're switching gears," said Clarissa.

"Um," the Administrator said, looking at his phone.

"And Marta's doing that?" Brenda asked.

The Administrator's phone suddenly rang again. He glared at the screen. Gingerly, he poked at it. We could all hear a man screaming. The man was Donald Trump. The Administrator sighed and walked out of the room once more, followed by the security ghouls.

As Mike began lecturing us again, I turned around and saw that every single miserable Bartleby in that room stared straight at me. I smiled weakly back at them and then looked at Khaled for help. But Khaled's face had turned red and tight, and he started quietly sobbing.

"And what's going to be great about the dynamic we're developing between oil and air, and coal and water, is how we're going to be able to harness corporate ingenuity and states' rights to develop a healthier planet for everybody," Mike said.

I stood up and made a vague gesture toward my pelvis that indicated "women's emergency." Mike and Clarissa pretended not to notice anything. I walked hastily out of the meeting, stiff-leggedly hurrying through the Reagan Building's intestinal series of corridors. Once out of sight, I ran through the halls, across Twelfth Street, and dashed into WJC North.

I entered my office and shut the door behind me. I trembled and grabbed the silver-framed photograph of my parents off my workspace. I did not look at it. I only pressed it to my abdomen and sat down hard on the floor, next to my chair. I rested my back uncomfortably against the various knobs and angles of my desk.

I closed my eyes.

It's important to be a good person, I thought, and to do good things that are not bad. But grudgingly doing something that you are told to do by a superior, after you make a sophisticated cost-benefit analysis and complain in a sarcastic tone, is different than doing a bad thing wholeheartedly, which could actually make you such a bad person that you'd be a stone-cold killer of other human beings, innocent human beings with fragile nervous and pulmonary systems, who are a lot like you are, or like you used to be.

It's important to be a good person and to not be a bad person,

I explained to myself. Being a bad person, though, is different than just doing one's job in a socially approved way with the endorsement of high government officials and a huge proportion, if not actually a majority, of American voters. If a person is directed to do things that are legal, then that is okay, because the laws have been vetted by reasonable people who are by definition not foaming-lipped homicidal maniacs. If a person rebelled against fulfilling their legal duties, say, by quitting their job and entering an uncertain labor market or burning down government buildings or racing naked through administrative offices shrieking dissents and obscenities, then that would seem unreasonable and like an overreaction, and unreasonable overreactions are stigmatized in this society as the deranged acts of the mentally ill.

At that moment, I wished that I had not wanted to be a writer and read all of those good books when I was young. I remembered that authors like Herman Melville and George Orwell and Jean-Paul Sartre and James Baldwin and Langston Hughes said the opposite thing from what I had just told myself, which is that you are bad if you do something that seems good or at least debatable but that you know in fact to be awful, the worst, the most evil, even though everyone else seems to like it. And if you do that bad thing, then you are the bad thing, you are the heinous one, you have committed a treason against some higher principle that cannot be cured by simply quitting and apologizing for past ill-judged actions. No, instead, you would deserve a terrible punishment.

In the hospital, I now understood with a stab of lifted blankness, I had learned a lesson that I later rinsed from my mind with legal training and lackadaisical adulting. Yes, in the cancer ward I had been filled with the crazed fury of the powerless and the murdered. I had tasted death, and I had known death, as if it had crawled up to me and smiled.

I clutched the photograph to me tighter as I remembered my parents' clenched faces, the sounds of their stricken praying. The past came rolling back to me in a hot, clear wave. It was almost as if my mother and father had returned from their vanishing and were accusing me of forgetting them, that I had ever loved them and that they had loved me. Within the midst of a total recall that felt more like a hallucination, I begged them to understand that I had done the best that I could in an impossible, horrible situation. But they wouldn't listen. Instead, their savage voices continued yelling at me from across hell. They sounded angry, disappointed in me, and somehow still very much alive. ✶

Several law clerks to Judge Alex Kozinski resigned Thursday, after the 9th U.S. Circuit Court of Appeals launched an inquiry into allegations of sexual misconduct lodged against the judge.

KEVIN DALEY, "Clerks Resign as 9th Circuit Launches Harassment Probe of Kozinski," *Daily Caller,* December 14, 2017

# Draft of a Letter of Recommendation to the Honorable Alex Kozinski, Which I Guess I'm Not Going to Send Now

December 16, 2017
Judge Alex Kozinski
125 S. Grand Ave.
Pasadena, CA 91105

To the Honorable Alex Kozinski, of the Ninth Circuit Court of Appeals,

I write this letter to give my most enthusiastic recommendation that you hire my former student, [NAME REDACTED], for a position in your chambers as a clerk. I have known [NAME REDACTED] since 2015, when she took my Criminal Law class here at [REDACTED] Law School.

[NAME REDACTED] proved from the very first week of the semester to be an extraordinary student: She demonstrated a keen legal mind by asking pressing questions that tackled the class's most difficult issues, such as why so many men in our casebook seem to get voluntary manslaughter mitigations when they assassinate their wives,[1] why battered women have such a

> NR
> Word choice.

> NR
> You're doing that overcompensation thing we talked about before; there's no need to fn letter of rec

---

1. *See, e.g.*, KADISH ET AL., CRIMINAL LAW AND ITS PROCESSES 463 (10th ed. 2017) (reproducing an abstract of Girouard v. State, 583 A.2d 718 (Md. 1991), which identified adultery as a "traditional" reasonable provocation in other jurisdictions); *see also* 2 W.

difficult time obtaining self-defense claims when they kill their abusers,[2] ~~and whether our rape laws[3] will ever actually protect women from the tsunamis of sexual assault and harassment that they apparently are doomed to endure in this country as a kind of blood-inheritance.~~

NR
Tone, run-on, relevance

[NAME REDACTED] then further demonstrated her intelligence and formidable work ethic to me the next year, when she enrolled in my Women and the Law seminar. She topped off a challenging and inquisitive in-class performance by delivering a spectacular final paper: Her manifesto, titled "Toward Reparations for Intersectional Women in the Age of the Anthropocene," topped out at 65 pages, contained 267 footnotes, and concluded with an original blank-verse poem ~~that argued for the impeachment of President Donald Trump on the grounds of his sexual harassment of Jessica Leeds, Samantha Holvey, and Rachel Cooks.[4] For this paper, she received an A-plus.~~

NR
I would emphasize the doctrinal strengths of her paper

NR
Regarding this week's events you might need to "read the room" more in this paragraph

It is on these bases that I recommend [NAME REDACTED] to your chambers, as she would prove an invaluable addition to any office of the law. Her work ethic, empathy, and astonishing capacity for legal exegeses make her a resource that you would well regret passing on. Moreover, since you are universally regarded as one of the most brilliant legal minds on the circuit, you have earned a status as a "feeder" judge[5] who could potentially gain [NAME REDACTED] a Supreme

NR
Is she on law review? Hopefully an editorial position? I'd talk more about that

---

LaFave and A. Scott, *Substantive Criminal Law* § 7.10(b)(5) (1986) ("We note that '[t]he modern tendency is to extend the rule of mitigation beyond the narrow situation where one spouse actually catches the other in the act of committing adultery,'" *cited in* Knight v. State, 907 So. 2d 470, 478 (Ala. Crim. App. 2004).).

2. *See* KADISH, *id.*, at 903 (reproducing an abstract of State v. Norman, 378 S.E.2d 8 (N.C. 1989) (refusing a self-defense claim to a woman who killed her husband, who had been severely battering her for years).

3. *See, e.g., id.* at 413 (reproducing an abstract of Commonwealth v. Sherry, 437 N.E.2d 224 (1982), which suggested that state rape laws proved so inept at punishing sexual assault that we should eliminate the traditional requirement that prosecutors prove a defendant's guilty mind).

4. ~~These three women are now asking Congress for an investigation. *See* Dan Merica, *Women Detail Sexual Allegations Against Trump*, CNN (Dec. 11, 2017, 6:46 A.M.), http://www.cnn.com/2017/12/11/politics/donald-trump-women-allegations/index.html.~~

5. *See* Lawrence Baum, *Hiring Supreme Court Law Clerks: Probing the Ideological Linkage between Judges and Justices*, 98 MARQUETTE L. REV. 333, 342 n.37 (2014) (you have provided twenty-six clerks to Kennedy).

a Supreme Court clerkship

honorable        sadfa;adjk;

NR
Alignment
problem

You are one of the best and brightest

NR
typo

You have sent several clerks to positions on the Supreme Court, such as the male Alexander ("Sasha") Volokh, who clerked for Alito before ascending to a professorship at Emory Law,[6] the female Theane Evangelis, who was sent "upstairs" to Sandra Day O'Connor and is now a partner at Gibson, Dunn,[7] the female Sandra Segal Ikuta, who also clerked for O'Connor and is now herself a Ninth Circuit judge,[8] and also the female Heidi Bond, a.k.a. Courtney Milan,[9] who

who

the list goes on

partners judges academics like me but at fancier schools etc[10]

It is true that [NAME REDACTED] is a woman, a woman of color, and that in the past several days it has come to the attention of the news media that your honor is accused of verbally sexually harassing a variety of female clerks and/or interns.

NR
No

Like, I guess, making the aforementioned Heidi Bond/Courtney Milan look at porn and then quizzing her about it.[11] Or saying garbage to Emily Murphy about being naked.[12] ~~All of the reports of sexual harassment that I have read are race~~

NR
No.
No.

---

6. *See* Emory Univ. Sch. of Law, *Faculty Profiles: Alexander Volokh*, http://law.emory.edu/faculty-and-scholarship/faculty-profiles/volokh-profile.html (last visited Dec. 11, 2017).

7. *See* Gibson Dunn, *Theane Evangelis, Partner*, http://www.gibsondunn.com/lawyers/tevangelis (last visited Dec. 11, 2017).

8. *See Sandra Segal Ikuta*, WIKIPEDIA, https://en.wikipedia.org/wiki/Sandra_Segal_Ikuta (last visited Dec. 11, 2017).

9. *See* Heidi Bond, *#metoo*, COURTNEY MILAN, http://www.courtneymilan.com/metoo/kozinski.html (last modified Dec. 8, 2017). Courtney Milan is the nom de plume of Heidi Bond. *Id.*

10. *See, e.g.*, Univ. of Notre Dame, *Jennifer Mason McAward*, http://law.nd.edu/directory/jennifer-mason-mcaward/ (clerking for you and then going on to clerk for O'Connor).

11. *See* David Choi, *Former Clerks Accuse Reagan-Appointed Appeals Court Judge of Sexual Misconduct*, BUSINESS INSIDER (Dec. 8, 2017, 9:21 P.M.), http://www.businessinsider.com/judge-alex-kozinski-porn-sexual-allegation-9th-circuit-2017-12.

12. *See* Maura Dolan, *9th Circuit Judge Alex Kozinski Is Accused by Former Clerks of Making Sexual Comments*, L.A. TIMES (Dec. 8, 2017, 5:45 P.M.) ("Murphy, who clerked for a different 9th Circuit Court of Appeals judge, said Kozinski joked to her in front of other people that she should work out naked at a courthouse gym because so few people used it."). Murphy now teaches at UC Hastings. *See* U.C. Hastings, *Faculty,*

~~neutral, so I can't tell about whether it's race and sex harass-~~
~~ment or sex harassment specifically pertaining to white women~~
~~or maybe also differently abled women or queer wymyn or~~[13]

NR
Relevance?
Spelling?
Clarity?

You don't seem to deny these allegations but instead have
said that you don't remember any of that happening,[14] sort of
like Reagan did when he had Alzheimer's and was being de-
posed during the Iran-Contra imbroglio.[15] But then maybe you

---

*Emily Murphy, Biography,* http://www.uchastings.edu/faculty/murphy/index.php (last
visited Dec. 11, 2017).

13. ~~*See, cf.,* Kimberlé Crenshaw, *Demarginalizing the Intersection of Race and Sex: A
Black Feminist Critique of Antidiscrimination Doctrine, Feminist Theory and Antiracist
Politics,* 1989 U. CHI. LEGAL F. 139, 140 (1989), which explains how the ways that
women of color experience workplace bias are erased by dominant approaches to race
and gender discrimination. On the intersectional woman's experience of sexual
harassment and the failures of courts to adequately address how race and sex must be
considered together in harassment cases; *see also* Kathryn Abrams, *Title VII and the
Complex Female Subject,* 92 MICH. L. REV. 2479, 2501 (1994) ("The acknowledgment . . .
that black women may be differently situated than white women with respect to
proving a sexual harassment claim reflects a recognition that even as women—that is,
those who are claiming sexual harassment—claimants are constructed by race as well as
gender. But the incomplete and flawed elaboration of that understanding by the courts
has created difficulties."). We must also, of course, consider the intersections of class,
queerness, and disability when deciding how to respond to the muddled newspaper
accounts of the complaints made against you. Insofar as clerks are experiencing
harassment at the Court of Appeals (at any hands), we cannot marshal a one-size-fits-
all outrage or fear but rather must worry about how the multivalent forms of sexual
harassment may be experienced by a class of clerks that hopefully exhibits numerous
forms of intersectionality. *See, e.g.,* Sheerine Alemzadeh, *Protecting the Margins:
Intersectional Strategies to Protecting Gender Outlaws from Workplace Harassment,* 37
N.Y.U. REV. L. & SOC. CHANGE 339, 368–69 (2013) ("LGBT advocates, feminists and
all marginalized workers, should continue to challenge, develop, and transform Title
VII sexual harassment jurisprudence to reflect and protect the fluid, evolving, and
intersectional gender identities that comprise today's workplace."). I don't know,
though: the other layer of oppression here may be in the paucity of intersectional
people who are clerking on the Court of Appeals in the first place, so that we are
struggling to get to a position where we can worry about the intersectional experiences
of abuse and dominance that we will face once there. *See* CHAMBLISS *infra* note 35.~~

14. *See* Dolan, *supra* note 12 ("'I have no recollection of that happening.'").

15. *Excerpts from Reagan's Testimony on the Iran-Contra Affair,*
N.Y. TIMES (Feb. 23, 1990), http://www.nytimes.com/1990/02/23/us/excerpts-from
-reagan-s-testimony-on-the-iran-contra-affair.html?pagewanted=all ("But that could
be my memory. I don't remember."). On the debate about Reagan's mental health, *see*
Jane Mayer, *Worrying about Reagan,* NEW YORKER, Feb. 24, 2011, https://www
.newyorker.com/news/news-desk/worrying-about-reagan.

do remember because when asked about these complaints by the *Los Angeles Times*, you didn't say, "Huh?" but instead replied, "If this is all they are able to dredge up after 35 years, I am not too worried."[16] And then you also said, "I have been a judge for 35 years and during that time have had over 500 employees in my chambers. I treat all of my employees as family and work very closely with most of them. I would never intentionally do anything to offend anyone and it is regrettable that a handful have been offended by something I may have said or done."[17]

It's cute how you use the passive voice,[18] as if this whole thing were a law school hypothetical—and then also appear to lay blame on your hypersensitive clerks for not getting the joke in the first place[19]

It appears that you understand that you are currently as safely ensconced in your position as a feudal lord in fourteenth-century Bohemia,[20] and that is why you are not Al Frankenishly

> **NR**
> Punctuation; annoying sarcasm. Intro signal for this fn not found in list in BB 1.2(a)

> **NR**
> This fn is full of surmise and conjecture! "Great cases like hard cases make bad law. For great cases are called great, not by reason of their importance in shaping the law of the future, but because of some accident of immediate overwhelming interest which appeals to the feelings and distorts the judgement." OWH Jr., dissenting in *Northern Securities Co. v. United States*, 193 U.S. 197, 400-01 (1904)

---

16. *See* Dolan, *supra* note 12.

17. Matt Zapotosky, *Prominent Appeals Court Judge Alex Kozinski Accused of Sexual Misconduct*, WASH. POST (Dec. 8, 2017), https://www.washingtonpost.com/world/national-security/prominent-appeals-court-judge-alex-kozinski-accused-of-sexual-misconduct/2017/12/08/1763e2b8-d913-11e7-a841-2066faf731ef_story.html?utm_term=.1c2a14817dd7.

18. *See* ANNE STILLMAN, GRAMMATICALLY CORRECT 289 (1997) ("In speech, the passive voice is often adopted by individuals wishing to minimize or evade personal responsibility for something.").

19. *OMFG*, Anne Lawton, *The Bad Apple Theory in Sexual Harassment Law*, 13 GEO. MASON L. REV. 817, 864 (2005) ("Judicial skepticism of sexual harassment claims is not uncommon. The concern is that absent tight judicial oversight sexual harassment law will become the legal dumping ground of hypersensitive employees.").

20. You are unlikely to be impeached, since at this moment you have not been accused of a misdemeanor, either high or low, *see* U.S. CONST., art. II, § 4. It is conceivable that you could be ousted for bad behavior, according to Saikrishna Prakash and Steven D. Smith, *see Removing Judges without Impeachment*, 116 YALE L.J. FORUM (Oct. 17, 2006), https://www.yalelawjournal.org/forum/removing-federal-judges-without-impeachment. *See also* U.S. CONST., art. III, § 1 ("The Judges, both of the supreme and inferior Courts, shall hold their Offices during good Behavior."). It's most probable that you will endure an aimless internal investigation, as you apparently did the last time you were found to be indulging in exploitative joshing. *See* Scott Glover, *9th Circuit's Chief Judge Posted Sexually Explicit Matter on His Website*, L.A. TIMES (June 11, 2008, 12:00 A.M.), http://www.latimes.com/local/la-me-kozinski12-2008jun12-story.html (addressing your collection of porn stored on a public website, which was the subject of a scandal in 2008). On judicial internal investigations, see the Judicial Improvements Act of 2002, Pub. L. No. 107-273, §§ 11041–44, 116 Stat. 1758 (2002) (codified in scattered sections of 28 U.S.C.) (providing the judiciary with the authority

to take and investigate complaints of judicial conduct "prejudicial to the effective and expeditious administration" of the bench). On the self-regulating character of the protocol, *see* Arthur D. Hellman, *When Judges Are Accused: An Initial Look at the New Federal Judicial Misconduct Rules*, 22 NOTRE DAME J.L. ETHICS & PUB. POL'Y 325, 333 (2008). On the ineffectiveness of this setup, *see* Lara A. Bazelon, *Putting the Mice in Charge of the Cheese: Why Federal Judges Cannot Always Be Trusted to Police Themselves and What Congress Can Do about It*, 97 KY. L.J. 439, 441–42 (2009) (discussing "institutional bias"). Of course, Judge Kozinski, if you had been alleged to have done more than just talking about pornography or naked Pilates, then it would be at least conceivable that you could be successfully kicked out by Congress. If, for example, you had subjected someone to unwanted sexual touching, then that could qualify as a misdemeanor sexual battery in California, which is where you currently sit on the Ninth Circuit. *See* Cal. Penal Code § 243.4(e)(1), https://leginfo.legislature.ca.gov/faces /codes_displaySection.xhtml?sectionNum=243.4.&lawCode=PEN ("Any person who touches an intimate part of another person, if the touching is against the will of the person touched, and is for the specific purpose of sexual arousal, sexual gratification, or sexual abuse, is guilty of misdemeanor sexual battery."). This offense has a one-year statute of limitations. *See* Cal. Penal Code § 802(a). Does that mean that you would then be impeached and removed? Unlikely—only fifteen federal judges have been impeached, and of those, only eight were convicted by the Senate. *See* Kenneth A. Klukowski, *Severability Doctrine: How Much of a Statute Should Federal Courts Invalidate?*, 16 TEX. REV. L. & POL. 1, 111 (2011). Those removed have been accused of accepting bribes, perjury, federal tax evasion, corrupt dealing with litigants, treason, crappy administration of an admiralty case, impressive intoxication, and heretical profanity. *See Senate Removes Federal Judge in Impeachment Conviction*, CNN (Dec. 8, 2010, 12:46 P.M.), http://www.cnn.com/2010/POLITICS/12/08/washington.impeach .judge/index.html (G. Thomas Porteous of the Eastern District of Louisiana, removed in 2010 for perjury); *Judge Walter L. Nixon Impeached after Perjury Conviction*, CONST. L. REP., https://constitutionallawreporter.com/2017/06/21/judge-walter-nixon-impeached -perjury-conviction/ (last visited Feb. 11, 2018) (Nixon, from the Southern District of Mississippi, removed in 1989 for perjury); Ruth Marcus, *Senate Removes Hastings*, WASH. POST (Oct. 21, 1989), http://www.washingtonpost.com/wp-srv/politics /campaigns/junkie/links/hastings102189.htm (Alcee Hastings, of the Southern District of Florida, removed in 1989 for conspiracy to extort a bribe); *see Harry Claiborne, 86, Is Dead; Was Removed as U.S. Judge*, N.Y. TIMES (Jan. 22, 2004), http://www.nytimes.com /2004/01/22/us/harry-claiborne-86-is-dead-was-removed-as-us-judge.html?_r=0 (Claiborne, of the District of Nevada, convicted of tax evasion in 1984 and impeached in 1986); Michael J. Broyde, *Expediting Impeachment: Removing Article III Federal Judges after Criminal Conviction*, 17 HARV. J.L. & PUB. POL'Y 157, 186 (1994) (Halstead L. Ritter, of the Southern District of Florida, was accused of bribery and evasion of taxes but was ultimately only removed for having brought disrespect to his court and having rendered himself unfit to serve as a judge, as a consequence of the alleged behavior); *id.* at 222, n.16 (Robert Wodrow Archbald, of the United States Commerce Court, removed in 1913 for improper business dealings with litigants); Michael J. Gerhardt & Michael Ashley Stein, *The Politics of Early Justice: Federal Judicial Selection, 1789–1861*, warbling about how ashamed you are[21] or Weinsteinishly

---

100 Iowa L. Rev. 551, 600 (2015) (West Hughes Humphreys, of the United States District Courts for the Middle, Eastern, and Western Districts of Tennessee, removed for treason in 1863 after leaving the bench to serve as a judge for the Confederacy); Jason J. Vicente, *Impeachment: A Constitutional Primer*, 3 Tex. Rev. L. & Pol. 117, 135 (1998) (John Pickering, of the District of New Hampshire, removed in 1802 for refusing to hear testimony and grant an appeal in an admiralty case, as well as for being drunk and cursing on the bench). None of these cases involve physical, and certainly not verbal, sexual harassment. There was one case where the House of Representatives passed impeachment articles involving physically venereal misbehavior—a.k.a. maybe rape: Samuel Kent of the Southern District of Texas was indicted in 2008 and 2009 on charges of abusive sexual contact, aggravated sexual abuse, attempted aggravated sexual abuse, and obstruction of justice, *see* Frederik, *Impeaching Samuel B. Kent, Judge of the U.S. District Court for the Southern District of Texas*, Daily Kos (June 21, 2009, 7:12 A.M.), https://www.dailykos.com/stories/2009/6/21/745120/-. Kent allegedly pinned his secretary against his door and kissed her on the mouth, put her hand on his crotch, touched and groped her "outside and inside [her] clothes," and committed unspecified "worse" acts. *See* Tom Cohen, *Victims Allege Years of Sexual Misconduct by Federal Judge*, CNN (June 3, 2009, 8:17 P.M.), http://www.cnn.com/2009/POLITICS/06/03/judge .impeachment/index.html ("Details of what [a victim] called 'worse sexual assault' were included in her written statement to judicial investigators."). However, Kent resigned before he could be removed. *See* Glenn Thrush, *Impeachment Judge Resigns*, Politico (June 26, 2009, 6:13 P.M.), https://www.politico.com/blogs/on-congress/2009/06 /impeachment-judge-resigns-019392. It also bears observing that Kent's demise happened in the Golden Age of 2009, one year after Barack Obama had been elected president—and not during the current hell-pit of an era when the president himself stands accused of sexual harassment, *see supra* note 4, and when the Republican National Committee helped fund the alleged child molester Roy Moore's bid in the Alabama Senate special election after Donald Trump endorsed him on December 4, 2017, *see* Rebecca Berg & Sophie Tatum, *RNC Is Getting Back into Alabama Senate Race*, CNN (Dec. 4, 2017, 11:40 P.M.), http://www.cnn.com/2017/12/04/politics/rnc-roy-moore -alabama/index.html. Also, the Senate needs a two-thirds vote for conviction, *see* Jason J. Vicente, *Impeachment: A Constitutional Primer*, 3 Tex. Rev. L. & Pol. 117, 128 (1998) (citing U.S. Const., art. I, § 3, cl. 6). But the Republicans currently enjoy a shaky 52–48 majority, *see* Megan Trimble, *Obama Robocall: Support Doug Jones, Don't Vote for Roy Moore*, U.S. News & World Report (Dec. 11, 2017, 10:31 A.M.), https://www .usnews.com/news/national-news/articles/2017-12-11/barack-obama-records-robocall -urging-alabama-voters-to-reject-roy-moore. So it seems you'd be okay if things ever got to that level.

21. *See* Mallory Shelbourne, *Franken Says He's "Ashamed" by Allegations, Will Return to Work Monday*, The Hill (Nov. 26, 2017, 2:49 P.M.), http://thehill.com/homenews /senate/361869-franken-says-hes-embarrassed-and-ashamed-by-allegations-will-return -to-work.

attempting to blackmail your victims with "dirt" that failed journalists dig up after being paid a hefty retainer.[22]

And if you're not going to be impeached, then shouldn't [NAME REDACTED] have the chance of clerking for you? And so then shouldn't I be writing her this letter of recommendation so that you can hire her and honorably ask her about pornography while at the same time providing her with exquisite legal training? Or am I abusing her myself by encouraging her to apply to clerk in your chambers?

But then she can make her own decisions. It's not like I'm forcing her, and we all have to make compromises in this life.

I mean, not only have I endured sex jokes and bullshit, but I have been sexually assaulted myself, which is why I got into the "Women and the Law" racket in the first place. I got raped by my boyfriend when I was seventeen and

I actually completely forgot about that for years until this #metoo[23] thing started happening, and then I remembered again, which is making this letter hard to write because I am becoming blindingly enraged.

But it's worth emphasizing that you didn't do that to the clerks. Which is to say I should acknowledge that you are not said to have touched anyone on the breast[24] or thigh or

**NR**
Writing her this letter of recommendation is PART OF YOUR JOB

**NR**
Exactly.

**NR**
word choice see Chicago Manual of Style rule 5.223 ("Careful writers avoid language that reasonable readers might find offensive or distracting").

---

22. *See* Oil Coleman, *Weinstein Tried to Hire Gossip Writer to Get Dirt on Accusers*, TMZ.COM (Dec. 2, 2017, 2:43 P.M.), https://pagesix.com/2017/12/02/weinstein-tried-to -hire-gossip-writer-to-get-dirt-on-accusers/.

23. Sandee Lamotte, *How #MeToo Could Move from Social Campaign to Social Change*, CNN (Nov. 9, 2017), http://www.cnn.com/2017/10/30/health/metoo-legacy /index.html.

24. Lindsey Bever & Paul Kane, *Sen. Al Franken Accused of Groping Again—This Time by an Army Veteran*, WASH. POST (Nov. 30, 2017), https://www.washingtonpost.com /news/powerpost/wp/2017/11/30/sen-al-franken-accused-of-groping-again-this-time -by-an-army-veteran/?utm_term=.50e979ff121d ("As Kemplin, then 27, posed for a photo with [Franken], she said, he put his arm around her and grabbed her breast, holding onto her for up to 10 seconds."); Nina Burleigh, *How Donald Trump Rules America's Garden of Dicks and Sparked the #metoo Movement*, NEWSWEEK (Nov. 9, 2017), http://www.newsweek.com/2017/11/17/me-too-donald-trump-harvey-weinstein -powerful-predators-facing-accusers-704658.html ("Trump allegedly touched the breast of Karena Virginia while she waited for a car outside the U.S. Open. 'Don't you know who I am? Don't you know who I am?' she said he told her after she recoiled.").

molested them as children[25] or raped them[26] or asked them to be your surrogate[27] or to have sex with you[28]

~~you just "may" have just said horrible gross things that make women feel infinitesimally small and insignificant and~~

25. *See* Michael Finnegan, *Roy Moore Dismisses Sexual Misconduct Allegations as "Ritual Defamation,"* L.A. TIMES (Dec. 10, 2017), http://www.latimes.com/politics /washington/la-na-pol-essential-washington-updates-roy-moore-dismisses-sexual -abuse-1512942626-htmlstory.html.

26. *See* Rebecca Keegan, *Paz de la Huerta Says Harvey Weinstein Raped Her Twice. Will That Bring Him to Justice?*, VANITY FAIR (Nov. 2, 2017), https://www.vanityfair.com /hollywood/2017/11/paz-de-la-huerta-harvey-weinstein-allegations; *see* Winnie M. Li, *As a Survivor of Violent Rape, I Believe #MeToo Is a Powerful Force for Victims*, THEJOURNAL.IE (Nov. 16, 2017), http://www.thejournal.ie/readme/social-media-sexual -abuse-impact-opinion-3701269-Nov2017/; *see* Halee Gray Scott, *#MeToo: I Was Raped by My Pastor*, WASH. POST (Oct. 16, 2017), https://www.washingtonpost.com/news/acts -of-faith/wp/2017/10/16/metoo-i-was-raped-by-my-pastor/?utm_term=.83139ed36300.

27. *See* Katie Rogers, *Trent Franks, Accused of Offering $5 Million to Aide for Surrogacy, Resigns*, N.Y. TIMES (Dec. 8, 2017), https://www.nytimes.com/2017/12/08/us/politics /trent-franks-sexual-surrogacy-harassment.html.

28. *See* Michael Levinson & Cristela Guerra, *Sexual Harassment Allegation Lead Millions of Women to Say #MeToo*, BOS. GLOBE (Oct. 16, 2017), https://www.bostonglobe .com/metro/2017/10/16/metoo-campaign-highlights-prevalence-harassment /NH4hDAFk6F7XXKgETSoojI/story.html ("One woman recalled a man in a park jamming his hand down her pants when she was 16. Another said she was accosted by her resident adviser in college. Still another said her boss told her he would give her a raise in exchange for oral sex."); *see U.S. Rep John Conyers, Civil Rights Icon, Allegedly Demanded Sex from Female Staffers*, WOMEN IN THE WORLD (Nov. 21, 2017), https:// womenintheworld.com/2017/11/21/u-s-rep-john-conyers-civil-rights-icon-allegedly -demanded-sex-from-female-staffers/.

NR
ipse dixit

NR
Hyperbole

NR
Re fn 32, why are you connecting domestic violence and failed self-defense claims to Kozinski's fumblings? This is not one huge related system of bad judgment or a vast conspiracy of omnipotent horrible men. Non tali causa pro tali.

NR
punctuation, hysteria

powerless,[29] which is a kind of spirit murder[30] for which you are at this point likely to be accorded a defense,[31] and also you don't have to worry about retaliation of other kinds because we exist in a law and society that systematically denies women the promise of self-help[32]

You are untouchable with your coolness, and despite the current female uprising that threatens to demolish your privilege right down to its "studs," I fear the coming backlash will save you you will probably die on the bench elegantly shrugging off stories of your lechery as if they actually burnished your nerdy reputation into a high gloss[33] that reflects the kind of regnant Casanova who always leaves in his wake a trail of broken disappointed woebegone bitter harridans who make baseless accusations

Judge Kozinski, despite all the terrible things that are currently being said about your conduct and character, I am still writing you this letter of recommendation in order that you

---

29. Cf. Allison Westfall, The Forgotten Provision: How the Courts Have Misapplied Title VII in Cases of Express Rejection of Sexual Advances, 81 U. CIN. L. REV. 269, 287 (2012) ("Sexual harassment makes women feel 'humiliated . . . embarrassed, and . . . angry.'") (quoting CATHARINE A. MACKINNON, SEXUAL HARASSMENT OF WORKING WOMEN: A CASE OF SEX DISCRIMINATION 47 (1979)). On MacKinnon's reorientation of the problem, see her argument that we should focus on inequality of power, not on women's states of mind, in Catharine A. MacKinnon, Rape Redefined, 10 HARV. L. & POL'Y REV. 440, 441 (2016) ("Like one wing flapping, consent analysis focuses endlessly on B—what she has in her mind or lets someone 'do to' her body. Inequality analysis, even in narrow form, starts where the interactions in question temporally start: with A, and what he does with his power.").

30. See Deborah Tuerkheimer, Street Harassment as Sexual Subordination: The Phenomenology of Gender-Specific Harm, 12 WIS. WOMEN'S L.J. 167, 190 (1997) ("[T]he harasser has caused me to suffer a spirit murder.") (quoting Deirdre Davis, The Harm That Has No Name: Street Harassment, Embodiment, and African American Women, 4 U.C.L.A. WOMEN'S L.J. 133, 176–77 (1994)).

31. See supra note 1.

32. See KADISH ET AL., supra note 1, at 903.

33. On your Wikipedia page, for example, Wikipedia crowd sourcers have cited your infamous 1980s appearance on the Dating Game game show where you appeared to force a woman to kiss you, but the Wikipedia people only smilingly call this a "surprise kiss," probably because your date was giggling, which under male supremacy always means not agonized disgust but instead consent. See, e.g., Alex Kozinski, WIKIPEDIA, https://en.wikipedia.org/wiki/Alex_Kozinski (last visited Dec. 7, 2017). See the clip at Kozinski on the Dating Game (and Squiggy, too!), YOUTUBE (Nov. 2, 2006) (last visited Dec. 7, 2017).

hire [NAME REDACTED] to your prestigious chambers. I do this because I want [NAME REDACTED] to have the same glittering opportunities that you have enjoyed. You clerked for Justice Anthony Kennedy on the Ninth Circuit and then Justice Warren Earl Burger at the Supreme Court. You were elevated to the Ninth Circuit by President Ronald Reagan in 1985 at the age of thirty-five, which made you the youngest person serving as a federal judge in the country. And then in 2007 you were named chief judge of the Ninth Circuit, a laurel that has brought you national recognition and puissance.[34] [NAME REDACTED] is a brilliant lawyer-in-training, and I know she could achieve similar herculean feats if she were given half the life chances as you, and that is just one reason why she should be toiling away for you in Pasadena next year.

But I also want you to hire [NAME REDACTED], a woman of color, for two additional reasons. First, because the presence of minority women clerks in the esteemed halls of the Ninth Circuit, or any federal clerkship, proves increasingly rare, and the scarcity of their influence at your level probably helps explain the damaged state of the law and nation at the present time.[35] Second, if you did not regularly hire clerks like [NAME REDACTED], then you would grow all the more emboldened to replicate self-serving Title VII decisions like *Swenson v. Potter*, where you set aside a jury verdict in a sexual harassment case involving a hearing-impaired Postal Service employee who worried that a coworker was going to rape her.[36] Or you'd feel extra free to replicate your dissent in *Washington v. Trump*, where you exulted that outland "foreigners" have no claim against the Muslim ban because they enjoy no due process rights.[37]

NR
run-on;
character
assassination

---

34. For the accomplishments listed in this paragraph, see Bio information on Alex Kozinski, ASSOCIATED PRESS, June 11, 2008.

35. *See* ELIZABETH CHAMBLISS, ILLP REVIEW 2017: THE STATE OF DIVERSITY AND INCLUSION IN THE LEGAL PROFESSION 16 (2017), http://www.theiilp.com/resources /Pictures/IILP_2017_Demographic_Survey.pdf ("The percentage of minority graduates with judicial clerkships, in particular, has dropped, from 10.2% in 1998 to 6.5% in 2014."). *See also* Crenshaw, *supra* note 13, at 140.

36. Swenson v. Potter, 271 F.3d 1184, 1198 (9th Cir. 2001). On Melody Swenson's hearing impairment, see *id.* at 1193. On her fears of being raped, see *id.* at 1189. *See also id.* at 1200, 1204 (Fletcher, J., dissenting.).

37. Washington v. Trump, 858 F.3d 1168, 1171–72 (9th Cir. 2017) ("First, the panel's reasoning rests solely on Due Process. But the vast majority of foreigners covered by the executive order have *no* Due Process rights. Nevertheless, the district court

Perhaps you have been able to tell from the foregoing, your honor, that I am finding it difficult to write the kind of functional letter of recommendation that my cohort is expected to supply in this setting, which should be full of abstract pieties and seeming objectivity. It also seems that I am fast losing faith in the institution that is supposed to protect the rights of humans who are not male and white and whatever else helps them become successful law clerks and/or sexual predators in this society.

NR
burn this letter.

So your honor
Judge Kozinski
you see
you see that all of this is untenable
and you should resign.
Sincerely,

Professor Sandra Martínez ★

---

enjoined the order's travel provisions in their entirety, even as applied to the millions of aliens who have no constitutional rights whatsoever because they have never set foot on American soil.") (Kozinski, J., dissenting) (emphasis in the original).

Californians recovering from wildfires in 2017 and 2018 will be able to apply for up to $12 billion of that aid, including farm assistance, highway money and flood infrastructure, according to an analysis from the office of Sen. Dianne Feinstein, D-Calif. Efforts to pass the bill dragged on for months. The Democratic-controlled House passed a bill in January and another last month that included billions of dollars for Californians recovering from wildfires. The holdup had been in the Senate over Trump's refusal to consider additional money to help Puerto Rico recover from Hurricane Maria, which killed an estimated 3,000 people in 2017.

TAL KOPAN, "House Sends Long-Stalled California Wildfire Relief Bill to Trump," *San Francisco Chronicle,* June 3, 2019

# Paradise

"I THINK WE SHOULD GO, DAD," I said, shielding my eyes from the wind. The sheriff had tweeted an evacuation order for Pulga twenty minutes before. It was quarter to eight in the morning, and the sky didn't look right. Ten minutes ago it had turned from bright blue to a thick, light, orangey-gray.

"I'm not going anywhere," said Wesley, my father-in-law. He looked eastward with his face crinkling up. He's a big bull of a man, about five foot eleven now. He's white and bald and wears glasses. He has a chipped front tooth and his son's blue eyes. He wore a Cowboys T-shirt and blue nylon shorts and black flip-flops. Eighty years old.

"That sky, though," I said. I am five foot two with a big ass and strong arms. I'm forty-four. My black hair frizzed all around my head. I wore black nylon shorts and a pink nylon top and no shoes.

We stood in the front yard of the house, which was on Edgewood Lane. Wes's huge black Yukon sat in the driveway. I'd parked my little green Prius by the curb. The winds whipped down the road. The crape myrtle bushes I planted on the sides of the house right after Mike died flattened and splayed from the hard gusts. The cottonwoods fringing the road shook like they were getting slapped by a huge hand. Dead, gold grass and dried leaves crawled along our front yard instead of a proper lawn. Back inside,

Jessie still dawdled, drinking her milk in the kitchen and playing with Henrietta.

"Shelly," I said. Our neighbor, a hefty yellowed-haired woman, had just walked fast out of her house wearing flowered shorts and a white T-shirt.

"Fernanda, they're evacuating Pulga," she said. Pulga's a little town maybe fifteen miles away from Paradise as the crow flies.

"I know," I said.

"You got Jessie?" Shelly asked.

"Yeah, I think we're going to go in like ten minutes," I said. Wesley shook his head.

"Wes," Shelly said, grimacing. "Sonny boy, smell that air."

Already, it smelled like burning, just like that.

"Fires here every year," Wesley said, tilting his head my way. "She can go."

"She is the cat's mother," Shelly said, pulling her phone out of her shorts pocket and jabbing at it.

Ten or twelve other neighbors came hurrying out of their houses. Martin, Tillie, Babs, Fred, Nancy, I can't remember. Already, Serena Hammer's Honda and Joe Tate's Chevrolet chugged down Edgewood toward Pearson and Skyway. The rest of us stood out there gawking for probably too long, making clucking noises and talking about the Carr fire in Nor Cal last August.

"Concow lines are down," Shelly said, gripping her iPhone. Concow's another town, closer to us than Pulga. "Can't get hold of my mother."

"Evacuation for Paradise," Martin suddenly hollered, from two houses down. He's another white man—but they're all white except for me on this street, so why keep saying it. His nose practically touched his iPhone screen. "They're telling us to haul out."

Shelly hustled indoors. People started moving back and forth between their houses and their cars. They lugged clothes, water, lamps, pillows, makeup cases, books, pictures, all this unnecessary crap.

I looked at Wesley. He sniffed.

"I'm not running," he said. "I built this house in 1982."

"Wes," I said. "Look at the color of that goddam sky."

"This is my house. You just live here," he said. "You and Jessie can go."

He started walking toward the myrtles on the left side of the house, where the hose was.

I ran inside.

\* \* \*

Wes didn't want his son Mike to marry me. It wasn't a secret. I'm Pomo and Mexican and grew up in the Evergreen Mobile Home Park with my parents, Lupita and Ben. Mike and I knew each other from around. We'd seen each other at Paradise High, where we graduated in '92, and then later at Butte Community. But Mike had been raised up on Edgewood. When he was young, he dated girls like valedictorian Renee Henson and cheerleader Willa Miller, whose parents lived on Pentz and Mountain View. I stuck to a crew of Native, black, and Mexican kids who played video games and got sent to detention when they shrugged at the white teachers. Mike was a blockhead back then anyway, and I wasn't interested. He played football, and I'd seen him soaking wet and drunk at house parties on Saturday nights.

Mike was above me because my parents worked as janitors at Paradise's Best Western and Chico's Oxford Suites. But his pa, Wesley Noonan, was one of the best lawyers in town. Wes set up a three-man outfit, Noonan, Gump & Penzer, up on Skyway, where he did estate planning for folks from Paradise to Chico. Wes was a big man, and not just physically. When he'd walk into Tattie's Café, where I bused and then waitressed during high school, diners would look up at him in an eager way. Tattie herself (she's now dead) would run up to him, wiping her hands on her apron and seating him, his pretty red-haired wife, Laura, and Mike, right away.

"I'll have the steak and a scotch," Wes would say to me, on the nights when I took his order. He looked me over once and then never again.

"Would you like that rare, sir?" I'd ask him, though I knew.

He'd sit there and sniff, like he was mad that the scotch wasn't in front of him already.

"He likes it well," Laura said, smiling. Mike would gawk at me a little bit and then blush and look down.

The twentieth time I pretended to forget that Wes liked his meat scorched, he set his jaw and smacked at a water glass so that it went flying.

"How many times do I have to tell you the same thing?" he snapped, while the water dripped.

"Dad," Mike had said.

Laura had begun to mop up the spill with her napkin.

"What's my name?" I'd asked him then.

Wes's face darkened with puzzlement. "What?"

"What's my name?" I asked again. I pointed to my nametag, FERNANDA. "Come on, I've been getting you steak for a year. You must know it by now." I just didn't like the way he did business.

Tattie came running over, wailing, "We've got this covered. The whole bill for tonight's taken care of, Wesley."

To do penance, Tattie made me keep bringing the table complimentary olives and fried cheese bites that came out of my check. But even though I fed that mope to the gills, I still got fired later that night.

* * *

Mike and I started dating eight years ago. I'd gotten a divorce and come back home from Dublin, Georgia, where my first husband, Scott, lived. Mike hadn't gone to law school like his father wanted but instead became a police officer for the PDP. He did K-9 patrol first with a German Shepherd named Logan and then with Henrietta. We were both in our midthirties around this time and so more free from our parents. My folks had moved back to Sonoma, where my dad's people were, and so I could stretch my legs a little. And Mike had become a grown man a world away from the drunk dummy who blushed and stammered at restaurants with his pop. He'd learned CPR, community policing. He was married for seven years and then divorced Willa in '01. He rented a little red house with Logan on Magalia Street and kept it tidy as a tea kettle.

I lived back in the mobile-home park in Evergreen where my parents had raised me, so we were still in two different worlds. But once I returned from Dublin, I joined a Facebook page, "Life in Paradise, Ca.," and I guess he saw me on it. We messaged back and forth about the "good old days" in PHS as if we'd known each other better than we had. After a while he asked me out.

"I always had a crush on you," he said, on our fourth date. Jesus, but had he grown up into a strapping sonofabitch with these biceps on him and thick, hard thighs. He hadn't turned my head back in the day, but at the age of thirty-six, after the rejection from my husband, I got sort of frantic for him.

"Do you remember that night at Tattie's with your dad?"

"Yes," he said and cracked up. "Hot diggity, I thought, watch out."

"I'll bet he was mad," I said.

Mike had green eyes with long lashes. He nudged up onto me, and I felt the sweet heat coming off his mouth and his face. "He's always mad," he said.

\* \* \*

The reason why I know that Wes didn't want Mike to marry me was because on our wedding day he sat in the front pew, just shaking his head. I didn't care. I was the happiest I'd ever been. Mike and I had our baby, Jessie, a year and half later. The first German Shepherd, Logan, died, but then we got smart-as-a-wizard Henrietta. We four lived like queens and a prince in that ugly little red house.

Laura would come over Sundays to see the baby, but Wes kept himself to himself except on Jessie's birthday and on the holidays.

The second Thanksgiving we were married, Laura hosted the meal. I remember how I got Jessie dressed up in blue velvet with a little Peter Pan collar. I wore a white-lace dress, which I'd found at the Goodwill on East Avenue and spruced up by bleaching it and mending the torn slip. Mike wore green sweatpants and a brown sweatshirt and said that belts weren't for turkey. We all bustled into Wes and Laura's huge house admiring the figurines and the Chinese whatnots. I worried that Jessie would totter around screaming and break something, but when Laura kissed her all over and Wes started laughing at her antics, I let myself relax a little bit.

After the main course but before dessert, Mike took my hand and led me through the house's hallway and down a short flight of steps. He brought me to Wes's bonus room / basement, which was lined in knotty pinewood and carpeted with dark-brown fluff.

"The pirate's cave," Mike said, snuggling his face in my neck. Here, Wes kept a collection of Chinese vases, wrapped in bubble plastic, and framed jerseys from the Cowboys and the 49ers. On a shelf, Wes had stored a big bronze General Custer in more of that bubble plastic. In another cabinet, I saw geodes and fancy autographed baseballs, a stuffed boar, and in the corner he'd lumped some white-supremacy survivalist hooey like expensive bottled water and boxes of freeze-dried chicken strips. Also, on the west side of the room, there was a big wall safe, which was all steel and had a *Mission Impossible* code box.

"What's in here?" I whispered.

"Oh, a fuckton of euros and dollars and gold bars, like for End of Days times or I don't know what," Mike said, wrinkling his nose at the contraption. He looked at me and started playing with the lace on my dress. "One of these days I'm going to break into this damn safe and then take you to Bermuda."

We started making out like a pair of wild wolves, while Laura clattered the silverware in the dining room and yelled out, "Pie!"

★ ★ ★

Mike never did take me to Bermuda. He died in '16. Heart attack. Laura had passed the year before, from cancer.

★ ★ ★

At Mike's funeral, Wes didn't hug me or pat my hand, and I wouldn't have wanted him to anyway. We sat there next to each other stiff while the police department marched up and down the aisles, offering me condolences. Wes didn't say anything then, but apparently he was already thinking about bailing us out. It was pretty plain that I'd go broke without the policeman's paycheck, what with Mike's miniature pension and my having to take care of Jessie.

A week after the service, Wes sent me an email.

"You 2 can live in the back room if you want."

Wes had more money for Jessie and me than my parents would have ever been able to scrape up. So I brought Jess and Henrietta to live with Wes at his ancestral manor. The house was a massive six-bedroom, way more than he and Laura had ever needed. It was just too big, layered with cream-colored acrylic carpet and Persian rugs. Wes had an LA architect build it to his specifications back in the '80s, though I don't know where all the cash went. Scattered around the salon and his office were the better examples of his celadon Chinese vase collection. Also, Laura had collected a gang of Lladró figurines, which she'd stored in a huge hutch in the living room. There was Limoges china in the kitchen and a squad of expensive books on Winston Churchill in the library. All that old-fashioned mahogany furniture of his looked as filthy to me as a family of warthogs. And then, of course, there was his man cave filled with baseballs, jerseys, bronze statues of Indian killers, the extra supplies, and his big wall safe with I guess enough money to start a new society after the sun exploded and the zombies rose.

At the little red house, I packed a few boxes and threw a lot of things away. Jessie and I drove our Prius to Edgewood and moved into a back bedroom. Laura's old sewing station became my daughter's play space. Right away I started doing all the cleaning and cooking and gardening. At night, I'd hold Jessie and try not to scream into my pillow over the loss of Mike.

"The baby's a keeper, but I know what you are," Wes said, the day we arrived. He marched me down to the bonus room and showed me the bubble-wrapped extra vases and the bronze fucking Custer. He gestured at the wall safe. "I ever see you trying to get into this thing, you're out." He took the time to point a finger at me, and I wasn't carrying Jessie in my arms, but if he'd gestured at my kid like that, I would have smacked him until his lip split. I didn't burn any calories on him insulting me, though. Mike's death had changed the girl who had once taunted Wes about knowing her name. I knew I had to eat the grits he gave me.

I nodded and said, "I get it."

His face shifted a little then, because he saw I wasn't interested in his junk.

"Now, I don't mean any ill feelings about it, understand," he said.

"It's okay," I said, just feeling like kicking that man until he grunted. "You're all right."

Still, Wes stopped being quite such a shit by the time the fire came. He adored Jessie, who'd just turned six. Every once in a while, he'd even thank me for my chicken dinners and also my vegetarian experiments with the increased fiber. And last year on my birthday, he took me to a new French restaurant that some Oregonians set up in the venue that used to be Tattie's. Wes had sat with me in a corner booth, silent and awkward, while I ate a steak and felt weird.

\* \* \*

I left Wes fiddling with the hose in the front yard and bolted into the kitchen. Jessie sat at the breakfast nook finishing her milk and petting Henrietta with her feet. As soon as I came in, Henrietta sat up, stiff and staring. But my daughter did not even notice the color of the sky because she's always daisying about like a princess petunia. I think she got her personality from her father, who was a lollygagger when he was a kid.

"Mom, Henrietta won't drink my milk," she yelled at me. Jessie's a gorgeous little creature with bronze skin and long legs. She has sleek black hair and incomprehensible green eyes that must mean that I have some white in me.

"Honey, just sit there, don't move," I said. Henrietta jumped up and padded over, standing next to me and looking around and breathing with her mouth open.

We had a little, white, plastic television on the counter. I searched frantically for the remote and found it by the coffee pot. While Henrietta pawed me, I grabbed it and started pressing. I flipped past bright, screamy cartoons to a black lady newscaster wearing a blue suit and red lipstick. The lady looked as serious as the pope while jabbering something. The screen suddenly split to show a white woman with a pert upturned nose who wore a big black jacket and had her brown hair flipping around her head from the wind. The white woman looked to be standing on traffic-jammed Skyway, which is the main road through Paradise and cuts all the way to Chico. The sky on the screen was a darkening bronze, and when I looked out the window, I saw that it was that color here too.

"Bobbie, I think there's an alert out for your region now," the black lady said.

The white lady with the wind-whipped hair nodded. "There's an evacuation alert for the community of Paradise, and there's already traffic on the road. So we recommend—"

From behind the white lady, you could see a bloom of gold and red suddenly shooting up through the brassy sky.

"Oh," said somebody off screen, maybe a cameraman.

"What?" the white lady said. I snapped off the television.

Henrietta and I ran from the kitchen to the hall and then to my bedroom, which I shared with Jessie. I lunged toward our green bureau and opened the drawers. From the top drawer I grabbed her clothes, and from the bottom one I snatched mine, but all just randomly. I had jeans and nightgowns lumped in my arms, and did I need sneakers? I dropped the clothes and ran to the closet and tore the door open and found my Kivas there. I put them on. I grabbed Jessie's little Mary Janes and put them in my shirt, in my sports bra. Then I ran out the room. Henrietta came flying out after me.

With the dog whining at my heels, I dashed down the hall again, making my way across the living room and then another hallway and then to a little carpeted stairway that went down to the basement / bonus room. The big safe gleamed from the west wall, all steel and with its nuclear code box where I just probably had to type in *L-A-U-R-A* to get to Wes's treasure. Beneath the safe, next to the bubble-wrapped Custer, there were three big boxes of Arrowhead water and some cartons of chicken strips. I had no idea what to take, but water seemed like a good idea. I could pour it on Jessie if there was fire. I lifted one of the water boxes up, using my back and hurting it, and then jostled with it up the stairs. I almost tripped over Henrietta but somehow stayed on my feet. I ran through the kitchen with my load as fast as I could and then out to the front yard.

Wes sprayed me and Henrietta as soon as I hit the lawn. He had turned on the hose full force and thumbed the nozzle so that it jetted out with a big, white fan of water, and the wind sent it shooting crazily everywhere.

I took the blast in the face and kept going. "Help me, help me," I said.

"Just go," Wes said. "This is my house and Laura's. I'm not leaving it to burn."

I blinked. My eyes were watering even without the help of the hose. The sky had turned a bright, bright gold. You could smell smoke, thick smoke, acid-smelling smoke. Everybody on the street was racing around and loading their cars.

"You could lose everything, Wes," I said. "Tell me the code for the safe, and if I can, I'll get your stuff and we'll pack it out of here," I said.

He looked at me funny. "I don't think so."

"Okay," I said. He could have called me Pocahontas right then and started dancing around in his Klan hat, and I would not have given a single tiny shit. I turned from him and ran straight to my Prius—the Prius instead of his giant Yukon in the driveway. It was a stupid move, but, like his weirdness with the safe, I'd learned not to mess with Wes's things and I was just operating on habit. I dashed to the curb in my Kivas and put the box of water down in front of my car. I grabbed at the Prius's back door, but it was locked. I started crying. I ran back into the house and raced around looking for my keys.

"Mom, Mom," Jessie yelled from the kitchen.

I swear to the Lord almighty that goblins must have taken my keys and hid them under the Dora the Explorer sweatshirt in the second bathroom, on the floor, by the shower stall. I'd had to stand in the hall with Henrietta growling at my feet and piece my actions of the night before and that morning back together. I wasn't thinking straight. I shouldn't have been focusing on those keys. It was a waste of time. I finally figured it out, ran to the bathroom, and thrashed around until I found them under the sweatshirt. Henrietta tried to help me by digging at the clothes. I jangled the keys into my hand, and we ran back out to the kitchen. I snatched up Jessie from the kitchen table, gripping her in both arms so that one of her shoes fell out of my bra. I ran back with her and Henrietta out to the front yard.

I think it might have been eight forty-five by that time, maybe nine or even nine fifteen. You could hear sirens. You could see towers of smoke from far off. I looked at the cars fleeing down Edgewood. Wes remained standing on the soaking lawn with a tsunami of water pouring out of his hose onto the myrtles, the cottonwoods, the dry grass, the house windows, the whole facade. Jessie had her face in my ear and started screaming. I looked at the Prius, and then I looked at the black Yukon shining in the driveway. If fire swept over our car, we'd have a better chance of barreling through in that monstrosity than in my flimsy eco compact.

I ran back to the house with Jessie bouncing up and down on my shoulder. I dashed into the foyer. There was a big mahogany secretary set up on the wall with little porcelain Chinese dishes that held keys and coins. I saw Wes's Yukon keys on their big, thick, plastic keychain in a little red dish. I balanced Jessie on one hip and grabbed them. Henrietta started barking. I ran back out to the front yard and dashed for the Yukon and clicked it open. I tossed Jessie into the beige leather back seat, and Henrietta jumped in after her.

Then I ran back to Wesley.

"Dude, listen," I said.

Wesley's face was folded up like a wallet. He stayed on the lawn pouring water on the house where he'd lived with his wife and seemed like he was ready to die there.

"Wes," I said.

"Oh, God," he said.

"Wes, Jessie and I need you in our lives to protect us and be with us as a family," I said, insanely saying any hokum that I thought he'd listen to. "You have to come with us. We can't make it without you."

He turned and looked at me with real, tender, human eyes, for maybe the first time.

"Okay," he said.

"Okay," I said. I was already running to the Yukon's driver's side.

"I'm driving," he said, dropping the hose.

"You're an old man," I yelled. "And you have to protect the baby from the fire with your body."

"Okay," he said.

We got into the car, slammed the doors. We left the Arrowhead water on the curb. Jessie began screaming again. I started the Yukon and jammed it down the driveway and almost crashed into a Camry that was speeding down Edgewood. Wes gripped onto Jessie in the back seat and didn't say anything about my freak driving. I screeched onto the street and pushed the gas so we zipped toward the end of Edgewood, where we'd turn the corner, onto Pearson.

There was a traffic jam, right at the stop sign. Pearson was one long clog of cars. Our Yukon idled four back from the intersection. I recognized Martin's brown Dodge in front of me and Nancy's gray something, I don't know, a four-door. Somebody else I couldn't make out had taken the front of the line, ahead of Nancy. Big, fluffy pieces of ash fell down from the sky, like snowflakes. I had to turn on the wipers just to push the crud off the windshield.

"No problem," I said, in a calm, normal voice, like I was at Starbucks and they'd accidentally put oat milk in my Frappuccino. "Just need this to clear, and then we'll be off."

In the back seat, Wes held onto Jessie, who sobbed herself hoarse. He kissed her many times on the cheek. "You're a very good baby," he said.

"I'm not a baby," Jessie wailed. She didn't know what was going on.

Henrietta sat quivering next to Wes. The dog began to nudge her way up past Wes and Jessie, then slid up in the space between my seat and the Yukon's big console where you keep your Big Gulps in its handy holes. She slipped through and lumbered onto the front seat next to me. Then she just sat there, looking out of the windshield, like a person.

I reached out and petted Henrietta on the nose and flashed on

Mike. He used to roll around with Logan and Henrietta, and the pups had opened up their mouths soft and pretended to bite him while he laughed.

"Yup yup yup," I said, rolling up all the automatic windows because the smoke and ash came flowing in. "We're going to be okay. We're going to be good. We're going to be fine."

We sat there. We sat there. The cars didn't move. We sat there. More ash flakes fell. I don't know how much time passed. The sky began to change again. Black smoke started to stream into the gold sky, like the design on a Chinese vase.

"Come on, come on," I said.

"Move your ass!" I could hear a man screaming, I don't know from where.

The car at the intersection moved onto Pearson. Maybe ten minutes passed, maybe more. A full, thick stream of cars waited behind me. Ahead of me, Nancy switched on her turn signal, which flickered at me like a sign from another, normal, world.

"Do you think it'll all burn down?" Wes asked.

"Yes," I said.

"My safe's fireproof, but I don't know to what degree," he said.

"All I care about's that child you're holding onto now," I said.

Maybe ten, twelve, twenty, I don't know how many more minutes crawled by.

"I'm never going to make back what I lose," Wes said. "I'm too old."

"Insurance'll cover you, and then Trump'll make you a rich man with one of those disaster packages," I rattled on. The sky was really starting to darken, and I could see a thick haze of smoke coming in fast on a current.

Nancy moved onto Pearson. I inched the Yukon to the stoplight. I turned on my turn signal like she had because we had all become robots.

"That asshole will leave us stranded," Wes said. "He'll piss on some more hookers and burn it all on golf."

I started laughing. Tears were streaming down my face. "You liked him, I thought."

"Only on Mexicans and Puerto Ricans," Wes said.

"Right," I laughed some more.

"Not you," Wes said.

"I don't care, it's okay," I said. "Because if we get out of this alive, I'm going to punch you till you sneeze teeth, you old sonofabitch."

"Okay," Wes said.

I turned my head over my shoulder to look at my daughter tucking her nose into Wes's armpit. "But everything's good, right, Jessie? Everything's good."

Next to me, Henrietta's jaws were working strange, like she was nibbling something. I saw froth on her lips.

"Everything's good," Jessie said. She clung onto grandpa but had stopped crying, I think.

"Here we go," I said. I got an open spot and moved onto Pearson. Pearson was filled with traffic. We sat there like on Edgewood, watching the known sky disappear. The wind whipped through the world. The pine trees standing tall above us thrashed and tottered against a heavens that quickly crowded in with orange-pewter clouds. We still had to move from Pearson, past the Elementary School, past the Gold Nugget Museum, past the park, and onto Skyway. From Skyway, we'd flee southeast to Chico, about forty minutes out.

We barely moved, just little bits, while it got hotter in the car. The sky got swallowed by busy blackness. The earth burned fast. The people used both lanes, of course. I didn't like to see the people in the lane to our left. Women and men bent over their wheels, mumbling to themselves, kids scrambling in the back seats. At one point I saw Shelly in her Dodge Caravan, which was strange, because I thought she had been long gone. She saw me, and we smiled at each other, our faces both shuddering. We looked away from each other. We looked toward the road ahead, which got worse as the minutes ticked away.

"Don't let her look out the window," I said to Wes.

At both sides of the road, the landscape turned into what looked I swear to holy Jesus like molten lava. Black-brown clouds streamed down through a bloody sky and onto a swell of hills that had fried deep black and were streaked through with flame. It was getting furnace-like hot in the car. It was close, like you couldn't inhale right.

Wes put his T-shirt over Jessie's mouth and said, "Breathe, baby, breathe."

"No! No! No! No! No! No!" Jessie started screaming.

Henrietta started moving back and forth on the seat, as if she wanted to pace but there wasn't enough room.

"No! No! No! No! No! No!" my daughter shrieked.

"You're all right! You're all right!" I yelled.

"Here you go, oh, my sweet sugar," Wes crooned. "Oh, my sweet sugar."

*Crack! Crack!*

"What was that?" I asked.

"Maybe some tires going, exploding," Wes said.

"I don't think they're ours," I said. I had no idea. Maybe they were.

We moved up Pearson, slow, slow. We got onto Skyway. The whole universe had turned into a place of red sky and pine trees swaying like demons dancing. Through the hot, hot windshield—the heat blew off the dashboard in waves and threw itself off the side windows—we could see walls of flames tearing up from Tacos El Paraiso and Bill's Auto Repair. We crossed Vista Way and saw that Noonan, Gump & Penzer had long orange rockets of fire shooting up from its roof and out its windows.

Wes turned his head to look at his old office burning. Then he looked forward again.

Jessie went quiet. Henrietta crouched down and did not move. We were all of us silent but breathing like animals.

"I'm sorry about the safe," Wes said. He started crying.

"Just make sure my kid doesn't get dead, you old buzzard," I said.

"Of course it's all for you. You're my dear son's wife," he said, sobbing, while clutching onto my daughter. "Everything I have is for you and Jessie. The money, the gold, the stocks, the car, the house—"

I kept my eyes on the road ahead. A wave of red-gold flame and sparks curled across the sky and earth ahead of us. Any minute now it'll be clearing, I told myself. Any minute, we can get away. Far off, I *did* see the sky brighten briefly and then go dark again. It brightened once more, then darkened out. Dark, then darker. Then bright once more. Then dark.

"It's going to be good, don't worry, don't scare her," I said, my whole mouth like sandpaper.

"Tell me you forgive me," he wept.

I watched the hellfire sweep across the trees to our right and kept my foot steady on the gas.

"Tell me," he said.

"I forgive you, you Custer-loving bastard," I lied.

I could hear the howling, eating sound of the fire. On the horizon, that tiny, pale clear spot opened in the sky again and flickered. The red underworld rose up to heaven, exploded in the pines, and whirled above us like naked stars. The pale spot of clear sky continued glimmering ahead, though, and I aimed for it, without praying and filled with something less like faith than a blind keeping-on. And what I hoped was not my last thought was, what a Native woman's got to put up with in this goddam life doesn't stop until the minute that she dies. ✶

Faulting the Trump administration for its failure to consider climate change late Tuesday, a federal judge temporarily blocked the auction of federal land in Wyoming for oil and gas drilling.

U.S. District Judge Rudolph Contreras said that, while the Bureau of Land Management had summarized potential impacts of climate change, it failed to provide the information necessary to understand the level of climate impact from oil and gas leases. . . .

Barbara Gottlieb with Physicians for Social Responsibility meanwhile said the organization was "proud" to have joined the lawsuit. "Fracking contributes to the destruction of a livable climate for all of us. It also endangers the health of people living near wells, pipelines, compressor stations and other fracking infrastructure," Gottlieb said in an email. "We can't keep disregarding the harm that comes from extracting and burning oil and gas. We already face a climate health emergency. The impacts are just too great."

BRITAIN EAKIN, "Judge Cites Climate Change in Block of Wyoming Drilling," *Courthouse News Service,* March 20, 2019, https://www.courthousenews.com/judge-cites -climate-change-in-block-to-wyoming-drilling/

# Abundance

*With thanks to Brad Watson*

I SAW THE GOLD HAZE in the sky, that night when Thomas and I got away and used his car. The roustabouts light the flare stacks to ease the pressures caused by the gas. They use a flare pen. My husband, Danny, showed me before. A man shoots a spark at the top of an invisible pile of vapors that rises up from the oil wells. The gas lights up in a bright thin flame, like a feather plume worn by the queen horse in a rodeo show.

I spied the hot blur from the misted window in the back seat. I raised my head while Thomas put his mouth on me. The light flashed into the darkness, and I closed my eyes.

\* \* \*

I met Thomas last winter when I brought Danny his stomach medication and other supplies at the Combs Ranch site, about ten miles away from our home. This was one of the periods when Dan lived at the man camp. The oil field's a busy place, with lots of workers, lots of machinery: there's the rig, the makings for the casings, the base fluids, the friction reducers, the sand and iron trucks. Danny tried to teach me about it all when we first got married and moved to Douglas twelve years back. I paid more attention to the people then. The wives, I mean. The men didn't mean that much to me.

We'd meet up every weekend in those days. One of the girls would bang together a barbeque or a burger night. We fillies gathered in the kitchen sipping bourbon while the men drank their beers in the backyard. Billie, Rufina, Felicia, Michelle, and I had a fine time of it. We'd get red-faced from the booze and talk nonstop about getting pregnant or about the little ones that had already been born. I remember the men as young and rambunctious, very brave, excited, but serious when they fretted over their work during nights off.

By the time I brought Danny his gear to Combs Ranch, we had stopped going to the barbeques or burger nights as much. We'd had three children and instead spent our evenings watching TV. Most of the folks that I still knew from before had grown old in what seemed like lickety-split. But business was good, better than it'd been before, because there was more of an opportunity for the company to get under the land. More chances to coax the oil up, Danny said. The fields now spread across Douglas into Fremont, Casper, Gillette, and Riverton, and there were lots of new young tuffs coming to town.

"This is Thomas," Danny said, at the rig site, when I handed him a white paper bag with his pills in it.

I shook the stranger's hand. He had a long, thin face and dark hair. His eyes were hidden by sunglasses, and he had a broad, crooked mouth. He looked about thirty.

"Hey there, ma'am," he said. His hand in my hand felt broad and warm and dry.

\* \* \*

I met Danny when I was eighteen, in Galveston. I'd graduated from high school and worked in an old folks' home. I'd had to get a job, but I'd also wanted to get away from my mother, whose problem with Lortab squeezed out most of the money from her SDI check. At Holden Estates, I cleaned the patients and let them talk at me. At first the old women's falling-to-pieces bodies gave me the worst fright. I had to hide it. And one or two could get aggressive, not knowing who they were anymore and hitting you. But after a while I got used to it.

Danny was eighteen too. He'd come to town from Salado. He was short but had a nice laugh. And he was a go-getter. He worked as the janitor for the home, but he always talked about the future.

"I'm getting out of this place to do oil rigs or construction," he'd say, mopping the floor and talking a streak while I brushed a patient's hair or rubbed their legs. "I'll learn the business and then get investors and start something of my own."

"I know you could do it," I'd say. "You have the fire."

"Sure I do," he'd say, mopping harder.

One day, he looked right at me, snapping his head up in a hurry.

"Do you really think so?"

I was washing the feet of this staring-into-space old mare with the worst toenails. "Do I really think what, Dan?"

"Do you really think I could have my own business?"

"Sure I do," I said, scrubbing away.

"Let's get married," Danny said, all in a huff and just falling apart from I guess a sudden need to shout out his love.

"Maybe we should go on a date first," I said, still holding that beast's feet.

"Okay," Danny said.

We dated for a while. After about six months, Danny officially asked me to marry him in an Italian restaurant, over spaghetti and wine. In the same conversation he said there was an opening at one of the mountain state oil plays, roughneck work.

So we got hitched and moved just outside Douglas.

\* \* \*

There's a bird here that some folks fuss about. It's a brown-and-white puff ball with fancy feathers. The bird makes this little burbly coo. I used to hear the creatures' call more when Danny and I were kids starting out here. These birds don't like people very much, and so they hightail from the new rig sites popping up. The flare stacks from the oil fields make the sky bright all over our neighborhood, at every hour. Birds can get confused and fly toward the shine in the sky. Some of them get burned up in the fire.

They're called sage grouse, and they're in the news all the time. Years back, I once spied a little family of them when I was walking the edges of the neighborhood, around a sagebrush patch about half a mile away from my house. The males looked so strange and walked so funny that I researched them on the web.

I like the sage grouse on account of their courting. They romance each other in these places called *leks*. Little hideaways out in the brush. The males put on the most ridiculous show. After a while, you see how it's beautiful. The critters have a *boop pi pooo doo* sort of cluck, and they fan out their back feathers, which are like peacock feathers but dark brown. After that, they pump out their breasts, which have long white pockets. When the male sage grouse bares its chest, the pockets open up and show a yellow color beneath. Like they're revealing their hearts.

The little brown hens peck at worms in the dirt and just eyeball them, patiently selecting their suitors.

★ ★ ★

I saw Thomas a second time, at the Safeway, over on East Richards. About a month had passed since that day on the field. I spotted him right away, by the steaks. We have some strapping men here in Douglas. Even so, his shoulders cut quite a figure.

"Mrs. Wojcik," he said. He mispronounced it *Wajik*.

"Good morning," I said. I pretended I'd forgotten his name.

"Thomas, ma'am," he said. He smiled with that thin crooked mouth. "Thomas Esposito."

"Esposito," I said, starting to laugh for no reason. "What is that?"

"It's Mexican, ma'am."

"Mexican, my goodness," I said, laughing some more. "Where you from?"

He laughed too. "Buffalo."

I stood him ten years. I looked at his hard, lined face, brown and tight around the bones. When I saw his long body, it made me feel the weight of the extra flesh on my thighs and the lower part of my belly. My eyes have sunk in a little since when I was younger. But my worrying about my looks didn't stop a pocket in my chest from opening up. Fool woman, fool girl.

"Call me Linda," I said.

Thomas smiled at me with a dirty, easy kindliness, as if he'd just taken my hand and led me to bed. "Why, isn't that a pretty name?" he said.

*　*　*

It's beautiful country out here, once you get past the houses and trailers, the rigs and the pits. The winter snows shoot you in the face like shrapnel but land soft on the trees and fill the streets like sweet smoke. Once the sun comes, the green hills ripple out, covered with tiny purple and yellow flowers. There's cows and horses and deer out in the remoter areas. Still, there's more rigs around Douglas now than when we first moved here, and more strangers too. The federal government used to have a no-sir attitude on oil and gas companies leasing the land beneath the surface, but the opportunity opened up with the new times we're in.

Some of the plains have been torn up to make way for the wells. I see the white scars cutting through the grasslands where I used to take our eldest when she was just a baby, to see the lambs. Now the lambs are gone, and the rigs make a high grinding sound as they pump up the oil while the men scramble around and shout.

But if you keep driving south, you can still find yourself a lonely field, where you can listen to the quiet and the birds. You take your sweater off and feel the air on your arms. After the long, pale winter you can feel your body sipping at the sunlight.

*　*　*

Dan and my girls and I went to church the Sunday after I saw Thomas at the Safeway. We've got Carmen, who is five, and Lila, who's six, and Samantha, who's eight. Carmen is blond and has a delicate stomach, like her father. Samantha and Lila are red-headed, like Dan's mother, Sue, who passed away eight years back from cancer.

Dan never got his own business, but he made foreman, so now he can come and go from the man camp. He'd slept at home the night before, and Sunday morning dressed up in his black suit with the bolo and his good brown boots. I put Carmen in her pink lace. Samantha and Lila wanted to wear the same thing, matching purple dresses I'd made them for Christmas last year. I wore a brown dress with brown leather pumps and my hair tied back with a green ribbon.

When I tied the ribbon through my braid, I got a very clear picture in my head of Thomas. I saw him leaning back against the meat counter in the supermarket, how his yellow T-shirt pulled against his shoulders. This vision made me twirl the ribbon around the wrong side of my head, and I had to fix it twice.

We got to First Baptist a little late and sat toward the back, shuffling and rustling in the quiet. My old friend Billie saw us sneaking in and gave us a wink.

"God sees all your sins and still loves you, remember that," Pastor Bill was saying. He was the younger one, in his twenties, and I couldn't take him very serious. "You just give the Lord your sins, and he will wash them away. He gave you this land, and he gave you your loved ones, and he gave you his Son's very life too, which is the most precious of all gifts in the world."

I nodded in my seat and let Carmen cling onto me. It was true that God had done his part for my family, because we weren't wanting. And I like the idea of Jesus's terrible love filling you up, from the bottom of your feet all the way to the top. But I'll admit I'm not much for that hellfire. I take what works for me, and I leave the rest.

Pastor Bill started quoting from Corinthians: "And God is able to bless you abundantly, so that in all things at all times, having all that you need, you will abound in every good work."

"Amen, amen," we said.

When we got home, I made us all a big lunch. I did the last of the preparations in the kitchen, looking out the open window at the smoke from the flare stacks drifting through the air. The well boys are supposed to push steam into the stacks to keep it cleaner, but that doesn't always get done. I closed the window, while out in the dining room, I could hear Dan cracking jokes with the girls.

"What's a cross between a wild turkey and a mosquito?"

"Tell us!" the girls wailed.

"A turkito."

I came in with the steak platters to see my daughters laughing and laughing, squeezing their forks in their fists and clamping down their eyes.

Samantha and Lila gobbled up the food, seared T-bones made with wild rice and a nice tomato sauce topping. Danny and Carmen just picked. I sat across from them at the table and studied Dan. He's thinner now than when he was a boy, and he has a few blue burst veins in his left cheek. Samantha and Lila favor him, and Carmen favors me.

"Doesn't Mama look nice today?" Dan said, looking at me and poking at his potatoes. "And these fine T's, honey, what's the special occasion?"

"I just thought you'd like something nice," I said, touching the ribbon in my hair.

I had a secret little flame pluming up in my body, which lit me up like a Chinese lantern. It had already started. My mind kept wandering, even there at the table.

"Who wants dessert? Peach cobbler."

* * *

Once Danny became foreman, we paid down our four-bedroom house and rebuilt the roof. We bought an extra car. In the early days I had an almost crazy fear of going broke because of my mother's mistakes, but I haven't felt like that for a long time now.

I'd seen women lose their minds before. I pitied them. I'd watched Felicia Jenkins tear up her marriage to Hans with a guitar-playing trucker she'd run across at the Waterhole. I'd seen Michelle Enders break up her family, losing her husband, Greg, and her two sons for a bowlegged waiter she met at the Flagstaff Café. I got a real close-up view to the wages of sin, and I'd hug my daughters and want no part of it. The women's natures seemed to hit them when they turned forty-five, a little later, and it brought them to ruination.

That winter I met Thomas I was only forty-one years old.

* * *

Billie Moorehead and her husband, Karl, threw Billie a fiftieth birthday party that June. Karl had worked with Danny for twenty years, and Billie and I had been girls together back in the early 2000s with Michelle and Rufina and Felicia. I wouldn't say that I have anything like a best friend anymore, but Billie and I used to be close. She's a large, powerful woman, with a crisp set of strawberry curls and very wide hips and long full breasts that are a real comfort to lean on.

"What doesn't kill me makes me weaker," she'd joke after a couple drinks. She'd lost a baby and had three miscarriages before hitting thirty-three. By her big five-oh, she'd laid her mother, father, two aunts, and a brother to rest. But she'd had five children, four boys and a girl, all of them grown now and working the derricks or in oil administration. And Billie had stuck it out with her man, Karl, who stood her fifteen years and had gone wrinkled and patchworked with scars since his problems with skin cancer.

When Dan and I came in through her door that night, Billie ran around with liquor bottles for top-ups and trays filled with the miniquiches you can heat up in the microwave. Karl was out back with the grill, getting help with the burgers from their sons. Billie handed me a bourbon and smacked me a quick kiss on the cheek. She gave me a hard little look and said, "Why, didn't you get dressed up for old me!"

"Oh, this is just one of my old standbys," I said about my outfit. I gave her a wrapped present of White Shoulders Cologne and Body Wash, but my head was swiveling around the room as I peered at the partygoers. There was Hans with his new wife, Lupita. There was single Greg. There was Philip Peterson, Rufina's quiet and broody southern husband.

Billie laughed and clucked at my chest. I'd put on a short dress made of slinky nylon and propped up my breasts with the aid of a fancy bra I'd fished out of the back of my drawers.

"Coming into your own," she said, nudging me with her big hip. "Well, good for you. Drink up, lady danger."

That's when I saw Thomas at the end of the room, talking to Rufina, a scraggly little sunburnt bugeater who'd already had too much to swill and laughed like a hyena at whatever he said. Billie tracked my eyes and nodded.

"Bambi is cute, and I'll bet he tastes even better," she whispered into my ear, so I could smell the bourbon.

Thomas turned his head and saw me. He looked straight at me and smiled.

"Oops," Billie said. "That boy's getting an eyeful of you in that dress tonight."

Thomas untied himself from Rufina and came striding over.

"Hey there, Linda," he said.

"Hello, Thomas," I said.

"I see you two have met," Billie said, her voice shifting gears into a lower speed.

"How'd those steaks work out?" Thomas asked me, leaning up on the wall and crossing his legs while drinking a beer.

"I know my way around a steak," I said, laughing again like I had at the supermarket.

"I'll bet you do!" Thomas reached out and clinked his beer with my glass. "I'll bet you know your way around a lot of things."

I stuck out my chin. "What's that supposed to mean?"

"It's a compliment, ma'am. You look like a capable woman."

"A capable woman?" I laughed some more. "Billie, does that sound like a compliment to you?"

But when I turned to nudge her, I saw Billie had walked away, to the back where Karl and her kids manned the burgers.

I drank my bourbon and then had another, and another. Thomas kept topping me up.

"Where'd you come from, Linda?" Thomas said. "California, I'll bet. Or New York."

"Why you say that?"

Thomas lowered his voice. "Those movie-star curves, if you don't mind me saying."

I went very serious and still, my heart smashing its way through the lake of liquor I'd guzzled down. "Now, you shouldn't talk to me like that. I'm a married woman."

"I won't talk like that if you don't want me to," he said.

But I did want him to, I did.

"Don't fuck up," Billie hissed at me later that night as Dan and I weaved our way out the door.

\* \* \*

I didn't see Thomas for a while then, more than four months. The men got busy again with assembling a new rig in Rolling Hills, about a hundred miles south. All the males just disappeared from town. Dan would come home on Friday nights and stay until Sundays. He got sick for about three weeks, though, having his stomach trouble. Carmen had the same thing. I'd run back and forth between them, toting ginger ale and wet towels and the Prevacid. Carmen cried a lot after she threw up, and to make her feel better, I'd play "Speechless" from *Aladdin* on my phone. Dan waved away the soda and the soup, but he gripped onto my arm in a silent thank-you. He never suspecting any of my treacherous feelings.

Finally, Carmen and Dan got better.

"Come here, kitten," Danny said one night in March. He smiled at me from the bed, and I saw the blue veins in his cheek like the neon star that decorates the Waterhole's back bar. "Come here, my little kitty cat."

I laid down while Dan patted me and kissed me on my neck, trying to be a husband to me. The doctors in Douglas had said that the stomach issue was probably allergies, though one female doctor in Laramie, a specialist, got interested when we told her about living so close to the oil fields. She thought it might be something to do with toxins or the flare stacks. I'd had a few years of panicking about health issues, but the Douglas medicals said that there was no proof that stacks or drilling really hurt anybody. Even so, I'd talked to Dan about quitting and moving, but he wouldn't hear about it.

"A person has to recognize the good when it shows up and hold onto it," he said.

So I didn't worry about toxins on the night when my husband felt well enough to pinch me and cuddle. Carmen had moved back to her bedroom with her sisters, playing with her dollies and getting angry at Samantha and Lila for leaving her out of their games. Dan rolled on top of me, and I looked up at the ceiling, where I saw Thomas's face as if it'd been painted there. I pictured Thomas's chest and his fist-hard muscles. I came up with scenarios where I'd gone to the man camp under the cover of night and surprised him in his bunk. I fast-forwarded to where he had me bent over and scratching at him. I wanted him to pull my hair and to say nasty things to me. Danny and I'd been married for over twenty-three years, and as far as I knew, he'd never gotten into a tangle with another woman. He'd done everything for us.

★ ★ ★

Thomas sent me a text in late April.

"How you doing Mrs. Im just checking on u—Thomas."

"How'd you get this number?!" I wrote back, scared.

"It's on the web baby all I had to do was type ur name in"

"Don't you call me baby," I tapped out, laughing in my bathroom.

"But ur such a pretty baby I can't help it."

* * *

I got these romantic notions in my head then. I started looking for the sage grouse nests, their leks. I wanted to see the males puff out so that the yellow hot spot opened up, on their breasts. I wanted to see the little brown hens pecking daintily in the dirt as if nothing was going on.

I'd do my aerobic walking around the empty areas that still remained, after dinnertime until dusk. I'd peer into the frosted patches of brush that hadn't been dug up. The skies would flush bright, then go dark, bright, then go dark. Those flare stacks beat like a heart in the weather. There used to be small flocks of grouse around here, like I said, back maybe seven years ago. But now I couldn't see any birds. I told myself that it was still too cold, and I hoped that they'd just tucked themselves deeper in the snow.

* * *

A week after I got Thomas's message, while I was on my way back from the Safeway, Samantha called me from the house and said Carmen had passed out in the living room. I raced home practically fainting and found Carmen sitting up on the floor by the sofa, looking drained.

"Let's go, Nugget," I said.

I called Billie, who said she'd look after the girls. I took Carmen straight to the ER, where we did a long round of tests. My daughter looked wrong under the lights, too white and thin, and I was sure they'd find cancer. I leaned over her bed and kissed her hands and prayed. I couldn't remember any prayer but that one Pastor Bill had gone on about in the winter, the one where God blesses you with all that you need. I said, "God, you give me what I need, which is this child to not be dying." It took some time to get the results, hours and hours, but they didn't come up with anything, so I guess Corinthians worked.

"Some kids just come out delicate," the nurse said.

We came home around two in the morning. I put Carmen to bed while her sisters hovered at the doorway and then disappeared. Billie went to the kitchen and made coffee.

"I don't like being sick," Carmen said and fell right asleep.

Billie and I went to the living room and held the hot coffee cups in our hands. It had started snowing outside.

"How you doing?" Billie asked.

"Like shit on a shoe," I said.

Billie sipped her coffee and gave me a plain-dealing look. "'Cause of the kid or 'cause something else?"

"What are you talking about?" I said, but I didn't meet her eyes.

"I'm going to give you a piece of advice," she said after a second or two.

"I've had a night of it, girl, give me some rest."

"Tell you anyway."

"I suppose you will."

"Don't do it, and if you already did, make your penance and get right," she said.

"Go home, Billie," I said.

"You think it ain't been hard for me with Karl and the cancer? And him getting to be an old man? And my losing those babies? You think I haven't had some dick come sniffing around? You want to wind up like Felicia and Michelle? Get right. Get right. Your daughter's in there. Get right."

"Go home," I said.

∗ ∗ ∗

The thing about sin is that it doesn't feel like anything wrong. It feels like the right thing, that you should be doing this. The earth gives its gifts. You're one of God's children, and what you're meant to do is bask in that abundance. Even when you look at the scars on the hill or the kid being sick or your tits pushed up friendly in a dress, you're in a state of grace. You move past the place of virtue and evil to a station where there's nothing but your own good reasons.

Two nights later Thomas and I curled up in the back seat of his Mazda, and I felt blessings rain down on my skin. I never, never, never felt my whole body open up like a wild bird's.

"What about when I do this?" Thomas whispered at me. It was muggy in the car from the heater and our breath. I stared hard into Thomas's eyes, which look nearly black in the nighttime. But when the flares went off, they turned brandy colored.

"Do that, yeah," I said.

"What about if I get down under here like this?"

"Yes, do that," I gasped.

The shame could come later. The disaster too. I leaned back and opened my mouth. The sky flashed gold, and the sky flashed red, and the mysteries released from the wells and spread. ✶

Georgia, Kentucky, Louisiana, Missouri, Mississippi and Ohio stopped short of outright bans, instead passing so-called heartbeat bills that effectively prohibit abortions after six to eight weeks of pregnancy, when doctors can usually start detecting a fetal heartbeat. Utah and Arkansas voted to limit the procedure to the middle of the second trimester.

K. K. REBECCA LAI, "Abortion Bans: 9 States Have Passed Bills to Limit the Procedure This Year," *New York Times,* May 29, 2019

# The Perfect Palomino

*With thanks to Pam Madsen*

THE DAY I DECIDED I was a Palomino my sister Monica locked herself up in the bathroom.

"Get out of there," Mom said. She was wearing her pink robe and had her hair tied up in a blue cloth.

"I'm going to do it in here," I heard Monica say. Her voice was a little muffled from her being on the other side of the door. "I got a spoon from the kitchen, and I'm going to just see if it does any good."

"Get out here now," Mom yelled.

"Mom, I'm a Palomino even though they say I can't be," I said, wandering up to her in the hall.

"Monica," Mom screamed.

"Oh, cut that hollering," Monica said.

"Monica, don't you hurt yourself," Mom kept shouting.

"Mom, Monica isn't going to hurt herself," I said, because I know my sister is smart.

"Holy God," Monica said.

"Get me the axe," Mom said to me, chewing on her lip. "It's in the garage, in the back."

"Don't get the axe, Chris," Monica said.

"Monica," I said through the door, "Emma says that I can't be a Palomino but have to be a Clydesdale or an Appaloosa."

"Why?"

"Because I'm too dark."

"Well, that's just racism," Monica said.

"That's what I said," I said.

Mom started hitting the doorknob with both of her fists, like to break it.

"Oh, Jesus," Monica said. "Can't I just have a little self-abortion here by myself?"

"Don't say 'abortion' in front of Chrissie," Mom cried.

"Mom," Monica said. "Mama. Stop having a fit. I'm coming out."

"She's coming out," I said. "Back up."

"Get the fuck out of that fucking bathroom right now, Monica Miranda Gutiérrez!"

Monica opened the door and stood there, dripping and naked. Her stomach looked popped out, tight, and shiny. In her right hand, she did hold a spoon. When I saw that she'd actually not been joking about that, I thought that maybe she would have hurt herself after all. Then I started to feel bad.

"Do you know someone who'll do it around here?" Monica asked Mom. "Like your friend Teddy, she seems kind of witchy and up to no good."

"Teddy's a nurse," Mom said, snatching the spoon from Monica.

"Yeah, but the crooked kind. She sells oxy."

"She does not!"

"You know she does, and it's either going to be me seeing her or taking a trip to New York, which I can't afford anyhow even though it's the cheapest place that'll take care of me."

Mom blinked up at the ceiling, thinking. "Is Arkansas a place where they say okay if you were *raped*?" Mom said that last word whispery and mouthing it even though I knew what it meant.

"Yeah, it's Alabama and Ohio and Missouri and some others that don't budge."

"You could say you *were raped*," Mom said.

"I'm not going to say that, because that's not what happened," Monica said, and a tough little look rippled across her face.

"It's an option," Mom said.

"No, it's not."

"Don't start up with that no tolerance policy of whatever is not the nicest thing, Monica."

"I'm trying to be a certain kind of person, Mom," Monica said.

"And you *are* a certain kind of person," Mom said. "You are certainly pregnant."

Monica ignored Mom and got a towel off the back door and dried herself off. Mom grabbed Monica's blue bathrobe from the bathroom floor and draped it around her shoulders.

"What's a Palomino again?" Monica asked now in a softer voice.

"Palominos are pale-gold horses with white tails," I said, clutching onto her arm. "They were bred to blend in with the desert so enemies wouldn't see them. The color is caused by a genetic whatchamacallit. It's an allele of this dilution gene that's called the cream gene that makes the horse go all pale yellow."

"Well, don't you know your horse science," Monica said.

"I read about them when I was studying to be in my girl gang," I said.

"Of course you did," Monica said.

"We'll figure something out," Mom said. "We'll fix it up when you calm down."

"Clydesdales are bay, which means brown, with little white spots," I said. "Appaloosas are spotted too."

"You are a perfect Palomino, Chris," Monica said, slipping on her robe and tying it up around her waist.

I hugged her, tight. I buried my face into her robe and said, "You're not going to have your baby?"

"Nope," Monica said.

"No, she is not," Mom said. "She is going to college."

I kept my face in Monica's robe and felt myself start to get the fits. So I calmed myself down by racing with the Palomino in my mind, golden colored like the sunrays and stampeding across the mountains of Appalachia.

"You don't have to go away to college," I said. "You could have that baby, and we could all live here."

* * *

Emma, Lucinda, Karen, and I were all eleven years old and in a girl gang of horses. We didn't ride the horses. We were horses. Emma was an Arabian even though she was white with blond hair. Lucinda was an Akhal-Tiki, even though she was white with darker blond hair, though I supposed it was more normal because Akhal-Tikis are sort of dark blond. But then Karen was white with brown hair and green eyes, but she was a Peruvian Paso, which is shiny black and sometimes gray.

"If you can be an Arabian and Karen can be a Peruvian Paso, then I can be a Palomino," I told Emma in our school's Gifteds Study Room, the day after Monica wouldn't come out of the bathroom. I've got big hair puffed up in separate ponytails and long horsey eyelashes and a Palomino's magic specialness.

"I'm not saying it because it's light and you're, like, not," Emma said, shrugging. "I'm just saying your personality is more like a Clydesdale or a nice Appaloosa."

"Why?"

"Because they're so sweet."

"It's racism."

"Peter Piper picked a peck of pickled peckers," Emma said, so Karen and Lucinda started screaming with laughter. "And anyway, I'm leader, and so I say."

"You're not the leader!" I said. I looked over at Lucinda and Karen, who were rolling around on the floor. "Say she's not the leader."

Lucinda danced around with her butt. "I think she's right."

Karen said, "Me too," and started copycatting Lucinda's wriggling.

"Well, I'm going to New York, and when I get there, I'm never going to talk to any of you again," I said.

Emma tilted her head. "Why you going to New York?"

But I already knew I shouldn't tell because from what Monica was saying, the law would set its monster men on her if anybody heard about the spoon and the baby.

"To get away from you," I said.

* * *

Monica, Mom, and I sat at the kitchen table and did some strategy.

"If I can get my hands on some pills, I could just do it right here," Monica said, resting her elbows on her blue-and-red calculus book from school. Monica's nineteen and a senior at Millikan High. I know she's a little old to still be in twelfth grade, but for six months, when she was in tenth grade, she got hurt and didn't feel good and had to take time off. She's fine now, except for the having a baby in her. She's tall and has long braids and shiny emotional eyes. She's a thoroughbred, which is the best kind of horse.

"Can you get them on the internet?" Mom asked. Mom has tilted mysterious eyes and beautiful long black hair. She's a thoroughbred too.

"I tried, but the lady selling them on the site said I was too late, same as the clinics here."

"Chrissie, go to your room," Mom said.

"No," I said.

"How much does it cost?" Mom asked.

"Maybe two or three for the surgery and then four hundred for one ticket, and then you got to stay over about three nights for the complications."

Mom threw up her hands.

"I know that," Monica said.

"That's college," Mom said.

"Yes," Monica said.

"Can't he pay?"

"He's gone to working rigs in Wyoming and hasn't returned any of my texts," Monica said.

I looked at them both hunched over. Their eyes looked hurt. I started crying.

"Chrissie," Mom said.

"Chrissie, Chrissie," Monica said.

I kept crying and started howling.

"Chrissie," Monica said. "Run around like a Palomino."

"Yeah, do your Palomino," Mom said.

"I'm not a Palomino," I sobbed. "Emma says I'm a Clydesdale or an Appaloosa."

"Do it, do it," they both told me.

I got up and started prancing around the kitchen. "The Palomino is the most special horse there is," I practically screamed because I tried not to cry anymore. "The Palomino was invented in Arabia, and it's gold and pale and yellow."

"Mmm hmmmm," Mom said.

"And in this war that happened, a second war," I said, trying to remember what I read about Palominos. "A World War, something."

"World War Two?" Mom asked.

"In World War Two the Palominos blended in with the sandy beach, and the soldiers rode the horses, and the enemy couldn't see them until it was too late."

"The Germans," Mom said.

"That's good, Chrissie," Monica said, staring at her hands.

I kept prancing through the kitchen even though they'd stopped looking at me. I whinnied and reared up like Trigger and Xena's horse, Argo, who were both famous Palominos, along with the war ones.

"Where are we going to get that money?" Mom said.

"Call Teddy," Monica said, thumping on her calculus book with her fist. "Call her, call her, Mama, call her."

\* \* \*

The next day Emma, Lucinda, Karen, and I prepared to go into battle. We went to McNally Middle School, in Fayetteville. Mom, Monica, and I weren't always from Fayetteville, but Mom moved us there after she and Monica came here from Alabama because of Mom's job and I wasn't born yet. Mom said that out of all of Arkansas, Fayetteville had the best schools for me and Monica and that even though it was a racist place, McNally gave us scholarships.

I was in the talented program with Emma, Lucinda, and Karen, and it was a racist program because there were only three black kids and four Mexican/Salvadorans in it. Georgie Marshall, Yolanda Frederickson, Gloria Peterson, Selena Hauser, Luis López, and Juana Morales were the other kids, but once I became friends with Emma, they wouldn't talk to me. I felt super bad about this for a long time, but once Emma decided that we were going to become horses, I got really excited, and then I didn't care anymore until the Palomino problem started.

"We're going to attack Kenny and Bobby after school," Emma said, at nutrition. "We'll do the Battle of Pea Ridge."

"The Confederates lost that one," I said, looking it up on my old and gross phone.

"No, they didn't," Karen said.

"You don't know what you're talking about," I said.

"The Confederates won," Lucinda said.

"No, Chrissie's right," Emma said. "But that's okay, because we're going to rape them."

"Oh, I don't know," I said, biting my nails.

"What's raping?" Karen asked.

Lucinda started giggling. "Raping is raping."

"You don't know what it is," I said.

"Raping is where you put your penises in somebody and they don't want it," Emma said.

I looked it up on my phone and showed Karen and Lucinda. "She's right."

We all went quiet, thinking.

"But we don't have penises," Lucinda said.

Lucinda, Karen, and I nodded, because this was true.

"If we're horses, then we can penises," I said finally.

"That's the spirit," Emma said.

"I'm a Palomino," I said.

"No, you're not," Emma said.

We set the showdown for three fifteen. Kenny and Bobby were next-door neighbors and always went home from school together by walking down Mill Road. Kenny was tall and pink-skinned, with brassy hair, and he wore loafers with pennies in them. Bobby was tall too and tan with dark hair, and he wore sneakers and an Aquaman backpack.

Emma, Karen, Lucinda, and I waited for them on Mill Road, whinnying and pawing our hooves on the concrete. Kenny and Bobby came walking around the corner. We reared up on our hind legs and snorted. It was four war horses against two unarmed men in the Battle of Pea Ridge.

"Ahhhhhh!" we yelled and went running for them.

"What the fuck," Kenny said.

"It's girls," Bobby said.

"Ahhhhhhh!" we kept screaming. We ran at them with our hooves up and our noses shooting fiery flames and our manes streaming in the wind. Emma jumped on top of Kenny and started wrapping herself around him and biting him. Lucinda and Karen ripped off Bobby's Aquaman backpack and then tore off his shirt.

But I didn't want to rape anybody. I ran.

"Come back here!" Emma shrieked at me while Kenny started punching her.

* * *

Mom and Monica said that I shouldn't come to Teddy's and should stay home and look at TV. There was some ice cream in the freezer, and I could stay up and watch *Miraculous: The Tales of Ladybug and Cat Noir* and *Star vs. The Forces of Evil*. But I screamed and cried so hard that they wound up taking me.

Teddy's house was in Mountain Ranch, off Betty Jo Avenue, about six blocks away from us. Her complex was big and brown. She buzzed us in, and we went up to the third floor.

"You brought Chrissie?" Teddy asked, first thing when she opened the door.

"Her shows are on around now, and if it's okay, she'll watch them on your set," Mom said.

Teddy was white with braids and a lot of blue eyeliner that I thought looked good. She was a nurse at a hospital here that I don't know what it was called. She was probably a Chestnut Belgian and wore a yellow T-shirt and blue jeans and bare feet with a turquoise pedicure that I wanted Mom to do on me. She smiled at me and said, "Hey, chickadee."

Monica put her hand on my hair and said, "Hey, Teddy."

"Hey, Ted," Mom said.

I didn't say anything.

"Sweethearts, just come on in," Teddy said. "What a world, what a world." She shook her head serious but friendly as she led us into the living room, where she'd laid out cheese and crackers and Diet Cokes. She had a TV set up in a wood furniture thing, which also had some books and vases in it.

"So," Monica said. She wore a big, flowy purple shirt with a black cotton skirt and sandals. Her face is beautiful like Zendaya's, but right then her cheeks had started to puff out bigger.

Mom wore sweatpants and sneakers and had her brown purse.

She took out her wallet and poured out some money. She gave it to Teddy, and Teddy didn't count it.

"What we've got here is a simple little operation that I do all the time," Teddy started saying. "We go to the back room and use just a little hose and some water. We also need some little sterilized instruments, which can help things go super smooth."

"Teddy, Teddy," Mom and Monica started yelling.

Teddy looked at me. "Oh, sorry."

"Let's just, kind of . . ." Monica's voice grumbled down into nothing, and she looked all around the room with one eye crinkling up.

"Have some Coke and TV," Mom said to me.

I looked up at the three of them and then went over to the TV and snapped it on. I got the remote and switched it until I found half an episode of *Ladybug*. I looked at them and ate a cube of cheese.

"I'm okay," I said.

Monica started shaking.

"Okay," Teddy said. She put her hands on Monica's back, and Mom put her hands on Monica's arms, and they pushed her toward a back room and shut the door.

I ate another cube of cheese, and I opened up a Coke. The *Ladybug* episode was one that I'd seen before, which was when Alya would stop at nothing to reveal the true identity of Ladybug, who was really Marinette Dupain-Cheng, who wanted to become a fashion designer. I watched the show and thought about how Marinette Dupain-Cheng didn't have red skin with black spots and that didn't stop her from being able to be Ladybug.

"No, no," I heard Monica saying through the closed door. "No."

"Stop doing it," Mom said.

"It's fine," Teddy said. "It's just a little water."

"It's not clean. Get off me. You're gonna kill me," Monica said.

"Monica, Monica," I screamed.

"It's all right, Chris," Monica yelled back. "Mom, go help her."

Mom came out with a horrible look on her face and wrapped me up in her arms. I cried and screamed some more while Monica came bolting out of the back room with a big wet stain on her purple shirt.

"I'm sorry, but no," Monica kept saying.

Teddy came out after, wiping her hands on a cloth. "It's okay, I get it. It's scary. You're fine."

"I'm sorry," Monica said.

"You're okay."

"I want to go home," I hollered into Mom.

"Sounds good," Monica said.

Teddy went back to the back room and came back with the money Mom had given her. She put it in Mom's hands.

Mom peeled off a few bills and gave them back to Teddy. "For your trouble, honey."

Teddy munched up her mouth. She shrugged and put the money in her jeans pockets. "Thanks, Marina."

We left.

* * *

"No, you cannot eat lunch with us," Emma said the next day in the cafeteria. She looked up at me with a big bruise on her right eye that had swollen it shut.

"You abandoned us at the battle," Lucinda said. She had a long red cut on her cheek.

"You're a coward," Karen said. She didn't have anything wrong with her.

Kenny and Bobby had been suspended for violence against women and girls. Emma got a talking to from the principal, and so did Lucinda and Karen, but they were allowed to keep going to school.

"You can't be that mad at me," I said. "You didn't tell on me to Principal Figgis."

"That's because you went AWOL, and so you're dead to us," Emma said.

"Fine," I said.

I took my lunch tray and wandered around the cafeteria. Over on the far end of the room, I saw the table with Georgie Marshall, Yolanda Frederickson, Gloria Peterson, Selena Hauser, Luis López, and Juana Morales. But when I walked over to them, they raised their eyebrows at me and laughed.

So I went over to the other corner. I sat down in an empty place and ate my Jack Cheese Fry Up by myself.

While I ate my cheese fingers in a corner, though, I was really shimmering like the sun had just come out and hit my mane so that it sparkled. I didn't actually drink milk like a human girl or wipe my mouth with a napkin like a regular mortal. Instead, I galloped by the sand dunes while the enemy tried to track me with their spy glasses. But they couldn't find me or hurt me, because I was the kind of special breed who could disappear into the background.

* * *

"I disappeared into the background," I said to Monica and Mom that night. We all sat at the kitchen table again, this time after a dinner of meatloaf and green beans and milk. "It's because I have that camouflage that protects me from the enemy."

"So what now?" Mom said.

Monica took her phone out of her pocket and poked at it. "Well, at least we're not in Alabama or Ohio or Mississippi, where the scarier baby savers live."

"Little mercies, I guess," Mom said.

Monica looked at her phone some more. "On Twitter even Trump says some abortion's okay, like when you're going to die or got bothered by your brother or were . . . *raped.*"

"You said that's an option, right?" Mom said. "Out here, in Arkansas."

"Mom," Monica said.

"Rape's where you put your penises in somebody but they don't want you to," I said.

Mom and Monica looked at me with little jerks of their heads.

"Great," Monica said.

"You're too young to know that," Mom muttered.

"Emma said it because when we were horses, she wanted to rape Kenny and Bobby at the Battle of Pea Ridge."

"Dixies lost that one," Mom said.

"That's what I said," I said.

"Emma's not going to rape anybody." Monica cacked out a bad little laugh.

"Don't hang out with Emma anymore," Mom said.

"She won't talk to me," I said. "That's why I had to sit in a corner at lunch and be a Palomino so that I had camouflage and my enemies couldn't see me."

Mom went quiet for a second and then said, "That's what we need. To evade the enemy."

"Mom," Monica said.

"They got this idea that if you've been raped, then you're something special," Mom started huffing. "But a hell of a lot of women have a mess of sex that they never asked for, and if they don't file papers, nobody cares about them. Use it, use it. Just say it. It's all the same thing."

"You know I've been knocked down before, and that shit is so serious you can't make up a story about it," Monica said.

"Ssshhh, sssssh," Mom said, waving at me.

"Thomas didn't rape me," Monica said. "He's a dick, but he didn't hurt me. I'm just up a creek." My sister munched up her mouth. "Why they only give you a few weeks? They cut you off if you take your time to think it through, but that's being a better person, I think, thinking about it, making sure."

"They don't care what you think, darlin'," Mom said.

"I care what I think," Monica said. "All I am is what I think and what I do."

"Baby, that's just something you read. Get your damn head out of a book and look at the world."

Monica kept her head bent and stared at her phone like she wanted to disappear into it.

I ate some meatloaf and kept my yup shut so they didn't send me to my room.

"Use the rape like a ticket," Mom went on. "Use it now when you need it."

"I think if you start playing games with the truth, then something nasty happens to you," Monica said.

"Something nasty happens to all of us," Mom said, her face turning shiny and twisted.

Monica didn't say anything.

"Monica," Mom said.

Monica still didn't say anything.

"Monica, do you want to be a secretary like me, saying 'Yes, sir,' and 'No, sir,' and 'Yes, ma'am,' and 'No, ma'am,' to people who barely remember your blessed name?" Mom said, tears spilling down her cheeks.

"Right now, seems to me like nothing in the world's going to save me from saying 'Yes, sir,' and 'Yes, ma'am,' for the rest of my life," Monica said.

"Money changes all that," Mom said.

"Not all of it." My sister shrugged, while Mom stared at her with wild Mustang eyes.

Finally my sister sighed and turned off her phone. "Yeah, all right."

* * *

Mom made a doctor's appointment for Monica set for a week later.

"We'll be back this afternoon," Monica said, while she put her jacket on by the door.

"Do your homework," Mom said, digging through her purse.

"I'm going with you," I said.

"No," Monica said.

"Yes," I said.

"No," Mom said.

"Yes, yes, yes," I said.

Monica shook her head. "Why do you have to go everywhere with us?"

"Because I love you," I said.

"She's getting separation anxiety," Mom said.

"What's that?" I asked.

"That's when I get too tired to fight," Mom said.

So I went.

The office was small, with white walls decorated with pictures of trees. Seven women and two men already sat on the sofas and chairs in the waiting area. The women all looked normal. There were no other kids.

"Gutiérrez," Mom said to the nurse at the desk.

We sat on three little chairs up at the front, by the nurse. The nurse was a black lady wearing purple eyeshadow and soft blue pants and a big blue top and was a Tennessee Walking Horse. She gave Mom a bunch of papers, and Mom started to write on them right away. Monica blinked her eyes fast at the pictures of the trees and chewed on the inside of her cheek.

"Don't talk to me," one of the women said to one of the men. The woman was black too. She had long, black, Peruvian Paso hair and wore green pants. She was crying. The man was white and wore brown pants and had a dog-like face.

"You'll feel better when it's over," the man said.

Another nurse, who was chubby and white, with big blue eyes covered with lots of black mascara and short, frizzy, light-brown hair, and who was a Clydesdale, came out from a side door. "Mulligan."

The black lady with the Peruvian Paso hair and the dog man got up and went through the door.

"Tell me about being an engineer," Monica said to Mom.

Mom kept writing on the papers and said, "You're going to go into robots like you always wanted and make little machines that fix people from the inside."

"Rehabilitation robotics," Monica said.

"That's right," Mom said.

"And after U of A, I'll go to Michigan or MIT and get a master's," Monica said.

"Yes," Mom said. "So just settle down."

Monica went quiet again looking at the tree pictures. All the rest of the seven women and two men got called, and more people came. The nurse who was a Tennessee Walker played with her phone and took two calls.

The white nurse who was a Clydesdale came out of the door and said, "Gutiérrez."

"Wait here, honey," Mom said to me.

"Can I come?" I said.

"Don't worry," Monica said. They left.

I sat on my chair and looked at the new people who had shown up. It was a bunch like the others, mostly women and a few men and the women being mad at the men.

"Just *shut up*," a white lady wearing tight black pants and who was a Miniature Warmblood said to another hound-looking man wearing an Ole Miss sweatshirt.

"Hey, little fidget," the Tennessee Walker nurse said to me. She opened up a drawer in her desk and took out some candy. "Want something sweet?" She reached over her desk and handed me a wrapped caramel.

"Thank you," I said. I ate it.

"Aren't these good?" she said, popping one into her own mouth.

"Tennessee Walkers can be any color," I said. "They all got flashy and unique four-beat gaits and their long necks are elegant and refined."

"Well, isn't that something," the nurse said.

Monica came hustling out. Her eyes had gone glossy and red, and she dashed through the office and out the front door. All the people bickering in the room went totally quiet and stared.

"Oh, Jesus," Mom said, coming out after Monica. "Sorry, sorry."

"It's okay," the Tennessee Walker nurse said. "It happens."

"Come on, sweetheart," Mom said. I followed her out.

When we go to our car, which is a black Honda, Monica had her arms crossed across her chest, and it looked like her forehead was swelling. Mom beeped the car so it opened. Monica got in the back seat and lay down. I got in the back seat too and curled up over her legs. Mom got in the front seat and started driving.

"It's all right," Mom said. "It's okay."

"You're not mad?" Monica said, crying.

"Don't cry," I said, hugging her legs.

"Of course I'm mad," Mom said. "But it'll be all right. We'll figure it out. Maybe we can make another appointment."

"Maybe New York will be nice," Monica said in a crackly voice.

Mom clamped her mouth down and kept driving. We were all quiet for a while except for Monica huffing raggedy while she tried not to cry so hard. I crawled all around her and cuddled up in her crooks. After about twenty minutes, she calmed down and tugged on my arm.

"Be a Palomino, Chris," she said.

"Yeah," Mom said, looking at us through the rearview. "Chrissie, do your Palomino."

I looked down at my legs and arms all tangled up with my sister's. I tried to horse up my mind, but I couldn't see that pale-yellow shine on them anymore. My pony magic was gone. My hands weren't hooves but just had fingers. My feet were girl feet in sneakers.

"I don't want to be a Palomino anymore," I said.

"Well, what do you want to be then, a Clydesdale?" Monica said.

"I want to be like you," I said.

Monica looked up and out the opposite car window. She looked tired and beautiful. Under my hands I could feel the tight, hard swell of her belly.

"No you don't, baby," she said. ★

We recommend Option 3 as the most effective method to achieve operational objectives and the Administration's goal to end "catch and release." This initiative would pursue prosecution of all amenable adults who cross our border illegally, including those presenting with a family unit, between ports of entry in coordination with DOJ.

KEVIN MCALEENAN, Commissioner, US Custom and Border Protection; L. FRANCIS CISSNA, Director, US Citizen and Immigration Services; THOMAS D. HOMAN, Acting Director, Immigration and Customs Enforcement, "Memorandum for the Secretary: Increasing Prosecutions of Immigration Violations," April 23, 2018, https: //www.openthegovernment.org/wp-content/uploads /other-files/Part3%20from%20CBP-2018-070727_Redacted.pdf

This practice of separating class members from their minor children, and failing to reunify class members with those children, without any showing the parent is unfit or presents a danger to the child is sufficient to find Plaintiffs have a likelihood of success on their due process claim. . . . A practice of this sort implemented in this way is likely to be "so egregious, so outrageous, that it may fairly be said to shock the contemporary conscience."

*Ms. L. v. U.S. Immigration & Customs Enf't ("ICE"),* 310 F. Supp. 3d 1133, 1145 (S.D. Cal. 2018), *modified,* 330 F.R.D. 284 (S.D. Cal. 2019) (quoting *County of Sacramento v. Lewis,* 523 U.S. 833, 847 n.8 (1998))

# Option 3

"**I**s IT DONE YET?" Gary asked. He stood at my door. Gary's probably fifty-two years old and about five foot five. He has brown hair and brown eyes and wears rimless glasses. Today he also wore a striped pink shirt with a solid-blue tie.

"Not quite," I said, writing at my desk, and I mean frantically typing garbage letters on my computer to look like I was working. I'm forty-eight years old, and I'm six foot four. I have brown hair and brown eyes. I have a mole on my left shoulder, and I need to do sit-ups. I'm a lawyer for the Office of the Principal Legal Advisor (OPLA), which serves the Immigration and Customs Enforcement Agency (ICE) out of Potomac Center North, on Twelfth SW. Gary is my bastard of a boss.

"I asked for it by two o'clock today," Gary said.

"It's not totally ready." I looked at the three massive accordion files on my desk and the three boxes of files on the floor next to my feet and sniffed helplessly.

"Do you have too much on your plate, Kevin?" Gary asked, his voice getting thin and high, like a woman's. "Is that the problem?"

"I'll get it to you by tomorrow," I said.

"Tomorrow at what time?" Gary asked.

"First thing," I said.

Gary nodded and turned to leave. I looked at the clock on my computer and saw that it already said 2:42 p.m.

"Or," I said.

Gary turned back around and looked at me.

"Look, it actually might take just a little bit longer." I rifled through the colossal amounts of papers on my desk. "But, since you're here, let me just ask you—"

"What?"

"About Option 3. It means that we're separating them when the parent's been arrested for illegal entry?" I scrabbled around my desk, trying to find Tab F in Folder XV because I thought it might have a synopsis of the protocol. "That's . . . human smuggling, when you arrest the dad or mom or whatever for 1325? Or . . . uh . . . 1324(a)?"

"Yes," Gary snapped. "Right, I don't know. It's what we're doing. You're the one writing the memo on it."

I slapped through some more papers. "Or it's human trafficking? Which is different from smuggling, sort of."

"It's zero tolerance, Kevin," Gary said. "That's the mandate. Read the file. I left you a memo based on notes of a conversation I had with the director. It's—yellow."

"What's yellow?"

He bugged his eyes out at me. "*What?*"

"Nothing, okay, I'm reading it," I rattled out, trying to find the appendix in File XVI, which maybe had the thing he was talking about.

"Get your shit together," Gary said and stomped off.

\* \* \*

As soon as Gary left my office, I started to research and write Option 3. According to Gary's emails and all-caps verbal instructions, the Acting Director of ICE wanted to share a first draft of this recommendation for family separation with the Director of USCIS and the Commissioner of CBP ASAP. Then we would shoot it over to the Secretary of DHS for approval and etc. He'd given me the assignment about two weeks ago. But I hadn't had time to do it yet because, in all honesty, Gary was sort of right. I really just did not have my shit quite together at the moment. Marjorie had a terrible flu and was also so mad at me. So I'd had to take a little family medical leave time to take care of Heather and Sabrina, particularly Heather, who is at a really delicate stage of development according to Marjorie. But Sabrina too, she's just eight years old, and I have to be there, as a father. And a husband. Whose wife is so pissed because, I have no idea why. I think it has something to do with me saying yesterday that maybe we shouldn't go to Lacie's party tomorrow, because she, Marjorie, didn't look that great, which Marjorie interpreted as something to do with me saying that she wasn't beautiful anymore after having the kids, which I absolutely did not mean. She's just sick! People don't look as good when they're sick.

Actually, on the family leave thing, I hadn't taken it officially, yet. I didn't even have time to fill out the paperwork. I'd just run panicked out of the office at all hours of the day every time I got a call from Marjorie or Saint Andrew's vice principal, like at eleven a.m. once, to get Heather from school when she started biting that girl. And then I'd also had to bug out every day at three p.m. to pick up both kids when their classes ended. After that, I'd take them to ice cream or to whatever until about four or so, so that Marjorie could get some sleep. Then, after dinner, I'd try to get some work done. The only thing was, Heather was having problems with screaming a lot, and Marjorie would need things like Vic's and Nyquil. And right before she'd gotten the flu, Marjorie had fired Conchita, because, who knows? Something somebody did. It was just a bad week. So, great!

I looked at the screen on my computer, which looked like this after my garbagey typing that I did to keep Gary off my back:

As;ldkfjas;dkfjas;kldjfas;kldjf;askldjfas;kldfja;lskdfj;askdfjasd;klf jas;kldfja;

I erased all that, and then I just had a blank screen again. I looked back down at the files on my desk and started to read through them, very rapidly and hopefully efficiently. I pivoted between stuff on credible fear screenings and did a quick Wiki on the Flores Agreement and then engaged a speedy review of the AG memo on zero tolerance that I'd actually not read when the front office globally first sent it around.

> ...I direct each United States Attorney's Office along the Southwest Border—to the extent practicable, and in consultation with DHS—to adopt immediately a zero-tolerance policy for all offenses referred for prosecution under section 1325(a)....

"Okay, not very helpful, just a bunch of regular blaaah," I whispered (Gary had left my door open, and secretaries and other line attorneys were meandering down the halls). I clawed through the files again and finally found a big yellow stickie just barely sticking out of the middle of File XV. I tore the stickie off and looked at it. It was in Gary's handwriting and I guess was my "memo" that he'd been talking about. I could have missed it so easily, he should have put it on the top of the file and stapled it there and put my name on it. But he didn't because he's an idiot and is stupid.

> Option 3 authorizes family separation in the event of an arrest of a parent at SWB on suspicion of a 1325(a)(1)–(3) violation. Find out legality and write up how it is legal and constitutional and also how we have humane controls and conditions in place at the whatever camps or prisons & things they're going to go in—find out what those are, too.

"Uh huh," I said, my mouth open and trying to remember what exactly 1325(a)(1)–(3) covered. "Something, something . . ." I began to type.

> Option 3 is an excellent idea for the protection of the borders and of smuggled/trafficked children, who are victims of sexual abuse. Option 3 is also legal because aliens basically have no rights constitutionally because Congress has very broad powers to control immigration, even when Congress's laws affect

delicate family dynamics, like when moms are mad at dads and won't help them out with child care or when people are trying to be good parents generally speaking but are having trouble doing so. *See, e.g.,* Fiallo v. Bell, 430 U.S. 787, 797–98 (1977) (ok to exclude illegitimate children and natural fathers from special preference immigration status).

"No, that's not good," I said, reading it over. I deleted it.

*Bzzzzzzzzzzz*

I looked down at my phone. Marjorie had just texted me.

"THEY R WAITING FOR YOU OUTSIDE OF THE SCHOOL RITE NOW"

"Fuck, fuck, fuck," I said. I looked at the files on my desk and on the floor. I couldn't carry them all out to the car. I took two of the big accordions, stuck them under my armpits, and ran out the door.

\* \* \*

"Hey!" I said, when I pulled up in front of Saint Andrew's, which is a beautiful and expensive private school with a huge campus full of Harvardish brick buildings and gorgeously mown lawns and is costing me my retirement.

"Hi, Dad," Sabrina said, smiling. Sabrina's eight, like I said. She's blond like her mom and has a triangular face that I love and sooty dark lashes and big blue eyes, also like her mom.

"Hi, hi. Heather, hi, honey," I said. "Okay, get in. Let's get in."

"Fffffff," Heather said, scowling at me. "You're late." Heather is seven and has also blond hair like her mother. She has a triangular face too, which is also like Marjorie's. Actually, neither of my daughters look anything like me or anyone in my family.

"Okay, let's get in," I said again, brightly. "In we go."

"What this?" Sabrina asked, climbing over the files I'd thrown in the back seat as she and her sister piled into the car.

"Oh, just some stuff," I said. "Push it to the side."

"There's not enough room!" Heather said.

"Of course there is," I said. "Just push it."

The girls kicked at the files, and I could hear the cardboard crunching and crushing as they smashed it onto the floor. It was fine. It was all on the computer, somewhere, though I wasn't sure if Gary had Dropboxed me all the things.

"Let's go get ice cream again," Sabrina said, when they'd settled in.

"I don't like ice cream," Heather said.

"Who doesn't like ice cream?" I laughed at her, trying to make eye contact in the rearview.

"Fat people like ice cream," Heather said.

"Where'd you learn that?" I asked, squeezing the steering wheel.

"I'm not fat," Sabrina said.

"Of course you're not fat," I said.

"Mom," Heather said.

"Mom, what?" I asked.

"Mom said it, that ice cream makes you fat," Heather said.

"No it doesn't," I said, cheerily. I was already driving down Victory Lane, without any idea of where I was going. Could I just go home and do my work? "Except, we can't get ice cream yet, because we're going to keep our appetites for dinner, right? We're just going to go home, right?"

"Mom texted me and said to stay away for at least an hour," Sabrina said.

"Okay," I said.

I drove us to the ice cream store, shop, whatever. Belson's. It's on Milbern Drive and has a little pink sign and tiny white tables and is filled with kids smashing cones in their fists and dropping balls of ice cream on the floor while their mothers and fathers and nannies stare out the windows. When getting out of the car, I extracted one of the crushed files from the footwell of the back seat and brought it into the ice cream place. Then we stood in line while children shrieked and smeared bloody-looking chocolate everywhere. I got Sabrina a vanilla and Heather a pistachio and a vanilla, and I got myself a big bowl of cherry and chocolate. The place was crowded with parents and squirts, and we barely got a table. But Heather sort of muscled her way into one before a grandmother or an extremely old mother and her dark-haired son got it, so we sat down. I immediately tried to do some research/writing as we all ate, by balancing the file on my knees and pulling out papers with my right hand and reading them and scooping ice cream with my left.

"I'm going to kill you," Heather told Sabrina, while licking her pistachio.

"No, you're not," Sabrina said. "Because then Dad would kill you."

"Okay, guys," I said, reading and only eating the cherry part of my ice cream. I'd found a good case, just, right away. Which was great. I started to really, actually, read it, and while I read it, I put down my spoon and pulled my phone off my belt to take notes. "Be nice."

"He would not," Heather said. "Mom would kill me."

"Yeah," Sabrina said, laughing into her vanilla. "Mom would kill you."

"Under the Illegal Immigration Reform and Immigrant Responsibility Act, the Secretary has broad authority to detain aliens who enter the United States unlawfully until we can remove them from the country," I yammered into the phone. "Inadmissible aliens and aliens who cross into the US illegally are subject to criminal penalties and deportation. See 8 U.S.C., sections 1325 and, Kevin, check, 1326."

"How would she kill me?" Heather said.

"She would shoot you with a gun," Sabrina said, quietly, while licking her ice cream.

"And if the Secretary seeks to deploy Option 3 by separating the children of inadmissible aliens and illegal, uh, crossers from their misdemeanor-committing parents, thus turning said children into unaccompanied minors," I went on, while Heather's face began to turn a bright shade of red, "that also would be well within her constitutional brief, because the enforcement of US immigration laws, on its own, does not itself violate substantive due process. *See, e.g.*, de Robles v. INS, 485 F.2d 100, 102 (10th Cir.1973). Further, ANY parental detention pursuant to the arrest of persons suspected of violating immigration laws can conceivably interfere with parents, uh, being physically with their children—"

"Mommy hates me," Heather said.

"I know," Sabrina said.

"You guys," I said. I looked around briefly and saw that the grandmother / old mom with the dark-haired son was staring at me or my kids, maybe because we'd stolen her table. She and her son were sitting at a table next to us, but it was a worse one, because it was smaller and jammed up by a wall.

I ignored grandma / old mom and pivoted back to my work. In verbally writing my memo, I was getting all of my information out of this one case I'd found in the file, but the case cited to a lot of other cases, and if I just cited to those cases and quoted the parts that were quoted in the case I was reading, then it would seem like I'd read them all. "As the First Circuit held in *Aguilar v. U.S. Immigration & Customs Enforcement Division of Dep't of Homeland Sec.*, Kevin, cite, 'such an incidental interference, standing alone, is not of constitutional magnitude. To rule otherwise would risk turning every lawful detention or arrest of a parent into a—'"

"AHAAAAAAHAHAHHAHAHAAH!" Heather started screaming.

"Shit," I said. I just realized that I'd been reciting into the recorder function of my phone, instead of the Notes function, and so it was just a verbal record that I'd then have to play all over again and then type out as I listened to it, instead of just having a nice rough Notes version that I could email myself and then clean up on my computer.

"Dad," Sabrina said. "She's doing it again."

"AAAAAAHHAHAHAHAHAHAHHAHAHA!" Heather screamed. She

threw her ice cream on the floor and then herself on the floor after it and then started to roll around in it.

"Okay," I said. I clicked off my phone and put it back on my belt clip—did you have to save recordings? I didn't do that or even know how to do that. I stuffed the papers back into the dented file and then stood up and put the file on the seat. I bent over and picked up Heather, who was making like a furious pistachio angel on the floor. I threw her over my shoulder and grabbed the file and put it under my free armpit. "Let's go."

Sabrina stood up. "Mom's going to be mad."

"Yeah," I said.

As we started to wind through the tables, the old mom / grandma with the dark-haired son looked at me again, or had been looking at me all of this time, like a stalker. She had black-and-silver hair and wide cheekbones and dark skin. She gave me the most scary angry lady look, but I've lived with Marjorie for fifteen years, and so it takes a lot more woman aggression than that for me to really take any notice.

"Table's free," I said, over Heather's screams.

"Jesus Christ," she said.

"That's not a nice thing to say," I told Sabrina, as we left.

* * *

"Hey, babe, we're home," I said, opening our front door. I threw my keys on the big Empire secretary in the foyer and the files on the floor. It was a full forty minutes later. I'd had to stop twice on the side of the road to deal with Heather, who had started tearing shit out of my folders and getting the pistachio on her sweater all over the car. She was better now, and it was like nothing had happened. The girls ran through the foyer, which was littered with toys and clothes and junk because Conchita was gone. I didn't even have Conchita's email or phone number, and so I didn't know how to get in contact with her without Marjorie knowing, and if Marjorie was mad at her, then if she found out that I was trying to mend fences to get the housekeeper back, that would be a whole conversation that I just didn't want to have.

"Did you bring dinner?" Marjorie asked. From the sound of her voice and tinny sounds floating toward me, I could tell that she was in the TV room, watching TV.

"Oh, uhhho, oh," I said, or something like that.

"No!" Sabrina said.

"No!" Heather said.

"I asked you to bring dinner," Marjorie said, still invisibly, from the TV room.

"Okay," I said. "Pizza."

"Yes!" both Heather and Sabrina shouted.

"Okay," Marjorie said, which was a great sign.

"Okay, okay," I said. I ran through the foyer toward my office, which had a PC that I didn't know how to make jive electronically or internetishly with my special one at work, which had a lot of government privacy blocks and was complicated. But I could draft something on this one and email what I wrote to my work address, which is what I usually did when I had to work on nights or the weekends.

"But I'm not going to eat too much because of Lacie's party tomorrow," Marjorie called out, while I grabbed the laptop, which was on a big mahogany desk that I'd inherited from my grandfather, who was an oil lawyer from Houston and had thought that government lawyers were illiterate cretins who didn't make any money.

"Do you really feel good enough to go?" I yelled back to her.

Marjorie didn't answer.

"Sorry," I said.

I got my keys from the secretary in the hall and went out again. Then I ran back inside and got one of the files that I'd thrown next to the secretary when I'd first come in. After that, I went out again a second time to go get the pizza.

* * *

"The only possible counterargument against the constitutionality of Option 3," I wrote on my computer while sitting at a picnic table in the outdoor eating/waiting area of Doohickie's Pizza Garden, on Tuckerman Lane, "would begin with the settled principle that aliens possess the constitutional right to substantive due process when on US soil. Mathews v. Diaz, 426 U.S. 67, 77 (1976). Such substantive due process rights include the right to family integrity. Quilloin v. Walcott, 434 U.S. 246 (1978)." Along with the laptop, I had brought the file that Heather had gooed with ice cream and ripped up. I'd opened it up on the picnic table, with the papers sort of spilling out and all crappy. "However, the standard for finding such a violation requires that the government action complained of 'shocks the conscience,' a standard that creates a high hurdle for any complainant, as only government behavior that is 'so "brutal" and "offensive" that it [does] not comport with traditional ideas of fair play and decency' will trespass aliens—"

"McConnell," the pizza guy said, walking out with two pizzas and a little electronic card-reading machine.

"Here," I said, raising my hand. I started rummaging through my pocket to find my wallet. I got out my Chase and stuck it into the little machine that the guy held out. He was like twenty years old and handsome and black with big shoulders and sort of perfect skin, and it made me think about my stomach.

*Brrrp brrrp*

"It doesn't work," the pizza guy said.

"No, it does," I said. "Just do it again."

*Brrrp brrrp*

"Sorry," the pizza guy said.

"It's okay," I said. I guessed I'd have to call that in when I had free time, which would be never. I took the AmEx out of my wallet even though it doesn't give as many points. I stuck that in.

"Okay," the pizza guy said.

We sat there and waited.

*Beep*

"Eureka," the pizza guy said, laughing.

"Oh, good," I said. I took the pizzas from him. "There's no sausage on one of them, right?"

He blinked at me. "I thought you ordered two Sweet Pigs."

"I did," I said. "But didn't I say, 'One without sausage'?"

He shook his head. "No." He shrugged. "It's okay. I can just get another one on the fire. It'll take like twenty, twenty-five minutes."

"I've got to get home," I said. "Do you have, like, a lot of bread?"

"Yeah, we have bread."

"Can we have some extra bread?"

"Yeah, totally," he said. He pointed at the file and the computer. "You working hard?"

"Oh my God," I said. "I'm doing this brief on this thing with immigration, where there's this huge constitutional question on whether you can . . ." I looked at his name tag, suddenly. It said "Pablo." "Like, whether you can . . . do stuff."

"Oh, yeah, that sounds hard," the pizza guy / Pablo said.

"Yeah," I said.

"I'll just get you some bread," he said.

A couple minutes later he came out with a huge bag of focaccia, and I went back home.

*　*　*

"It's fine, I didn't even want to eat a lot," Marjorie said. She was in a good mood. She wasn't green anymore and had taken a shower. She'd lost probably six pounds from the flu and looked like a different person. We were sitting at our dining table eating the pizza, except that Marjorie didn't eat pork because pigs wag their tails, and so she was eating the bread and drinking some wine.

"I don't want to eat a lot either," Sabrina said, digging into her slice of Sweet Pig.

"Me'en either," Heather said, actually not eating.

"God, this tastes good," Marjorie said, drinking from her glass.

Marjorie is five foot three and has light-blond hair and blue eyes and a triangular face. In her hand, she held a big glass of white wine, which she kept refilling from a bottle that she'd brought out from the fridge and opened up before I'd got home. "You know that feeling, after you've been sick, and then you can finally drink? My God."

I wasn't drinking that much. I still had to write my fucking memo. "Yeah," I said.

"Heather screamed today," Sabrina said.

"Not a lot," Heather said.

"Oh yeah?" Marjorie said. She didn't care. She looked at me with renewed interest. She probably wanted to have sex with the wine and not feeling so bad. She grabbed a chunk of the focaccia and chewed it and swallowed it and then had two huge gulps of wine. "Oh my God, this is so good."

"I have to write a memo tonight," I said. I'd already had a glass of wine and eaten two slices of Sweet Pig. I just wanted to go to sleep.

"On what, babe?" Marjorie asked.

"We're going to start separating kids from their parents at the border," I said, rubbing my eyes, but my hands turned out to be not clean from the pizza, so then I had to wipe my whole face with a napkin.

Marjorie was still smiling at me. "What?"

"It's a new initiative. They're calling it Option 3," I said. I rubbed my eyes again and then had to wipe my face again with a napkin. "It's to combat human smuggling, or trafficking. It's to protect things."

"But you're not, like, *separating* little kids from their parents," Marjorie said.

"Yeah, yeah, but it's not forever or anything. And the cells are good, they're clean," I said.

"Oh," Marjorie said. She drank some more wine. She looked at the kids, who were looking at me. Her face sort of rippled and then sagged. In the next instant, she smiled brightly. "Hey, what's this I hear about somebody yelling today?" she asked abruptly, in a mock-angry voice.

"Heather did," Sabrina said.

"*Heather?*" Marjorie said. "Heather would never do that."

Both girls started giggling.

\* \* \*

A few hours later, after I'd done some work on my memo, I went to bed. Marjorie wasn't sleeping. She was lying down and staring at the ceiling. I looked down at her pretty body and started to feel affectionate. I sat down on the bed and kissed her mouth and then her cheek, because she moved her head.

"I thought you were tired," she said.

"I am tired," I said. "I'm beat."

"Yeah, I'm still a little sick," she said.

"Oh, I thought you were feeling better," I said. "Does that mean you're not going to go to the party tomorrow night?"

"No, I told you, we're going," she said. "Lacie's pissed at me for not going to the christening, and so I have to show up."

"She'd understand," I said, getting into bed and curling up against my wife.

"No, she wouldn't," Marjorie said.

We lay there for a few minutes with me petting her hair.

"That thing you're working on sounds weird," she said.

"Mmm hmmm," I said. "Gary is being such a dick."

"No," she said. "The kids. The little ones not being with their folks."

"No, I know," I said. "It's really something, what they're doing."

"Well, what you're doing," she said.

"Me, I'm just filling in the dots," I said. "It's not my call." I swallowed some phlegm. "And it's for, you know, protection, of the kids."

"Right," she said. She stared at the ceiling for a few seconds, until it started to get a little awkward, and I didn't know what was going on.

"What's up?"

She sighed. "Oh, nothing." She kissed me on the temple.

"So you're not mad at me anymore?" I murmured, snuggling deeper into her neck.

"For what?" she asked.

"For, I don't know," I said.

"Don't get started," she said.

"Yeah, all right," I said.

"I'm always mad at you," she said, laughing a little.

"You *are*," I said. "You're like Heather. But I just love you."

Then she started saying something else, but I don't know what it was, because I guess I fell asleep.

★ ★ ★

The thing that I'd said at dinner about the cells being clean and good was actually just a guess, because I hadn't done the research on it yet. The next morning, though, I looked it up, and it was fine. In 2008, the CBP had put out a memo detailing the national policy on short-term custody and hold rooms, which required that containment spaces be clean and sanitary and that pregnant women and moms and children got fed every four hours. There were mandates for sanitary beds and clean linens and toilets and soap. And children typically would get diverted under the regs required by the Trafficking Victims Protection and Reauthorization Act of 2008, which required that Health and Human Services give the children to the Office of Refugee Resettlement within seventy-two hours of determining that the minor was unaccompanied. I couldn't figure out where exactly the kids were getting stored in that three-day period, but it wasn't that long, and the ORR has a more shelter- or home-like situation than normal jails, and it didn't have locked pods or anything like that. So the "shock the conscience" standard seemed not really in play, maybe.

Anyway, that's what I wrote up for Gary, though it took more time than I expected. I did have to wind up transcribing that recording I made at the ice cream shop. Also, I had to make sure to check the negative treatment of all of the cases that I'd cited but hadn't necessarily read, and four of them were overturned, and three others had red flags, so I had to write around that. I was sort of scrambling at the end of the day to get it all done, but at six p.m., I was able to email it off, with a smiley face and a "Here you go." Gary answered it with another smiley face, and so I thought that was good.

After I sent it, I went to the bathroom and peed and washed my hands. It was already six thirty by then. I was already late for meeting Marjorie at Lacie's party on time, so I got my jacket and jetted.

* * *

"It's just totally beautiful," Marjorie was saying, after just having emptied her glass. I had entered Lacie's big, mock-Tudor house on Connecticut Avenue and wandered through the crowded house until I got to the huge backyard. It was Friday at about seven fifteen, and all of these people were there. Marjorie used to be a lawyer with Morrison & Forester until she had the kids, and she still had all of these friends from law school and practice and also from her days in clerking. She liked to hang out with them and get a break from mommy time. Lacie was a younger friend of hers, whom she'd known at Morrison. She was a big, tall blonde with a nice laugh and a new infant and a husband who did Superfund defense, which is what apparently had paid for the epic aquamarine necklace she had on right then.

"It was my push present," Lacie said, fingering the blue baubles around her neck. "If you had gone to the christening, you'd have seen it."

"I know," Marjorie said. "It killed me to miss it!"

"Kevin!" Lacie said, when she saw me. "Hel-lo!"

"Hey, Lace. Hey, ladies," I said.

"Hey, babe," Marjorie said, threading her arm in mine and kissing me on the cheek.

"Let's get you a drink," Lacie said. She made eye contact with a waiter who reminded me of the pizza guy / Pablo, and within seconds I had a chardonnay in my hand.

About five other women were standing around Lacie and Marjorie, and all of the ladies were eyeballing the necklace, which had this huge center stone that made it probably cost like $300,000 if it was really real, which I would know because Marjorie likes jewelry and I've priced a lot of it on eBay. There were men at the party too, but they were drinking among themselves in little huddles and not talking about the jewelry. Lacie's guy was rich, but a lot of people here were like me, in government.

"How did he give it to you?" one of the women asked, a youngish brunette in tight white slacks.

"He just gave it to me in the hospital, like in a cardboard box that had the red Cartier box *inside* of it, so the presentation was ruined," Lacie said.

"Still, it's so pretty," said another woman, a middle-aged blond lady wearing a dress with little purple flowers on it.

"Yeah, it looks good on you, Lace," I said.

"Hey, are you two going to have another baby?" Lacie asked, still gripping her necklace.

She was looking straight at me, but I didn't understand that she could be talking about us, because Marjorie had told me in extremely certain terms two years ago that we would never have another child, and she illustrated her point by putting her hands in an X formation in front of her vagina. "Who, us?" I asked.

"Maybe," Marjorie said, squeezing my arm harder. She was flushed and her eyes sparkled, but there was a thin fake shine over everything, and I wasn't really sure how tonight was going to shake out.

"You know, Marjorie," Lacie said, "you're so lucky to be married to Kevin. He's a man's man, but you can see he has that tender side too."

Marjorie looked at me, still smiling, and her eyes did seem to soften for a second. "He's great with the girls."

"What have you been up to lately, Kev?" Lacie asked.

"Oh, hell," I said, taking a sip from my glass and then another one. "I've been working like a bear on this one issue. Immigration." I drained my glass and flagged down the pizza guy for another one.

"Oh, immigration," all the women said in serious voices.

"Um," Marjorie said.

I got my new wine glass from the guy and drank half of it, in like one swallow. "My boss has been riding me. It's this really tough case about—"

"Um, wait," Marjorie said, grinning and squeezing my arm.

I hesitated and drank some more, watching the tiny but scary shifts in her expression.

Marjorie's eyes remained glittering, and her smile stayed just as wide. But she very lightly shook her head *no*.

"Sorry, what?" Lacie asked.

"Oh, it's just . . ." Marjorie said. "Didn't you say it was classified?"

I continued looking intently at my wife's beamy eyes and stone grin and began to think about how, when I'd left Baker & McKenzie to come to work for the administration, she'd been excited. It's been a fun, happy time, full of deregulation and the promise of power and loads o' money to be made after my public-service stint or maybe even during. But then, later, it seemed less good, with the social hate and the actually really low pay. These memories fiddled with my mind a little, so that Marjorie's face flickered in front of me and then seemed to morph all at once into a smaller, sweating, squalling version—Heather's face, as she'd pitched a fit on the floor of the ice cream store the day before. I flashed on Heather making a pistachio angel as she furiously flailed her arms and yelled. I contemplated my child's red, dumb mug and her squeezed-shut eyes. You couldn't spank kids these days. You just had to wait it out. When I was young, I'd gotten spanked plenty by my parents, and for behavior far less disgusting than my daughter's. But I was glad that things were different now. Gentler, more civilized. I loved Heather more than anybody else on the planet, and the thought of her spitting with stupid rage and her screaming made me suddenly feel so tired I could have just lain right down, right there on the grass, with the ladies' high-heeled shoes sticking their spikes into the earth by my ears while my wife looked down on me, disappointed.

"Oh, it's nothing," I said, draining my glass while the women all nodded at me. "It's just this thing at work." ✲

The agents take them in their wet clothes, at first, to the "*hielera*," the "icebox," a refrigerated building, a large processing center, where they had to try to sleep on the concrete floor or sit on concrete benches under mylar blankets, prodded by agents all night and day, deliberately kept awake.... After the Hielera, they went to the "*perrera*," or "doghouse," a place where families were put in cages, cyclone fencing between them as though they were animals.... The detention center in Dilley is run by CoreCivic, a company that contributed $250,000 to President Trump's inauguration.

MARIN GARBUS, "What I Saw at the Dilley, Texas, Immigrant Detention Center," *The Nation,* April 22, 2019, https://www.thenation .com/article/dilley-texas-immigration-detention/

Correctional Officer...$15.63 per hour...Senior Correction Officer...$42,261 per year.

"CoreCivic Salaries in the United States," *Indeed.com,* accessed June 20, 2019, https://www.indeed.com/cmp/Corecivic/salaries

"I can't imagine being the person who grabs a hold of a child and takes them. I don't know where you have to go in yourself to be able to do that job," [the baby's foster mother] said.

CAITLIN DICKERSON, "The Youngest Child Separated from His Family at the Border Was 4 Months Old," *New York Times,* June 16, 2019, https://www.nytimes.com/2019/06/16/us/baby-constantine -romania-migrants.html

# Zero Tolerance

YEAH, I TOOK HER. It's my job. So, of course I took her. She was supposed to go to the doghouse, the segregated cages, but I put her somewhere better. The mother didn't like it, but that's really not my problem. If you don't like it, then don't come here, that's what we say.

I'm sorry, excuse me? Yes, that's what I'm telling you, I was told to bring her to holding C.

I'm just trying to answer you honestly, which is what I was told to do.

I'm a senior corrections officer at the Dilley Detention Center. It's my responsibility to manage and contain the aliens who come to our facility.

Now, you don't have to [*indistinct*] me like that. I'm sitting here trying to be professional, and I expect the same thing from you, Mrs. [*indistinct*]. Fine, Sharon [*muffled*].

* * *

If you don't like that I did my job like a professional, it's because you're living in a fantasy world. I hope the lady's getting this part down too. Because that's what we should be talking about at trial, the lawsuit, whatever. We should be talking about that and not about me taking the youngster and putting it in another sector. No, we should be talking about how this entire system is rigged, and you guys with your law degrees and your total ignorance about the world don't have the faintest clue what you're involved with here. But I do.

\* \* \*

No. No.

No. I want to talk about something else.

What you don't understand is the number of people that we're supposed to process. What people just don't understand is how little we are paid and the overwhelming amount of work that we've been assigned to do. We have to maintain order in an unmanageable situation. And we have to do our duties under the law, which is zero tolerance. It's no tolerance, which means that the work load is just going to be just that much more insane. When I first got here in 2014, we were processing 480 aliens. And now's it's up to 2,400. Do the math. And they're putting all of it on us. And most of us don't have enough money to feed our own children well or to take them to nice places or to give them nice things. We're exhausted, frankly. That's what people don't understand.

Also, come on, let's be honest. The aliens that we're managing are themselves criminals. In most cases, I'm saying. I don't know how many aliens pass their credible fear screenings. But it isn't a lot. From what I understand.

\* \* \*

I'm from here, South Texas. I graduated from Dilley High School ten years ago and then took the job at the Center because it pays more than half again as much as I was earning waitressing. I waitressed at the Subway on the interstate and got paid $7.25 an hour. Do you know how much that is? $14,500 a year. You're standing there behind the counter with your hands hurting so bad because you have to cut up all of those chilies all day. You'd get paid more if you poisoned yourself in the grape or strawberry fields like an immigrant or had no respect for yourself and did something worse. Because women, sometimes, around here, when they get real broke, they'll go low. I didn't want to do that. And I didn't.

But really, I was ready to do almost anything. I was that desperate. I already had my son, my baby. Nat. So I had to think about him. Mom helped me take care of him, but Nat's dad, Raymond, didn't really help much. So, of course I'm going to jump at a job with CoreCivic. Are you kidding? I get paid over 42K a year now. Which sounds like a lot. And it is a lot more than when I was at Subway. But now that I have two kids, and Jerry is out of work, it's peanuts, man. My rent's $1,500 a month, which is all on me since Mom got sick and lost her job. So, forty-two, let me tell you, it's nothing.

* * *

What happened was that Edgar pointed the aliens out to me and said, "Take care of it." So I did. She wasn't the first. And it's not like she died or got hurt. They just sent her to Chicago, I think. Because there have been deaths, at other facilities. But we are working so hard to keep these conditions up to par that nothing like that has really happened here. It never happened except for once, and that's after it was out of our hands, and that particular infant received adequate care.

In this case, Edgar said to take the child to holding C, and so I did go get her. It's not that complicated.

Did I *feel* anything? What kind of answer are you exactly looking for?

* * *

When I first got here, I was falling all over myself to take care of the women and the children. I wanted to do the best job and get promoted, and I did, but not because I was getting diapers or aspirin. But when I first got hired, I'd see the mommies and babies, and I didn't really get what the situation was, the overwhelmingness of it. I'd see them like individuals. I'd be like, this one's named Graciela, and this is her kid Pedro, and this is her daughter Yolanda. Or, this guy's name is Victor, and his kids are Rudolfo and Cecilia, and his wife's Serafina. I'd notice the color of their eyes, and if any of them were sick, which they all were, because they'd been in the water and then captured, and they get scared and all jacked up.

I remember this one case, back in '15, back when I was still with Raymond. This was when Obama was president, so don't you forget that. You think that Dilley was invented in January of 2017.

So in '15, there was this alien named Graciela, who I was mentioning, and she had this kid, Pedro. I mean, she had two kids, but Pedro was the one with the problem. Pedro was about one and a half years old, which was around the same age of Nat, so I knew how old he was when I saw him. Pedro was runty with huge brown eyes and this shiny little face that changed expression all the time. Oh, he was cute. We put them in the icebox with the others, and that Graciela was hard as a brick and didn't complain. She got her kids and put them under her sweater and sat in the corner and just waited.

But what I noticed was that Pedro started crying after the second day, and he didn't stop. And my reaction wasn't, "How can I get this kid to shut up?" Because that was Edgar's reaction. He was back here then too. We were both just correctional officers in those days, though he'd already been at the Center for four years already. Now I'm a senior corrections officer, and he's a sergeant. Anyway, Edgar was like, "Jesus Christ, get me out of here." Because little Pedro was making such a racket. Edgar put his jacket over his head to block out the sound. "I hate my life," he mumbled at me through the jacket, until our sarge at the time, Milly, told him to cut it out.

So the baby's crying for two days, but Graciela wasn't doing anything about it. Nothing. Just nothing. I think she was from Guatemala. Here, they're all like from Guatemala or Honduras. And I don't know how they raise them there, but those girls are tough, like too tough. Like unnatural. Because Graciela was just staring at the wall with no expression while her daughter's lying around all filthy and her son's screaming bloody murder.

I felt that scream tear through me, I swear. Because I'm a mom. I'm a natural mom. I feel those things. I felt them then—I felt them for her kid. Because that's the type of person I was. Before everything became so overwhelming. Anyway, I ran over to the kid finally, and I put my hand on its face, and it was burning hot. It was just flaming hot.

I said, "This kid has a fever!" But Graciela, she was just checked out. I don't know what was wrong with her. She didn't make a move and only looked at me with these empty eyes. I grabbed the kid from her and ran him to the infirmary, and they had to do a surgery on him super fast because he had an infection.

"I guess he had septicemia," Edgar said later, shrugging. "Good on you, Georgia," he said.

So I saved that kid's life. I did that. So why don't you put that in your pipe and puff it.

* * *

Yes, Edgar pointed me to an approximately five-year-old minor who was in the apparent custody of an alien who said that she was seeking asylum. But what she really was, the alien, was suspected of illegal crossing, which is a federal crime that entitles her to deportation unless she can pass the credible fear screening. And until she passed that test, the child was going to be separated from her, because we didn't even have any proof that she was a blood relation of the alien or not being trafficked. So the child becomes an unaccompanied alien, right away. Which is why we have to remove them, for their safety. Also, we have to separate the families, that is, the aliens, in order to deter future aliens from coming here with their kids. That's why it's zero tolerance. Because we have to do something about this assault on the border that we've been experiencing for just years and years. The aliens have an incentive now to show up here with all of their babies and then get released into our society. And it just can't happen that way anymore.

* * *

Excuse me, ma'am, but do you really see any other way? Are you saying that you want open borders? Have you really thought about what that would mean? Where do you live? I see. That sounds nice. Do you have your own house? No, really, do you have your own house? Like, with a mortgage and everything? Or do you live in some shitty little apartment with your sick mom and your out-of-work husband? Hmmm? You want to take a break? Is she going to shut off the little recorder there? Hmm?

I'll bet you're so excited to have this case. Talking to big bad me.

So, you live in the big city, and what that means is that you have zero percent of any kind of clue what it means to be overridden by these tidal waves of aliens who are hurting themselves and their children and us by just flooding into the territory and expecting every kind of service and benefit, while people like me, who obey the law, have barely anything at all. And I mean barely anything.

\* \* \*

My salary, as I've said, is $42,271. After tax, Social Security, Medicare, that's about $35,400. For five people.

My rent is $1,500 a month, which is $18,000. Food bill's about $670 a month. Car, with payments and insurance is—

I'm sorry, is this boring you? Did I get off topic? Oh, really? We're not here to talk about me?

That's what I'm saying.

\* \* \*

I started to see the professional side of things about, I don't know, maybe a year or so after the Pedro incident. Our intake started to really pick up. Like I told you, now we're at over two thousand units. Sometimes, honestly, it seems closer to three thousand a year. They just keep coming and coming and coming. And on the staff side, I'm getting higher wages than the lowest rank. Our beginning correctional officers get paid just a little over fifteen dollars an hour, and most of my subordinates have their own sad stories, let me tell you. Divorces, domestic violence, bankruptcy. Alcoholism. A lot of depression. So we're all just managing here as best as we can.

You've been to the facility. You've smelled it. And it's loud, right? It's so loud all the time you can't hear yourself think. Try to think of what it would do to you to work in those conditions.

I'm saying that it is just not possible to keep seeing the aliens as totally regular folks, like, as individual, single people with their own little lives and what have you. You want something to exist that just can't. They all start to look the same, and they sure as hell all have the same story. They're all crying, and they're all staring strange with blank faces, and they're all sick, and none of them belong here. And it's our job to make sure that they get contained in safe conditions, so that when the judge sees them or they get deported, they're still in one piece, and so are we.

* * *

I think that I noticed the change in myself, the necessary change, necessary for my own self-preservation, in about 2016. Maybe earlier. The way it works here is that first we put them in a large containment facility that is known for its cool temperature, and then we put them in another facility that has more separated or segregated cages. Yes, the icebox and the doghouse, that's what they're known as.

We don't want them to go to sleep in the icebox. There's a policy reason for that. If they're sleeping, or they look like they're sleeping, then maybe we're not going to know if there's a serious medical problem happening. So we want them to be alert. We don't kick them. We don't kick them as a policy. I'm not saying that I myself have never personally seen anyone kick an alien, that is, nudge them with their feet, so as to keep the alien awake. That's not kicking them. That's keeping them alert so that we can see if there's a medical problem.

When I first got here, I would cry when I'd see Edgar and the other guards kicking them or handling them with their feet, and I would worry about how cold it was and what have you.

But you get used to it. It's the job. You're asking people to do a job that requires a certain amount of mental strength. You can't be running around having nervous breakdowns about this one not having a sweater or this other one having a fever. You just can't. Because then you will lose your job, and that's four people who depend on you now not having anything to eat.

Do you think that prisons and alien camps can be run by bleeding hearts that are sobbing over every little thing? That is just not possible from the guard's point of view.

So I started to move them with my feet too. And when they didn't want to stay awake, I'd get mad at them, just like Edgar got mad and like every other guard would get mad. You get angry. You see the scared and deadness on their faces, and, I'm sorry, but in the end it doesn't touch you anymore. It just doesn't. That's how it works. That's how it works in war, that's how it works in prison, and that's how it works in alien containment facilities. There are certain hard truths that keep this country running that civilians just don't want to know a damn thing about.

So I'd move them with my feet, and I'd keep them awake. And I'd see my other guards doing the same thing. We were all doing it. And when the aliens did something awful, like attempt suicide, at first, of course, it's a shock, and you run about like a chicken with no head, but in the end, if you laugh a little, it's just to survive this ridiculous life.

Listen, my father was in the Marines. He was at Ganjgal. He told me, in war, soldiers laugh at the enemies that they see skewered on a bayonet or who get taken down by phosphorous. And in alien camps, at the end of the day, there's some dark humor here too.

★ ★ ★

I've probably removed, I don't know, three hundred minors from aliens? I have no idea. It's probably more.

What did I feel when I did that? When I took the alien in this case from its mother or the other alien minors from their mothers? You want to know about the first time I did it?

Well, Sharon, when I first took a child away from its mother or its purported mother, I suppose that what I felt like was shit.

Okay? Because it's a real to-do. Everyone is screaming and crying, and it is honestly a fucking nightmare, particularly from a parent's, a mother's, point of view. And, you know, some of my people were from Mexico originally, so it's not like, it's not as if [*indistinct*].

Because, because—can we stop for a minute? Can we stop? I want to stop. I want [*muffled*].

* * *

Okay, so, on May 2, 2018, I, Georgia María Beckett, was informed by my superior, Edgar Williams, to separate a minor child from a suspected illegal crosser who had been detained in the South Texas Family Residential Center in Dilley, Texas. I see from the papers here that her name, what I now understand to be the mother's name, is Delmy Morales. And I guess the girl child's name is Idania. I've never heard that name before. Idania.

They were in the icebox, the room with the cooler temperatures. I had earlier brought them a blanket and some ham sandwiches and two bottles of water. I didn't have enough blankets for everybody in there, but I did try to get them to the aliens with children. A hundred or so people were in the icebox. Delmy and this little Idania were sitting on a bench by the far west wall, and I entered the box and approached them. The mother knew. I could see she understood what was happening when she looked at me. Her face got extremely furious, and she started crying right away.

Sometimes, when the mothers get like that, they can get sort of crazy. It can get physical. Now, you see that I'm not that big, but I don't want it so that I'm always having to call male guards for backup, because then it's going to swing back on me, and I'm going to get a reputation for not being able to do my job. So I have to sort of stand really tall and talk really loud. You can't let anyone believe that anyone but you is in total control. So that's what I did with the alien with the child. I stood in front of her, and I said, in the Spanish I learned from high school and at home, "You're going to have to give her to me now."

And the mother, the alien, says, "Please don't."

But I'd already got my hands around the child's middle, her stomach region. The child was small—they're smaller in Guatemala than you've got in Mexico and certainly in the US. Just a little itty tiny bitty thing, with delicate bones. So it was a difficult operation. I was worried that the little one would get hurt. It's happened. The parents go wild and wind up injuring the minors.

So what I said was, "We're just going to get the doctor to check her out. I'll get her right back to you."

But the mother's screaming, "I heard you are liars and that you will be stealing her from me. Do not take her, please, please, please, please."

So it wasn't easy. And in the end, I did have to get a male to sort of stand by and look on in a threatening way so that the mother would give up the child without my tearing it from her arms. And in the end, the mother just gave up. She knew how it was going. She didn't want to hurt her kid. She just gave her to me. Oh, and then, yeah, she, the mom, was screaming and crying. And the baby, just screaming and screaming.

I didn't put the minor in the doghouse. We had a back room where there was a nurse, and I just left the child with her. The mother screamed for a long time and had to be sedated. From what I understand, the mother was deported back to Guatemala after failing the credible fear, and the child was sent to a Chicago shelter. Heartland Alliance, is what they're called, the facilities there.

That's what happened.

\* \* \*

So, what, that's it? We're done? I think I'm allowed to tell my side, here. I think I'm allowed [*muffled*].

\* \* \*

No, no, no, no. Here, listen up. You listen up. My two sons are Nat and Johnny. Nat's six now, and Johnny's three. No, no. I'm just going to talk here for a second now. I'm just going to talk. I've listened to you plenty.

I have two sons, Nat and Johnny. And I love them more than I can say. More than there are words. And so I want you to look and see the human in me, if you can, Sharon. Do you see me? Do you see the mother in me? Because I am a human too, and I am a mother. And if you for one second forget that I am, then you're the one who's going to be doing wrong. I'm an American woman, and I work sixty hours a week, and I have two sons, and I love them more than anything in the world. So you can look at me from your high horse, and you can judge, and you can ask all your questions with that face on you like you've never had a difficult day in your whole damn life, but when you are trying to understand what is happening in Dilley, don't you ever forget that about me. Because that's what you should be worrying about. People who are asked to do things that are so, so hard and for such low pay. A woman who is asked to do these things. Me. What? No, that's what you should worry about, Sharon. Because people like me, little people in this country, they're the real story. ★

Schey said many of the children his team and other partnering organizations have interviewed showed signs of trauma and emotional distress.

DANIELA SILVA, "'Like I Am Trash': Migrant Children Reveal Stories of Detention, Separation," *NBC News*, July 29, 2018, https://www.nbcnews .com/news/latino/i-am-trash-migrant-children -reveal-stories-detention-separation-n895006

Maslow's hierarchy of needs . . . [are] those that ensure survival by satisfying basic physical and psychological needs (physiological, safety, love and belongingness, esteem); and . . . those that promote the person's self-actualization; that is, realizing one's full potential, "becoming everything that one is capable of becoming," especially in the intellectual and creative domains.

BASSANT PURI and IAN TREASADEN, *Psychiatry: An Evidence-Based Text* (Boca Raton, FL: CRC Press, 2009), 214

# The Hierarchy

### (Physiological)

EVERYTHING'S GREAT. It's good. The food's good. No, I'm happy. I just think it's funny, this place. Dilley's Restaurant, I never heard of it before. I don't know, the name. The name's funny. Yeah, go ahead and have it. It's good. I'm just not that hungry. No, of course! I'm not mad. I'm just tired.

\* \* \*

Honey, I don't want to get into a fight. We're not having problems. No, I am not emotionally unavailable. I wish you wouldn't say that.

I'm just not like you, always wanting to talk about every single feeling that I have as soon as I have it.

You're getting all worked up about something that doesn't have anything to do with you.

What does it have to do with? Have some more pizza. Have some more wine.

Fine, it has to do with my mother. But you know I don't like to talk about that.

I'm upset because of that thing that happened when I was really young. I'm just sort of weirded out right now because coming here has brought up all this stuff that I went through with my mom. I'm talking about when we first tried to get over here.

I mean, when you picked this place, didn't you even once think about it? How I would react?

*Dilley's Restaurant?*

I'm not sure why you would think it was okay to bring me here.

How do you not know what I'm talking about? I told you about it when we first got together. I told you about it when we were talking about having kids.

Dilley, you know. Dilley, Texas?

\* \* \*

I did explain it to you. I told you on our second date, so that you would understand completely what you were getting into with me. I said, "My mom and I had this thing where they separated us when she came over, and it was really hard. And it was at the Dilley Center, in South Texas. I got separated from her, and they sent me to Chicago, and I spent several months with a family whose names I don't even know, because I don't remember any of it, except for very little."

And that's why Mom later had those problems, and she and I had our problems. And why I didn't want to have kids.

\* \* \*

I know that you can't tell that she has it rough mentally, but that's because you don't know her like I do. But you do, too. You see how tense she gets even now when we're over there for dinner and it's time to go home. And how she can't relax, how she'll start crying sometimes. It's worse now that she's older and her memories are coming up on her so intensely. She used to be very, very strong. Just strong as hell. But now, she doesn't have to be so tough. Also, I guess she can't put up as much of a fight against things that hurt her mind.

I think that's what happens when you age. Your memories come back really vividly, and it's like they're almost happening right that second, like you're reliving them.

We do have Alzheimer's in the family, but I'm not sure that's it.

\* \* \*

The first time I realized that it was a serious problem was probably when I was seven, and I think that's my first complete memory. Like my first full memory.

We were over here already. We'd sued the government for splitting us up, but we lost the lawsuit that would have gotten us money. The civil lawsuit. We'd gotten sponsorship, though, and had made it over. We were living *here*, in San Antone, already. She'd gotten a job making food for the laboring crews who work-wed around the Plaza.

Oh, she was tough. Normally. She'd be on her feet making empanadas and stews for fourteen hours a day. And if any of the guys gave her trouble, she'd just look at them with this wicked glare, and they'd stop. And you know how small she is. Well, how small we are. But they could tell that she was not a woman to mess with, and then they'd get really polite. Most of them. Some of them called her bruja, la chica fea, all that mess. But it wasn't the men that made the problem.

It was a social worker. A teacher at my school apparently was worried about how I was doing. I still wouldn't talk a lot then. My mother later said that, for a long time, after she'd gotten me back from Chicago, I wasn't the same. I was slower. I don't know if it was intellectually. I mean, I hope not! That I was withdrawn. There were a few weeks they thought I might be deaf.

Anyway, so the social worker gets a tip from the teacher and comes over to our apartment to check up on us. And my mother's standing there in the doorway talking to her—one second she's standing there, making nice with the lady, and the next second she's ripping my arm out of the socket because we're running through the apartment. She pushes me out of the back window to the fire escape. And we're running down the fire escape, and she's screaming. The police arrested her. They were confused. They thought it was child abuse. After that, we were separated again for like ten weeks, while the public defender was sorting everything out. I got put in that home.

But, no, it wasn't child abuse. On her part, it wasn't.

No, you can't call that child abuse. That's not—she was the one who was abused.

Well, you were raised in Minneapolis, and so, I don't think you really can know.

⋆ ⋆ ⋆

Are you done eating? Baby, let's go.

I just want to go.

## (Safety)

No, I don't really feel like—I'm just tired.
Babe. Babe. I'm just, like, so tired.

All right.

Yeah, it feels good. It feels good. Okay.
Yeah, yeah. Okay. Right? Good.
Good.
Yeah, it's good. Yeah, I love you.

## (Love and Belongingness)

Hey, Mom. Hey, hi. Can you hear me? Yeah, how you doing? Everything okay? Your message was a little. I didn't call because I just got busy.

Oh, that? No, not because of that. The test was fine. I just had to do my annual. It's just a regular checkup, like the kind you get.

Yes, yes. I pray every day. I pray. Just like you taught me.

Mom, Mom. Mom.

Hey, Mom, okay, I'm going to come over. It's okay. Please, I'm sorry I didn't call back. Just don't get upset.

I'm going to come over later tonight, after work.

Yes, I'm at work right now. I'm at the office.

## (Love and Belongingness)

See, Mom? Alive and well. No, I'm not hungry. Okay. Okay. Sure.

Do you want to watch TV? I don't know, whatever's on.

I love you, do you know that? I love you. I love you. I love you, do you know that? Everything's fine. Everything's fine. I just have to go, to get back to Rex. He's fine. He'll come next time. I just have to go home.

I love you. I love you. Okay? It's okay. I love you.

## (Safety)

Well, they had fucking concentration camps here, and that's where we were. And that's why I got so tense at the restaurant. It's not because I don't love you anymore.

Why do you want to hear about it again? I did, I told you already. It was a concentration camp, and they put us in it, and then they sent me away from my mom. And we'd come here because there were gangs in Guatemala, and one of these gang guys had raped her, several times. But that apparently didn't qualify as a reason to get asylum. And I don't know why they separated us. Just to be cruel. Just for the hell of it. Later they said it was illegal, unconstitutional.

\* \* \*

I don't know if my memories of it are real memories or memories that I picked up from Mom talking all the time about it.

It was in Dilley, Texas. In some huge facility. It's still out there. They haven't dismantled it. Over thirty years later, and they're still housing people there.

It smelled and it was crowded. They put us in a pen like we were animals. And you didn't get bathroom breaks and, and—it was like that. It was unsanitary.

They gave you these frozen bologna sandwiches and water. If they fed you at all. And they wouldn't let the adults sleep. I don't know why. And they kicked you and they laughed at you. And there were some people talking about suicide. Everybody there was all the way scared and screwed up from what they'd been through already. Some had been raped and beaten and stalked by gangs. Political persecution in other cases. Not everybody was Latino. Some were Romanians, and some were from Congo.

It was a woman guard. She took me from Mom and sent me to Chicago.

In Chicago, well, it was nice. I guess it was very, very nice. Compared to what Mom could give me.

And when I got back to Mom, apparently I didn't want to be with her. I screamed and I bit her. I cried for the other mother, the foster mother. And I did that for a long time.

## (Safety)

Rex, if you have a problem with me, then why don't you just leave? You're just exhausting me. Really, I can't take it anymore. I just can't take you anymore, being all over me and demanding everything of me. Take, take, take. That's all men do. Just taking.

No, don't touch me.

No, don't touch me! You don't even listen to me!

You don't even care, if you loved me, you would care. You would care more about me.

You would see that I don't want to talk about it! I don't want to talk about everything all the time!

It wasn't child abuse. Yes, you said that. Yes, you did. Yes, you did.

You said that. That you don't remember is making me insane. You said my mother abused me, but you don't understand what we went through.

Just stop.

## (Safety)

So you're not talking to me anymore? Can't we just forget last night? I've been stressed. That's the issue.

Why are you looking at me like that? That hurts me when you look at me with those kind of eyes, because I can see what you're thinking.

Let's just forget all that. I was just in a bad mood.

Come on, I was just in some bad mood. You know how women get.

Yes, it is. It's normal for women to get bitchy sometimes. It's just something that you guys have to put up with.

Hey, come on. Can't we laugh about it?

Of course I am. That's what I'm saying. I'm sorry I was like that.

I'm sorry. No, I really am. I mean it. I'm sorry. Please. Okay? Just forgive me.

Please, sweetheart, darling, please.

I know I'm not—I wasn't, I wasn't nice to you.

I love only you. Only you. There's only you. If I didn't have you, I would die. I wouldn't be able to live. Please, I swear, I'll never talk to you like that again.

I don't want to get a divorce. Don't say the word "divorce" ever again.

I need you so much. I love you so much.

I love you so, so much. You're my whole life.

I don't know what I was thinking. I was crazy.

Don't leave me. Say it. Don't leave me. You won't leave me.

You'll never leave me.

Swear it, promise it.

## (Safety)

Dear Nigel,

I am so sorry that I forgot to send you the memo. I completely blanked. It won't happen again. I'm attaching it here. I crunched the data on the T5215 project, and it looks good on cost. We're actually coming in $3,260 under budget, which I think the client is going to love.

Again, I apologize for not sending this last week. I've had some family issues occupying my attention, but I think that's all cleared up now. Still, there's no excuse, and I know that.

Yours sincerely,
Miranda

### (Safety)

Sorry, I'm in here! Just hold on.

Yes, yes, I'm coming out!

I wasn't in there for that long.

Well, sometimes mascara runs. Thanks for letting me know.
Also, there's another bathroom down the other hall.

### (Love and Belongingness)

amy girl how u been long time no talk

u want 2 get some drinks next week on me

i don't care wherever u want

### (Safety)

Rex, you won't leave me. Say it. Say that you won't leave me.
Say that you won't do it.
I don't know, I don't know why.
I've got chest pains. They're really bad. I think I have to go to the doctor. It's not normal to have chest pains like this.
Tell me you won't go. Tell me, tell me.

\* \* \*

I will, I'll take a pill.

It's like I feel the panic, but I can't feel it. That's what Valium does. You know you're scared, but you don't feel it. But you do feel it, or you know it. You know it, but you don't feel it.

The doctor says I shouldn't take too many of these, because it's bad for your brain health. Like, when you get older.

### (Self-Esteem)

I bought this for you, Rex. It's red silk. Do you like it?

I was thinking of you all day. I thought about your big hands. The way you touch me.

Do you want to touch me?

Maybe I won't let you.

Maybe it'll be look but no touching.

\* \* \*

Whoo! Come on cowboy, show it to me, show it to me.

Show it to me, Daddy. Show me.

Right there, you know where it is.

Or do you want me to do that? Do you like that?

Say it, say it. Say it.

\* \* \*

Rip me apart, just rip me apart. Just kill me.

I love it. I love it.

I want it. Just eat me up. Use me all up.

You can do anything you want to me.

### (Self-Actualization)

Aims, let's have another one. It's on me. All right, it's on you.

God, this is great. Just what I needed.

I mean, the wine's good. But what I'm talking about is, just us. Hanging out. Just chilling.

Just fucking chilling for a change, you know?

Oh, he's fine. We're fine. It's marriage.

You know what I think? Sometimes, I think, you can just slip out of your past like a goddam snake. Like out of its skin. Do you think that's possible?

Like, on a night like tonight, hanging out with you. It's such a pretty night. We're just two girls. Not a care in the world.

I mean, all that worrying and whatever, who gives a damn. Let's just chuck it. In the trash. Like, you can just be brand new sometimes. I think you can decide that you're just not going to be in that pain anymore.

Yeah, my mom. No, I know you know, Aims. I know you do. That's kind of why I texted. Just needed to see my old Aims.

Yeah, it's that old anxiety. It just came back. I haven't thought about it for, like, two years, and then last week, it was like, bam.

And I got worried that maybe I'll never get over all of that. Something I don't even remember that well. Like, I don't remember the camp. I do remember Chicago, though. I didn't want to leave that family. That's what I've been thinking about. How I didn't want to go back to my mom, you know, because she was just so scared all the time, and the other family was normal. Also, they gave me presents—a doll, a little ring. A dress. So I wanted to stay with them and not her.

The guilt. It's just, it eats you.

And I love her. Of course I love her. I love her more than anything. But you just feel disconnected sometimes, from yourself.

I don't know, they take you away, and then you're just not the same. And sometimes you worry you're not going to be the same forever.

\* \* \*

But it's still possible to just be you. To be a person separated from that crap. To be something else than a person that's had something done to you. On a night, hanging out, chilling, I can feel that.

They can go to hell, right? Go. To. Hell. Go to hell.

★ ★ ★

Let's do something crazy. Amy! Come on, Amy! Let's get a bottle and just go driving.

Let's party. Let's have fun. We'll get into trouble. Like the old days.

Let's just fucking crush it. Night's young. We could do anything at all.

We have to live for now. Right, Aims? Right on.

Right on, Aims. Let's get a top-up. I want a top-up.

Yeah, this is good. Being here with you makes me feel like I can breathe for a second, like we're okay, and everything's fine. ★

A manifesto tied to the alleged El Paso, Texas, shooter included ranting about Hispanic immigrants "replacing" European-American culture and pre-emptively defended President Donald Trump from media criticism. Patrick Crusius, 21, of Allen, Texas, was arrested Saturday . . . after he allegedly gunned down dozens of people, killing at least 20. The manifesto was posted to the website 8chan about an hour-and-a-half before the El Paso Walmart shooting began. . . . "My ideology has not changed for several years," the purported Crusius text reads. "My opinions on automation, immigration, and the rest predate Trump and his campaign for president."

BENJAMIN FEARNOW, "Don't 'Blame Trump': Manifesto Tied to
El Paso Shooting Rants about Democrats, Hispanics Invading Country,"
*Newsweek*, August 4, 2019

# Walmart

"Honey, please stop."
"Mama. Mama."
Saúl won't stop screaming in the back seat of the car. Even though Peter said not to worry about it, I have to get peppers, ground beef, milk, buns, and salad if I'm going to get dinner on the table tonight. So I dressed Saúl in his Pikachu sweat suit and strapped him into his car seat. We're heading to the store. I can't see him while I'm driving, which you'd think I would appreciate when he's shrieking like this, but it's just making me more nervous.

"Honey."
"Mama."
Sometimes Saúl gets quiet when he's in car. He likes the rumbling sound. But maybe he can tell that I'm messed up. I think that's why he's upset. Although he's always upset, right? It's normal. I've helped plenty with Olga, so I've learned how a two-year-old can fuss. He doesn't know what happened anyway. And Mom said it was fine. That I wasn't acting strange or hurting my child.

Going to the one on Alameda. Obviously not the one on Gateway. That's still closed.

What do we need again?

I can't remember.

Do I turn right or left?

Oh, it's just right here. Okay.

Parking lot's full. Lots of cars, lots of families. People are out shopping like it's regular and fine. They're not hiding in their houses. It's important to understand when fears are real and when they're not real, at least not real right now. And, yeah, security everywhere. Police and security. They'll take care of any problem. Because the Gateway store didn't have any guards on duty, I guess.

Peppers, meat, milk, buns, salad.

"Come on, babe."

"Mama. Mama."

"In you go. In the shopping cart."

"No."

"It'll be fun!"

"No."

"I love you. Love you so much."

Making myself walk up to it. Past the police, into the cold, cold market. There are tons of women here. That's good. Because women know. They can sense it. Psychically. Although Grandma didn't know it, and she was part witch, I always thought. Like we had special powers in my family. But she didn't have a premonition that day. She goes to Walmart, and then that guy shows up.

It's weird being in here. Even if it's not the one.

"Mama."

"There are the tomato cans you like, baby." He loves these pyramids of tomato cans. "Here's a little tomato can. Play with that. Isn't that pretty?"

Okay. Buns and meat and water and dinner and things that people eat.

I'm tired.

*My most precious baby. My most precious beauty, my beautiful. I love love love love love love love love love love you, you are still my little girl.*

"Hey, ma'am, may I help you?"

"What?"

"Do you need any help?"

Lady's talking to me. Name tag. Works here. I used to go to the other one, so I don't think I know her. Tall with a ponytail. Older than me. Looking at me with nice eyes. She can tell.

"Where's the meat?"

"At the back. There's a meat counter. I can take you if you want."

"Oh, no, that's okay. We can find it."

"That's a beautiful boy you have here."

"Yeah. He's my little one."

"He's a little beauty. A little beauty. Are you a little beauty?"

"He's shy."

"Of course."

"He's a good boy," I say.

"Let me show you the way," she says.

"Okay."

"Tomato," Saúl says, while we pass a security guard who has a gun on his belt. Maybe I should get a gun. Or Peter should get a gun.

"Tomato, that's good," I say.

"Tomato," the lady says.

"Tomato."

"That's actually a tomato can," I say.

"Tomato," Saúl says.

"Here you go," the lady says. I look at her name tag. It says "Tonatzin."

"Thank you," I say. I look down at the refrigerated meat. It's pink and red. It's pieces of glistening steak and flesh. It's ground up with white pieces of fat in it. It has blood on it.

"Thank you," I say again.

"I'm right here if you need me," Tonatzin says, squeezing me on the shoulder and then walking away.

"Help you?" There's a young Latino guy behind the counter. He's, what, twenty years old. Little fluffy mustache.

"Um, let's see," I say.

When I was really young, she took care of me, because my

mom was always working. Peter makes enough so that I can take the next year off, but my mom couldn't, and so my grandma was like my mom for a while. Forever.

"So many choices," I say, while Saúl talks about dogs or frogs. I try not to look at the blood.

"We have a special on liver," the kid says.

We would lay in bed, and I'd look at her hands. Because they had wrinkles and veins in them, which I thought were beautiful and exotic. I would say, "Why do you have all of these bumps?" And she'd say, "Because I'm an old lady. The old lady who loves you." She'd say it in English or Spanish. I'd run my fingers over the papery skin on the tops of her hands, tracing the brown spots and speckles.

"Hamburger," I say. "Two pounds please."

"Two pounds coming up," the kid says.

I see her hands when I last kissed her. Eight days ago, when I identified her. Her fingers were white and curled, like she was still trying to hold onto me.

What happened to her is something that I can't see in my head without losing my mind.

The kid behind the counter is weighing the red, shining meat on the weigher thing. He looks over at me. His eyes shift.

"This says two and half, but I'll just write two," he says.

"Okay," I say. I look down at Saúl, who's still talking and playing with his tomato can. It's a tomato paste can. It has a drawing of a tomato on the label.

I take the cold package from the kid's hands. It's wrapped in white paper. The meat inside is soft. I can dent it with my fingers, but a little meat juice comes out. I put it in the shopping cart and wipe my hands off on my slacks.

"Where's the milk?" I say.

"Over there, aisle sixteen," the kid says. He points.

I steer the cart and walk over there. Past more women. Everybody has normal faces. No one's crying. We look at each other, though. In aisle sixteen there's a short Latina with red hair staring at the refrigerated yogurts and sighing.

After the service, Marisol was holding Olga and sighing like that. She said, "I don't understand."

And Mom said, "There's nothing to understand. It's just evil."

"That's not good enough," Marisol had said.

"Please calm down," I'd said. "You're just making everything worse."

The lady with the red hair says, "Oooooohhkay." With her right hand, she opens the refrigerator door and takes out two lemon Yoplaits and puts them into a black plastic basket that she's holding with her left hand. She seemed fine when I first looked at her, but now I see that her eyebags are puffing out, like when you get stressed and age ten years in a minute.

She closes the refrigerator door and stands there, still glaring at the yogurts through the glass.

I look at the milk.

Saúl's saying, "Mama." He's not screaming it.

"Yes, yes."

"Mama, I want NOW, let's NOW," he says. He starts laughing.

The lady looks down at him and then at me. She blinks when she sees my face.

"This is no world for a child," she says. She reaches out her hand and pats Saúl's cheek, gently, with two fingers.

"Is whole fat better for toddlers, or is it nonfat?" I say. "I can't remember."

"Whole fat," the lady says.

"Whole fat," I say.

"Some people say they shouldn't drink milk at all because of the allergies," she says. "But I always drank milk and my kids all drank milk, and we were fine."

"Right," I say. "Like peanuts."

"Peanuts can kill," the lady says.

At that second, I'm not in the Walmart anymore. I'm at home, and I'm seven years old. Grandma was doing one of her spiritual things. She'd sprinkle me with holy water and tell me to close my eyes and imagine a large pink ball of energy around me. The large pink ball was like a defensive shield, she said, like in *Star Trek: Voyager*, except it was made by the angels. If I meditated very hard, I could make the pink ball grow huge, so that there was a massive space of safety around me that no one could enter.

"You are surrounded by light," Grandma had said, sitting in front of me on her knees. "That's God's love, Teresa."

"I think I have to sit down," I say.

The lady slides her eyes over to me. "Okay."

Saúl is singing in his seat. I sit down on the linoleum, pressing my back to the cold glass wall of the refrigerator case.

"Are you okay?" the red-haired lady asks.

"Yeah," I say.

After a couple of minutes, the lady with the ponytail, Tonatzin, walks up to us.

"Hi, hon," she says in a tense voice, wrinkling her forehead.

"Give me a second," I say.

"She just sat down," the red-haired lady says.

"Are you light-headed?" Tonatzin asks.

"I don't know," I say.

"We were talking about milk allergies and peanut allergies," the red-haired lady says. "Maybe I said something wrong. I am having a lot of anxiety. I was going to go by Cielo Vista that day, the day there's the shooting. And I went to the Albertson's instead. Because I had to get my shoes fixed, with the shoe man. If I hadn't needed to get my shoes fixed, I would have gone to the Cielo Vista one."

"You got lucky," Tonatzin says.

"No kidding," the red-haired lady says.

"That guy's going to fry," Tonatzin says.

"I know a hundred people who'll push the button," the red-haired lady says.

"You want a glass of water?" Tonatzin says to me.

"I don't want anything," I say.

"Is there a problem?"

I look up. A white man in a blue security-guard uniform is walking up to us. I'm shaking like I did before I gave birth. I close my eyes. I try to imagine a huge pink bubble around my body and around Saúl's body. But there's no God and no pink bubble and no angels and no witches and no nothing but Saúl and the Walmart and these two women.

"I should have gone to another store," I say.

"Everything's fine, Gerald," Tonatzin says. "Go away."

"You okay?" Gerald says.

"Just need a second," I say.

"Is she sick?" Gerald says.

"Give us a minute," Tonatzin says.

"Get out of here with your damn gun," the red-haired lady says.

"All right," Gerald says. He walks away.

The two women stand above me, guarding me. Saúl starts screaming, and I don't do anything. Tonatzin takes him out of the seat and tries to hug him. But he thrashes and screams harder.

"Mama."

I stand up. I'm dead, in my heart. I take Saúl and bounce him and show him the tomato can. He stops screaming, and I put him back in his seat.

"What are you here to get, hon?" Tonatzin asks me.

"Dinner," I say.

"Dinner," the red-haired lady and Tonatzin both say. They look into my cart, at the hamburger.

"She was talking about whole-fat milk," the red-haired lady says.

Tonatzin opens up the refrigerator door and takes out two gallons of whole-fat milk and puts them in my cart.

"I got to get some salad," I say.

All three of us walk down the aisle, and Tonatzin guides us to the produce. I put a wad of lettuce into a bag. I get some carrots.

"Just meat?" the red-haired lady says. "What are you going to do with the ground beef?"

"Oh, buns," I say.

"Get a tomato," the red-haired lady says.

Tonatzin gets two tomatoes and puts them in a bag and then puts the bag in my cart.

"Let's get the buns," the red-haired lady says.

They walk Saúl and me to another aisle in the middle of the store. We look up at five rows of bread and buns and rolls in shiny plastic sacks.

The red-haired lady reaches up and gets a bag of hamburger buns and puts it in my cart.

"Soda?" Tonatzin says. "Cake? Cleaning supplies? Bottled water? Electronics?"

"No," I say.

The red-haired lady and Tonatzin walk me up to the express checkout.

"Just because of some shoes," the red-haired lady's saying.

"You never know," Tonatzin says.

There's a girl doing the register. She's about sixteen years old. Her long, glossy black hair is tied up into a ponytail like Tonatzin's. She's wearing thick black glasses. Her nametag reads "Luz."

The red-haired lady and Tonatzin put my stuff onto the conveyor belt. Luz rings it all up. I look down. I don't have my bag on me.

"I don't have my bag," I say.

"Where's your bag?" Tonatzin asks.

"I don't know." I think. "In the car."

"Okay," Tonatzin says. "We'll wait here. Go to your car and get your bag."

Saúl's chattering at me. I turn around and go outside and walk past the police. I start crying. I go to the car and open up the door and, howling like an animal, get my bag from the passenger's seat. Then I walk past the police again, heading back. Some of the police are looking at me strange, and some of them are turning away from me, to give me privacy. In the Walmart, there's a long line behind where Tonatzin and the red-haired lady are standing with Saúl. Saúl's sobbing because I left. I stop crying when I see him crying. Tonatzin is trying to get the people in the line to go to checkout stand six or four. The red-haired lady is talking about shoes again.

"The heels on my pumps were all worn down," she says.

I pick up Saúl and cry some more into his neck. Then I get my wallet and hand Luz my card.

"You have to put it into the thing," she says, looking at Tonatzin with a scared face.

The little machine with the chip reader, is what she means. I put the card in the slot while balancing Saúl, who's screaming, on my hip. The machine beeps, and I sign the screen with the plastic stick. Tonatzin squeezes past me and helps Luz bag up my stuff in a paper sack and puts it in the back of my shopping cart.

"Go somewhere else," the red-haired lady says to a tall bald man who's holding a six-pack and complaining about the wait.

"This is the express checkout," he says.

"Bug off," she says.

I put Saúl back in the seat in the shopping cart. He's jerking his arms and hollering.

Tonatzin and the red-haired lady walk me out of the Walmart, the red-haired lady still holding her basket.

"What I think is that you can't fight destiny," the red-haired lady says. "What you have to do is be very, very grateful for every day that we have. For every second of life. For every breath. You need to breathe in the good air and remember that we are alive. And that everything happens for a reason. Because why else would we be standing here and not be dead like those poor people? Because there's a plan, a secret plan, God's plan, and we aren't important enough to understand it. Why else would I go to the shoe store and not to the Walmart that day? And why else would those mothers and abuelas and children go to the Walmart and not go to the shoe store? Because of fate. Because of the angels. Because of heaven. Because of demons. Because of hell. Because of Satan."

"That's enough," Tonatzin says.

Saúl's crying is splitting my head open. I look at the two women and try to smile.

"Thanks for helping me," I say.

"Aw, sure, honey," Tonatzin says. "Whatever happened, I'm so sorry."

"My grandma didn't go to the shoe store," I say. "She died."

Tonatzin's face crumbles.

"Go home and pray," the red-haired lady says.

I take hold of my shopping cart's handle, but I don't walk to my Mazda. I squint into the bright sunlight bouncing off the glossy tops of the cars and the police officers in the parking lot. Tonatzin and the red-haired lady don't move. They stay there patiently, watching me. It seems to me, in that moment, as if time expands, like a pink bubble, so that my grandmother is not dead and I'm not dead, and no one has died. Like time doesn't exist, almost, because we're just here, here in the parking lot, which is the same as being at home, or being nowhere. The world's opened up, and when I look inside, it's empty. My son is roaring at me. He's bending over so that the Pikachu on his sweatshirt is getting cut in half. Saúl's face is as red as a tomato.

"Everything's going to be all right," the red-haired lady says.

"Not really," Tonatzin says, hugging herself.

I wipe my face with the back of my hand. There's meat juice on it.

"I can't feel anything," I say. ✴

Known as Michigan's "godmother of school choice," DeVos has been one of the top funders of Detroit's charter schools, which, as a *New York Times* op-ed commented, "even charter advocates acknowledge is the biggest school reform disaster in the country." As the *Times* reported, half of Detroit's charters performed only as well, or worse, than traditional public schools in the city, which are some of the most challenged in the country.... Perhaps it's not surprising that for-profit companies run 80 percent of Michigan's charters, far more than any other state.

ZACHARY JASON, "The Battle over Charter Schools," ED. (Harvard University), Summer 2017

During Tuesday's hearing, Sen. Jeff Merkley (D-OR) asked DeVos about whether or not her department would continue to provide federal funding to schools that had anti-LGBTQ policies. At first she tried to dodge the question by asserting, "Schools that receive federal funds must follow federal law." But Merkley pressed, leading DeVos to say, "In areas where the law is unsettled, this department is not going to be issuing decrees. That is a matter for Congress and the courts to settle."

ZACK FORD, "Betsy DeVos Abandons LGBTQ Students, Won't Protect Them from Discrimination," *ThinkProgress*, June 6, 2017

The company, Neurocore, which has received more than $5 million from Ms. DeVos and her husband, Richard DeVos Jr., to run "brain performance centers" in Michigan and Florida, lost an appeal before an advertising-industry review board, which found that the company's claims of curbing and curing a range of afflictions without medication were based on mixed research and unscientific internal studies.

ERICA L. GREEN, "'Brain Performance' Firm DeVos Invested in Is Hit for Misleading Claims," *New York Times*, June 26, 2018

One picture of private prisons ... includes barely edible food, indifferent health care, guard brutality, and assorted corner-cutting measures.

CLYDE HABERMAN, "For Private Prisons, Detaining Immigrants Is Big Business," *New York Times*, October 1, 2018

# The Overton Window

OUR MANDATES are more far-reaching now than under previous administrations, but we must still ensure that our supervisors do not forget their essential responsibilities. We have extended extraordinary latitudes to our more gifted stewards, and our policies encourage them to innovate learning, health, welfare, behavioral, and performance modules within the more generous potentials allowed by public-private partnerships and developments in constitutional law. Nevertheless, we at the Department of Education lead from the top and require our administrators to cultivate the same sound bodies and regulated minds that we develop in our nation's youths. If an administrator moves too far beyond the Overton Window—that old, handy helpmeet for policy makers—we will not hesitate to pivot his platform back to acceptable settings.

To that effect, during my investigation of Harrison Carver's stewardship of the Landingsburgh Program (#180232SC), which I conducted 2/12/38 at the behest of the Secretary, I concluded that certain benchmarks have gone missing

it appears that in Landingsburgh our standard framework has been modified to accommodate

it seems that Carver has not

I'm afraid that Carver has

I'm afraid

* * *

The day the Secretary told me to check up on Carver started cheerfully enough. I had woken early to make pancakes and waffles for my husband and three children. We live in Chevy Chase, Maryland, in a modest four-bedroom home with a large, grassy backyard that gives the kids plenty of space to play and calibrate. I'm at the office a lot because of the demands of my job as first assistant to the SOE. Still, when I can, I like to spend high-impact time with my family, which I use to manage their personal parameters and do homey things, like cook for them.

"Eat up," I'd said that morning, spooning strawberry jam into a sauce boat while I still stood in the kitchen.

James, my husband, sat at the breakfast table with my eldest, Sheraton, and our twins, Tina and Ulrike. They munched and muttered gentle joshes at each other while drinking orange juice and spearing sausages.

"Why don't you sit and eat with us?" James asked, as he finished his pancake stack. He's a tall, well-built fellow with large green eyes and a short nap of brown hair, like a puppy's. We met at a Dupont Circle nightclub in '22, when he studied for his UCPAE at Georgetown and I had not yet started my job at the DOE. James now works as an accountant for Cheshire Inc. in DC. We've been married for sixteen years.

"Sheraton likes the strawberry. I'm just fixing it up," I said. My name is Petra Eager, and I'm a medium-built thirty-eight-year-old woman with blond hair and brown eyes. James and I go running regularly together, and so I have kept my figure despite riding a government desk for sometimes eighteen hours at a stretch.

"Your mother fusses over you," James said, reaching out to ruffle our son's daisy-blond hair. Sheraton's twelve years old. He's a quiet, gentle, sweet boy with clear green eyes and a delicate constitution. He has a small learning disability—he's two clicks behind in reading, which classifies him as an A/B—which we countered by sending him to one of the specialized charters in DC that Carver had founded so many years before: Middlebrook Elite focuses on Comprehension and Self-Awareness, and Sheraton had been flourishing there. The girls, Tina and Ulrike, are hale, hearty, russet-haired beauties who excel at sports and science, and so we'd placed them in another nearby school, Marlborough, which is Well Rounding them in arts and relationships. They're solid As.

"Thanks, Mom," Sheraton said, smiling at me.

"I want the strawberry before Sheraton gets it," Tina said.

"No, I do," Ulrike said.

"Don't eat all the waffles," Sheraton said.

"Enough for everybody," James and I said at the same time.

That's when my phone started to beep. I reached over to the kitchen counter, where I'd placed it before mixing the pancake batter, and picked it up.

"Need to see you ASAP," the Secretary's message said.

\* \* \*

An hour later, I stood on the blue-and-gold eagle carpet that spread out from beneath the Secretary's huge desk. The Department of Education is headquartered in the Lyndon Johnson Building on Maryland Street. It's a big, boxy, latticed-looking structure, built in the early '60s. After the presidential Extension in '23, there'd been some talk of replacing it with an Addison Mizner–style palazzo that brought together Spanish and Venetian influences, but this plan was quickly scuttled by the Secretary as too accelerated an aesthetic modification. I agreed with her, as during that period, we had already implemented a host of reforms that proceeded on the quick track, and I knew from personal experience that it takes a little time for people to get used to change. You can't spring it on them all at once.

"I need you to go look in on Carver," the Secretary said, tapping her painted nails on a rectangular blue whiz drive that lay on the blotter before her. She's dark-haired, didn't look any bigger than a minute behind her huge desk, and bears a tanned and attractive visage adorned with light makeup and tasteful dermatological work. Her easy-does-it appearance is deceiving, though, as she has revolutionized the school system into a for-profit charter landscape through brute force of willpower and an advanced sense of ends-means.

I wore a plain beige suit with a white silk shirt, brown pumps, and a lilac scarf at my neck. I remained standing, though I could feel my face crease slightly with confusion. "You want me to monitor Carver?"

"Yes. He's still in Landingsburgh."

"Which has the best metrics in the nation," I said.

The Secretary waggled her fingers at me, a sign of tension. "You know that he made it a condition that we leave him alone as long as his numbers stayed up—and he's been an independent agency since, when?"

"About ten, eleven years, ma'am," I said.

"That long," she shook her head. "Well, he has kept his stats high. Plus, he started generating liquidity, especially after he began to caucus with other bureaus."

I nodded, familiar with all of this. "But?"

The Secretary looked at me over her glasses. "We've been hearings things. Sort of strange rumors. The governor's complaining."

"About what?"

She waved a hand. "That he's depressed, there's emotional issues, something."

"Does the governor want him out?" I asked.

"Oh, no!" she said. "Oh, no, no. But his reports have been only trickling in, so we don't really have eyes on. I've informed Carver's assistant that you'll be coming." She pushed the whiz drive toward me.

I stepped forward and took up that little burden.

"Listen, this doesn't leave the room," the Secretary said. "But we haven't heard from Carver in four months. So you need to go out there and see what's going on."

"Yes, ma'am," I said.

\* \* \*

Carver was a great man in his way, as we all knew. Army, Harvard, Stanford. Medal of Honor, Magna Cum Laude, NEH Fellow. Before he came to us, he developed his penchant for problem solving by captaining an F/A-18C Hornet during the Iraqi Civil War and helping to retake the Mosul Dam. He then set his sights on education. After receiving his MA at the age of twenty-seven, Carver began teaching in the Maine school system, impressing his superiors by lowering 7–12 truancy by three classifications and 9–12 depravity by eight stages through Core Values tutorials enforced in 4×4 block schedules. Within two years of being tapped by the Secretary to lead the DOE's Rehabilitative Services Bureau, Carver implemented the Clean Bodies, Full Hearts, and Healthy Minds programs for the nation's students, which tests the subjects on various skill sets and then assigns them a category ranging from A to SubD. His innovations activated a +17 rise in national intelligence and a full rank uptick in self-management metrics observable in units scoring beneath 192 in the General Test.

When Carver ran the RSB, I had just been hired by the Agency. This was in '24. The Secretary (her contract's been re-upped eight times) assigned me to the Office of Safe and Healthy Students as a GS-5 assistant supervisor with responsibility for the C class students in the Midwest. Even there, in the Agency's low-lier precincts, we had heard of Carver's successes and sought to emulate him. He'd not only succeeded in privatizing the national athletics and humanities curricula but also launched the trailblazing "I Am" and "Listening Traits" pedagogies, which it is no exaggeration to say that he single-handedly invented.

The first time I laid eyes on the man was in the summer of '26, when Carver gave the keynote at the six-day New School conference. Carver strode to the podium in quick but fluid moves and radiated an aura of bracing confidence. He'd raised his arms and stared at us with his well-deep, misty eyes for a moment, so that a hush lowered down upon the room. Then, in the most mesmerizing and honey-dark voice I'd ever heard, he said, "Our job is to love and protect our nation's children, who have been entrusted to our care during a dangerous age of crime and laxity. To fulfill our covenant, we must remember *always* the hard truths that without mandatory decency there cannot be harmony and that without costs, there cannot be benefits. So armed with this knowledge, we must exert the authority we hold over these little souls by virtue of God's grace and expend it toward unbounded and efficient good works." He pounded the podium, his face aglow with conviction. "And only a system rooted deeply in public choice can achieve this!"

After the roaring and applause, my colleagues huddled together, trading notes. "He increased productivity 89 percent in SubD Belligerents in his Cincinnati Focus Group," a GS-11 from Federal Student Aid murmured. "In New Jersey, he organized delivery systems that optimized Emotional Resilience in B's by six stages for the entire region," a G-6 from the Office of Civil Rights breathed.

"He's a remarkable man," I agreed.

Like my other colleagues, I kept an eye on Carver's accomplishments throughout his career. The Secretary had encouraged a culture of Best and Top Notch, and Carver embodied those ethics. We wanted to embody them too.

* * *

I grew up in Dane County, Wisconsin, the daughter of Sheraton Hauser, a strict but loving father and English schoolteacher at Jefferson High. I wanted to be just like my dad, and so I earned my master's in '22, teaching in a Dane County middle school. I entered a challenged system where the classes were massive—units running sometimes into the seventies or eighties—and the facilities were infested with asbestos and lead. The Publics were then nearly defunded in the overhaul of '22. At Dane, we had Acute Incidents on a nearly daily basis and two mass shooting in four years, which I understood to be fostered by the combustive interaction between the pupils' desperation and saturnism and an increasing citizen discontent with the use of tax dollars to teach outlanders.

After losing six children in a conflict between White vocationals affiliated with a patriot alt-chan site and Hispanic students, I decided that I wanted to be part of the revolution that created safe classrooms and optimized children's civic characters and brain performances. As soon as I saw the advertisement for the Office of Safe and Healthy Students, I applied. It was lucky too, because after the Second Emergency, we started to see a tidal wave of exciting ideas for how to address children's behavioral health challenges and government overspending. In those years, almost all of the innovations came from Carver's own fertile mind, and it always gave me a thrill on the rare occasions I saw him wandering the Agency halls, barking orders into a phone and exuding the centrifugal magnetism of a rising star.

* * *

The Secretary promoted Carver to General Counsel in '26, and he acquired authority over three thousand schools located in Vulnerable Districts across the United States. Carver soon enough began to focus most of his energies on the "school-to-prison pipeline," a term developed by the Left to chastise educational and law enforcement technologies that were said to have disparate impacts on SubDs, who were more likely to be people of certain races. Carver did not shy away from this phrasing but rather began issuing a blizzard of increasingly excitable-sounding memoranda wherein he promised that he would not only eliminate the pipeline but also decrease SubD juvenile delinquency at the same time. Carver worked continually toward this goal and achieved a breakthrough quickly enough in '27. This is when he implemented his groundbreaking Growth Model, which saw his Vulnerable District conservatories becoming an all-inclusive learn-live society. Delinquency in all grades fell to between 22–46 percent at his franchises, and, what's more, the juvenile felony convictions for his SubDs also plummeted. Perhaps most excitingly for Congress, after an initial start-up period, his Academies also began to pay for themselves.

Carver managed this miracle by marshaling the powers of eminent domain and also cultivating synergies between both federal and local governmental pub/pri organs—the hospitals, the police, the housing authorities, sanitation departments, and, increasingly, jails and immigrant camps. Every few months, whenever Carver needed the Secretary's approval for a new merger, he'd fly up to DC. He marched through our offices, his warm brown eyes shining as he chattered about setting up ICE and Marshal satellites in the surviving remnants of the Publics or setting up trial-balloon administrative guidelines on child labor.

"Don't miss the boat on this, Gwen," Carver would enthuse to the Secretary, smacking his hand on her desk. "This is going to be a game changer."

"I'm sure it will be," she'd reply, smiling at him indulgently. "But not everybody likes to move as fast as you do."

My job was to do the paperwork that leveraged our programs off the ground. I had to keep in mind advances in constitutional law, administrative law, and the less-dynamic international treaties, while always balancing the ROIs so that the human outlays and deficit issues would never become so overwhelming that Congress would shut us down—but that was unlikely anyway. At the Agency, we kept a keen eye on the Overton Window, that concept developed by Joseph P. Overton (deceased) of the Mackinac Center for Public Policy, which alerts to the range of ideas currently permitted to be spoken aloud in political discourse. If reforms are too radical, they stray outside the allowable aperture, and censorship is likely to follow. So we always took care to curb

Carver's more fanciful ideas, such as his Adversative version of the "I Am" and "Listening" Exercises, which employed intense images and fluids. As in all government institutions that harbor visionaries, we had to protect him and us from punishing budget cuts and troublesome social movements and insurrections.

Still, the Overton Window seemed to be rapidly expanding. Since the Second and then Third Emergencies in '22–'24, and our resulting new twelve-member Supreme Court, there had been a host of alterations in the legal and educational landscape. *Roper v. Simmons* had been overruled, to be replaced with *Cruz v. Macias*, allowing capital punishment for minors. Then, there'd been the striking down of *Graham v. Florida* and its substitution with *Adams v. Texas*, permitting mandatory LWOP for under eighteens. The national educational platform also reacted to the butterfly effects of the cut in the corporate tax to 4 percent and the release of Puerto Rico and the Virgin Islands, which together created an exodus that flooded the already filled-to-bursting public schools and generated more shootings, stabbings, possibly or probably rapes, and other related problems.

A multiplicity of previously unheard-of new regulations began to cross my desk, and it was my task to see them fulfilled according to the rule of law and best practices. During these long, long years, when Carver began to recede from everyday view and explicit influence, I will admit that I myself had to work on my own personal Overton Window. Sometimes, the practicalities that I was saddled with executing seemed initially vile and flat-out disgusting, at least from the vantage of the girl who had once worked so hard to teach kids their ABCs in Wisconsin. When I read the new US Guidelines on schools' use of corporal punishment after the National Relaxation, for example, I had a brief nervous episode that saw me running across the Mall in a panic. I consulted my psychologist (recommended by the Secretary), who helped me destimulate with biofeedback processes and a new regimen of vitamins and mineral packets.

When the Secretary ordered me to effectuate Carver's early-regime recommendations for allowing the charters to block LGBTQ kids, I once again glitched, taking to bed with "the flu" for three days. I'd had friends in my youth, during my own high school days, whom I had cared for deeply, and their memories made my coordinates temporarily swing shut. I finally came back to work only after another adjustment in my biofeeds, which allowed me to type up the paperwork, reams and reams of it. By the time I'd finished drafting and line-editing the five-hundred-page report, I found that my Overton Window had expanded to allow in the necessary light.

There were other episodes like this, though they seemed to decrease with the years. When the Secretary winnowed Non children from White charters in '31, I spent at least a week fighting off a thick, spiritual sickness that seemed to cling to my lungs and my very skin, but then I submitted the issue to a complete cost-benefit breakdown and almost never worried about it again. By the time the Secretary tasked me with setting up UNCRC-compatible furnished camps for Mexican and other Hispanic minors in the wake of the '33 Wall and the Puerto Rico catastrophes, I had worked with the Masters Level (Gentle) "I Am" and "Listening" protocols and also, with my doctor, tailored my self-nourishment calibrations. These measures helped me power through my workload and kept my Window in good working order.

* * *

Far before Carver's monoculture disruptions wholly transformed the American educational landscape, though, he made an unexpected decision. The Secretary had invited him to the post of undersecretary, which was a training ground for the head position itself. But he declined. Carver asked instead to withdraw from national policy and take over the territory of Landingsburgh, a good-sized but bankrupt Midwest city with considerable street-violence issues and a nearly destroyed school system. He wanted to set up a Next Gen experimental holistic organism known as the "Consolidated Academy," which would integrate all organizational components so that the educational infrastructure connected to the total ecology of a distressed metropolitan area. That's the way he explained it anyway, in one of the lengthy emails I was cc'd on, and I can't say that I understood exactly what he was talking about. The Secretary was not impressed either, at least at first. But when he threatened to quit government work entirely and move into private enterprise, she relented.

So Carver moved away from the capital to Landingsburgh, and in '28–'29, he set up his new system. He presided reportedly over two to three hundred schools all across the region, arranging with the Secretary to develop his Growth Model with "all necessary space and freedom" (so he wrote). This, he insisted, required that public and even in-house access to the mechanics of his stewardship should be restrained. He wrote us increasingly lengthy emails, wherein he argued that the only way data confidentiality could be assured would be if his mission were allocated a Sensitive Classification with an accompanying alteration in the criminal code regarding complaints against his didactics and other forms of civil unrest.

The Secretary allowed this mod on a six-month trial. She then extended it *in perpetuum* when his numbers across all benchmarks leapt by 67 percent and the top brass of his civic copartners in HHS, ICE, and BOP (I lost track of all of them) sent us glowing reports on his contributions. I helped out with most of the licenses—the installation of a small judicial firm at his Consolidated Academy, for example, and his waiver permitting partnerships with disciplinary and immigration sectors. Still, the Sensitive Classification allowed Carver to hammer out many of the finer details himself.

The whole project was a success. Landingsburgh itself soon began to flourish, with pioneers from Los Angeles, New York, Chicago, and other major cities moving to the area, encouraged by the city's auctioning of abandoned houses and rapidly increasing work opportunities. Carver's influence spread to other vectors as well, and I heard of even more lucrative syntheses of unclear origins and specifics, which were easily authorized once crime statistics in the city fell to the lowest bracket in the country.

It was now '38, and while we on the Hill bare-knuckle brawled with the small remaining gangs of House Democrats and protest cells, Carver had remained in Landingsburgh all this time. He stayed away from DC because he was a perfectionist who would never leave his life's work, the Secretary explained to me in a low, admiring voice, on those nights when we stayed late at the office and she'd share her rare confidences. He'd dedicated himself to refining his methodologies and optimizing an efficiently faithful pedagogy, she went on. He was the cat's meow, and he was the bee's knees—and that remained her fixed idea of him until she'd started to hear the rumors about the shift in his demeanor and the tone of his emails changed.

That's when she'd called me into her office and ordered me to go to Landingsburgh and report back on what I found.

* * *

I came home from my meeting with the Secretary and began to pack for my trip and get read into the assignment. My plane would take off the next morning, so after I'd cooked dinner for my family, tucked in the kids, and had a special cuddle with Sheraton, I spent the deep evening hours looking through Carver's file. All in all, the documents on the whiz drive the Secretary had given me totaled about seven thousand pages. A lot of them had been cc'd to his assistant, a substeward named Melinda Gerber, who had taken over communications with the Secretary at least two seasons ago. The other materials gave essential details on Landingsburgh and assorted minutiae concerning infrastructure, sewage and security contracts, teacher's wages, etc.

I took a quick look at the old maps of Landingsburgh in Appx F of the file, which for some reason had not been updated with more recent charts. Landingsburgh radiated around a corporate downtown, which was half-circled by a series of neighborhoods. Perhaps its most prominent feature was the massive, multicomplex prison system that filled the western quadrant of the city and could house upward of thirty thousand units. The elegant, boxy, and well-equipped LFDC had been built in the style of Le Corbusier and commissioned upon Reagan's Executive Order 12292 after the '85 floods and consequent riots.

I turned from these materials and spent the rest of my time on Carver's correspondence with the Secretary. A missive early in '24 seemed to set out his general philosophy:

> ... and if we have the bravery to make the hard choice, we might recalibrate the curriculum to institute the values of tenacity, joy, and optimism that will return these needful generations to the bounty of industry that is their national inheritance.

In '27, he seemed to have deepened his commitment to privatization:

> ... the state is not equipped to truly look after the welfare of the country's youths. But the invisible hand was designed to be swift and accurate in its solutions, if not to crush inefficiency with the same brutal economy as nature herself. As I have said to you repeatedly, the market is a machine for living, not for wasteful and hypocritical proselytizing.

But by '33, his writings seemed to have become accented with the melancholia that the Secretary had alluded to in her briefing with me:

> I stared all day out the window, thinking of the paths that have led me here. Melinda chats merrily of my past successes, but the route I took toward this destiny remains shadowy and filled with failures. At the end of the day, I know that I've made men out of boys and women out of girls, but I must learn not to expect any thanks.

His last message, four months back, was only one baffling line:

Eliminate the externalities.

* * *

The next morning, I boarded my flight to Landingsburgh and touched down two and a half hours later. As I possessed a government pass that gave me Special Assignment Status, I moved swiftly enough past the blockades that the Academi police had set up at all ports of entry in response to coordinated riots in Union City, Georgia, and Boyle Heights, California. I was also met by an armed escort. This man, named George Underhill, was tall, thin, White, dark-haired, and approximately twenty-six to thirty years old. In lieu of the suit-and-tie uniform of DC scholastic administrators, he wore a black jumpsuit of immaculate and very plain design, which he'd decorated only with a plastic badge bearing his name and a picture of his face.

"Hello, ma'am," George said in a low, astonishingly beautiful, and honey-dark voice, while grabbing my bags and quickly maneuvering me into a black sedan. "We heard you were coming and trust you had a good flight."

"I'm here to see Carver ASAP and get a briefing on his progress," I said briskly, settling into the back seat while he lumped my bags next to him in the front seat and took his place behind the wheel.

George did not answer me. He only pulled away from the airport and began to drive us toward the city on smoothly trafficked freeways.

I had never been to Landingsburgh before, but I had heard horror stories about it. In the '90s, the city had been overwhelmed by encampments and languished from a devastated corporate center that was ringed by the dilapidating neighborhoods. The only architecture of note was the city's famous prison complex and its former Art Deco glories that now littered downtown. Most everything in the financial and higher-income sectors had been burned in the fires that had followed the '80s flood. As I leaned back in the car seat, checking the Eyes Only National

Data on my phone and unsuccessfully attempting to make small talk with George about Carver's health, I gazed out the window at the slowly changing landscape, expecting to be greeted by wastelands and slums.

I was pleasantly surprised. Just outside the airport, we passed a delightful green space, filled with trees and parkland that looked usable by families. I detected no blighted townscapes, no tent cities. Instead, past the parks, I saw unmistakable signs of prosperous small businesses and trim, tidy homes that appeared very well cared for. The suburbs gave way to corporate districts that also looked populated and busy and were ornamented by shrubs, flower beds, and glossy green trees that shone under the state's uncertain weather.

"Landingsburgh's looking good, better than I thought it would," I said.

George nodded his head encouragingly but said nothing.

"I'm speaking to you, boy," I said. "Don't you answer?"

"Oh, I'm sorry," George said, flustered. "I didn't realize that was a direct question."

"I'm saying I thought that Landingsburgh had more rough edges," I said.

"Carver accounts for our prosperity as an example of virtuous circles, ma'am," George said, in his deep and very polite voice, while looking at me intently with large clear eyes that reflected in the rearview.

"What do you mean, exactly?"

"I'm sorry, ma'am, you'd have to read Carver's writings about it," George said. "He's the one who knows about all that. And I don't want to talk out of turn."

George continued driving. We passed another tidy suburb and pocket of well-oiled industry. Then came a long stretch of vacant land, stripped down to red dirt. Men in hard hats scurried back and forth on the area, and I saw trucks, backhoes, bulldozers, loaders.

"What's that?" I asked.

"Car industry's coming back," George explained.

At around the center of the city, I was again astonished. I knew from my brief study that Landingsburgh's incinerated business district had hosted once-stunning but now-shattered Albert Kahn and Charles Noble–designed arcades. But instead of seeing ruins, I descried a cleared area bounded by a chain-link fence and occupied by miles upon miles of parking lots. Shining, small cars filled the spaces. Non attendants or crossing guards, who all wore green jumpsuits, were stationed every five hundred feet or so. And many people wearing jumpsuits of varying colors wandered to and fro, coming back to their cars to drive home or heading deeper inside.

"Is this one of those huge malls?" I asked, looking up through the car window. In the wide span of the gray and cloud-dusted sky, I saw suddenly a curl of what seemed to be dark haze or some sort of black, spiraling smoke, which I wrote off as the product of a nearby refinery. "Why is everyone wearing the same kinds of clothes?"

"That's our uniforms. This is the schoolyard parking lot, ma'am," George said.

"Schoolyard? But why is it so big? There are at least three hundred schools all over the city."

"Isn't it normal size?" George's face remained placid and amiable as he maneuvered the car toward the entrance of one of the lots. Its gate opened out into a small sentry station employed by young, green-suited Non guards who waved us in once George flashed him his badge.

George drove us through the seemingly endless lot. I saw that the space was cut through by a serpentining track, which carried electric red-and-white cars that picked up the jumpsuit-clad workers at regular intervals. But George did not park and lead us to a tram stop. He continued driving through the forest of vehicles, which ended eventually in the outskirts of a large and pretty campus that had its own small roads leading to buildings boasting fresh white paint and red-tiled roofs. Children in blue jumpsuits played beneath trees or in posh playgrounds, while adults in pink jumpsuits watched on. Non sanitation workers in yellow suits bustled along, sweeping; Non maintenance workers wearing purple suits attended to a utility pole and its cables; other employees exited a nearby tram and walked in varying directions with steady gates and purposeful miens. George continued maneuvering us past this lively, pastoral scene until we reached one of the red-tiled buildings. A woman in a gray jumpsuit and a long fall of ash-blond hair waited on the curb for us, waving as we pulled up.

George stopped the car, ran to my side, and opened my door. I got out.

"Mrs. Eager," the woman said, stretching out a hand. She had round, glowing cheeks and bright white teeth and was perhaps twenty-eight, twenty-nine years old. "We heard you were coming and hope you had an excellent flight."

I shook her hand. "And you are . . ."

"Melinda Gerber, ma'am, and I am so pleased to make your acquaintance."

"Yes, of course, thank you for arranging the meeting."

"We want to make sure that you are very comfortable here and that we show you some of our amenities."

"I'm here to see Mr. Carver," I said abruptly. "That's my only order of business."

"Oh, Carver's an abiding influence at the Academy, Mrs. Eager," Melinda said. "You can see him all around you, in a way."

"Yes, but where is he? I need to go to his office and have a meeting with him now."

Melinda's beautiful face crinkled slightly with concern. "George, do you know where Carver is at this moment?"

George turned red and looked confused. "He's still back in FW," he said, or something to that effect.

Melinda smiled. "Ah, that's fine, George. Mrs. Eager, we'll

find him, very soon. He knew you'd come eventually. But for now, I was wondering if you wished to see our Gifteds facilities. We'd love to show you around."

I looked at the spacious parks and towheads playing in the swing sets that surrounded the red-tiled buildings. The children laughed and gamboled like deer. The clouds parted, and for a moment, the sunlight brightened the black, curling scar of smoke that continued to cut through the sky.

"What's the land grant?" I asked, admiring the vast facility. "I don't remember the filings being this big."

Melinda placed her hands on her hips and looked out at the scene. I noticed suddenly that she looked tired, with a sallow tint to her skin. "We've expanded this sector to nine hundred acres."

"How many units?"

"Here, about twenty-eight thousand."

"It's incredible how you've been able to scale," I said. "Your *numbers*."

"It's because we started with a rock-solid plan," she said, her lips lightly shuddering. "Carver said that we'd achieve escape velocity once we locked down the variables, and he was right. He led us out from the wilderness and into a world filled with harmony, enlightenment, rational color schemes creating security and identity . . ." She yelped a short, high laugh. "Not that it hasn't been hard going sometimes. Not that we haven't had to make sacrifices. But it's all been worth it."

I studied her. "Is he working you too hard, Melinda?"

She shook her head with great seriousness. "There's no such thing, Mrs. Eager, not when you're executing brain training in total, pure love and unwavering faithfulness."

The poor amanuensis's tone was certainly fevered, yet I already knew that Carver had a tendency to inspire such flights in his people. I had to admit that I was deeply intrigued by the developments here. I decided I could spare a few minutes to take a peek.

* * *

I have spoken already of my son Sheraton's struggles with reading comprehension. Sheraton was my firstborn, and his was a hard birth. He'd been a breech with a cord problem, and his heart had cratered twice during my labor. The doctors placed him in the pediatric ICU for about six weeks, and some very anxious days passed when we didn't know if he'd live. It was a tough time.

He fought hard, though, the little critter. My sweet little baby. I knew immediately when I saw his tiny face that I would honor him with the name of his grandfather, as my dad had recently passed away.

What with my father being an English teacher, maybe it was ironic that Sheraton had a problem with reading. I don't know if he suffered from a mild form of ADHD and related cognitive atypia because he hadn't had enough oxygen during his delivery. Lots of kids struggle, and for many different reasons. We addressed the problem by placing him in Middlebrook P–12, which has a six-to-one student-to-teacher ratio and offers the age-appropriate Loving Variants of "I Am" and "Listening" Exercises to enhance A/Bs' Comprehension and Self-Awareness. I'd taken special care to ensure that the curriculum did not feature the more rigorous Pain Management and Self-Assessment protocols. Though studies showed that A/Bs who had endured these programs had often gone on to succeed brilliantly in the fields of business and medicine, neither James nor I could withstand the idea of our son being frightened to the point of loss of bodily governance or threatened in ways that he would later have to integrate into his adult memory processes.

Sheraton was a sensitive child. He suffered from nightmares about invisible vampires and bloody-handed murderers that he couldn't redirect into healthy cognitive loops despite the "I Am" and "Listenings" trainings. He also had mommy's-boy tendencies, which I'll confess that I encouraged. I loved to take him in my arms at night, after James had gone to bed and the girls were ensconced in their bedrooms like duchesses. I'd kiss him all over his dewdrop face and tell him that he was my little angel prince-ling from a far-off planet sent to Earth to make my life perfect. "Hey you, hey you," I'd say, a little song of mine. "Hey you," he'd sing back to me. "Hey you."

Even though I coddled Sheraton, I had nevertheless come to understand that a certain amount of unpleasantness was inevitable in every program that we'd installed. Without mandatory decency there cannot be harmony, as Carver had taught us. There is no discipline without discomfort. There is no pride without shame. A certain amount of cost-benefit had to shape every choice curriculum. We had learned to accept as a common fact of life that all of our sons and daughters must learn about the terrifying love of our Creator, the importance of bowel control, and the difficult if necessary workings of hate if they were to avoid being classified as SubDs, whom the studies deemed as inexorably fated to a 91 percent incarceration rate (what Carver had so audaciously insisted on describing as the school-to-prison pipeline that he would jettison).

When my son would come home weeping and shaking, I clutched at him and felt my heart break. But I believed that our methods were the right ones. My Window didn't open up far enough for me to understand there could be any other way.

* * *

This long-held belief system of mine may explain why I spent almost the rest of that day at Carver's Consolidated Academy in an attitude of bliss. As George tailed behind us, Melinda led me into a huge network of red-tiled buildings, and I saw assembled there small groups of attentive, mostly blue-eyed boy *and* girl children who together learned lessons in Geography, English, Love One Another, Calculus, French, Civics, Political Theory, God Thought, and Right History without any assists except for books and benevolent pink-jumpsuited teachers. There was no fear, no violence at all. Only two or three times, I saw students leap up in an excess of enthusiasm, flailing their arms with excitement. But these incidents passed without coming to any crisis. Each time this happened, the educators came over to the pupils and patted them tenderly on their heads, and the children instantly sat back down.

"This can't be the whole school," I asked Melinda, while George stood silently three or four feet behind us. "These units are displaying so much emotional control that they can't be below Bs."

"Actually, this campus does goes from A all the way to SubB. We just make small variations in the aptitudes," she said, glancing sideways at me and giving me a small, watchful smile.

We began walking through yet another one of the buildings' whitewashed corridors. We stopped by a red door, which Melinda cracked open so that I could spy inside. This classroom, like so many of the others, was decorated with soft sofas upholstered in merry primary colors. Twenty students ranging from the ages of eleven to twelve sat at small desks and looked at their open books. A black-haired but fair-faced female teacher wearing spectacles stood before the class, gesticulating with measured gestures.

"And what happened during the Second Emergency?" she asked.

A slim girl with a long brown braid raised her hand. "We had to get rid of all the disease."

"And how did we do that?"

"By cleansing ourselves of disinformation."

"Excellent, Lauren," the teacher said.

I scanned my eyes back and forth across the cheerful room, looking for monitors and the bio aids.

"There haven't been any breaks—aren't you running programs on them?" I whispered to Melinda. "Aren't you hosing them?"

Beaming, Melinda made a sign to me, and I closed the door. "No, they don't need it. We've been able to select them and amend their nutrition so that they don't require any interventions." She began quickly walking down the hall, toward the rear of the building, whose doors led back to the parks. "We have them do sports for two hours, reading for three hours, socialization and fraternity during playtime; we have them in science labs, drama workshops . . ."

Excitedly thinking of Sheraton and how as an A/B he would qualify for these classes, I followed her outside. George still peaceably ambled behind us.

"Our children are leading the country in reading acuity, mathematics, devotion, and slow brain-wave production," she said, speaking rapidly and her eyes shining a tad too brightly. "They're last in ADHD and sexual perversity."

"I know all that," I said. We stood under a jacaranda tree in the lowering light and the rising chill. George lingered behind Melinda and looked off toward the smoky part of the sky. "But I hadn't realized that you have both genders in the same classroom. There's so much *diversity*. It's a miracle."

"It's no miracle," Melinda said, her pale eyes locking onto mine with an intensity that I remember from Carver himself. "It's what happens when you truly realize that our society has run itself into perdition. And it's only then that you make the deep, hard subtractions in the consumer surplus. And that's when you create a new age."

"You sound like Carver," I said.

"He's been my mentor," she nodded, as pink flush began to spread up from her neck to her eyes. "He was, and has been, my everything."

"I see," I said, after a moment's recalibration.

"No, you don't." A small note of hysteria crept into her voice. "You couldn't."

"Melinda," I said, "I hope you don't mind me saying so, but I think you, yourself, might need an 'I Am' session."

Melinda looked around desperately at the campus. But the façade she had maintained all day cracked. Dark, masacaraed tears began dripping down her cheeks. "You never supported him."

"What are you talking about?" I tilted my head. "We've given him everything."

"Why didn't you come before? Couldn't you tell that he needed more resources?"

I blinked at her and felt my patience give way. "Okay. This has been great, but I'm done. I'm here to see him, not to get this tour from you."

"Oh, Mrs. Eager," she wept, wiping her made-up eyes and making herself look a fright.

"*Where is he?*"

For a second, anger rippled across her face. "No."

"If he does not submit to this investigation, there will be consequences," I nearly shouted. "I swear to you, the Secretary is going to rain down controls on this place if he doesn't meet with me today!"

Melinda burst into tears afresh. "I know it."

I turned from her, toward the parkland, where the children had now disappeared. The sky began to darken very quickly—what time was it? And the black, curling haze that continued to waft thickly up into the sky seemed to have spread.

As I turned back to watch her with mounting anxiety, Melinda shuddered with suppressed sobs. She would obviously be of no more help. But just as I resolved to leave the playground and roam the school's administrative sector in search of Carver, something now occurred to me, something more important than whether I saw him that day.

"Melinda, you said this whole campus was all A/Bs," I said. "Where are the other students?"

Melinda continued crying.

"Jesus, Melinda, where are the other students?"

"Don't blaspheme," George said behind me, suddenly and harshly.

I turned and stared him down. "The Cs, the Ds, the SubDs, where'd you put them?"

George glanced at Melinda, who pawed the tears off her red face.

"George, look at me," I said. "I am your boss. *I* am your supervisor."

He swallowed and nodded. "Yes, ma'am."

"Tell me where the other kids are."

His eyes shifted toward Melinda again. He sighed. "I'll show you, Mrs. Eager."

\* \* \*

George brought me back outside, and we got into his car. He drove us for maybe three miles, past the bucolic campus and deeper into the complex. The trees here grew less lush, and the grassy lands grew barer. Trucks now began to appear on roads that cut through the shabbier landscape. Some of the vehicles had labels that read "C/SubC" or "D/SubD." Others read "F/W." I sat stiff in my seat, trying to ignore an unpleasant pressure developing in my chest. George drove calmly forward and looked blankly out the windshield.

I looked ahead too. After perhaps ten minutes, a large, concrete building, built in the boxy Le Corbusier style, appeared before us. White bricks rose in huge blocks and extended into tall silos that were cut through by thin, rectangular windows that could not capture much daylight. Jumpsuited employees of the Academy flowed in and out of its guarded doors.

George stopped the car on an incline, and we got out. Farther up, on a steeper ascent, there stood another similar and larger concrete building. Beyond that, I could only spy a darker and thicker spiral of smoke rising into the sky, which seemed to be the same black pollution that I had first seen in the parking lot and that had followed me all the way here.

"This is the prison," I said, shaking my head. When George didn't answer but just gazed at me passively, I pointed at him. "George, this isn't the school; it's the jails. I've read about these buildings. These are Landingsburgh's prisons."

"This is the school, ma'am," George said, shutting his car door.

"School for whom?"

He tilted his head at me, pausing. "Permission to speak candidly?"

"George!"

For the first time, I saw an unpleasant expression cross his features. He pointed at the structure that stood directly before us. "This one is for the Not Cleans, but don't tell Melinda I called them that."

"What are their formal classifications?"

"They're Cs and SubCs."

"Show me."

George and I endured a short hubbub of badge inspection at the entrance. He then brought me through the door, leading me to a spare, pale interior that was staffed with more guards as well as a receptionist who sat behind a thick glass wall. We took an elevator up three levels. Exiting, we walked down a brightly lit corridor, whose glare picked out the shadows under George's eyes. Finally we reached a tall metal door, which George opened with an electric card that he took out of his pocket. We entered into a long hall filled with halogen lights that filled the room with a dazzling, alarming brightness.

I stared. This massive gallery was filled with both White and Non children who sat at common tables made of white plastic. Individual laptop computers had been placed before each child. The pupils watched images that played on their screens while also listening to instructions on white elongated devices that poked out from their ears. They all wore white jumpsuits. The standard rubberized neurologic caps used in brain-training drills had been placed on their heads. But drips had also been inserted into their arms, so that all the students had plastic tubes extending from the veins in their hands to metal IV stands holding saline bags. Non guards in green jumpsuits had been installed around the room's perimeter, though that wasn't standard for a c or even SubC system.

"Charm," I heard the students saying, all together. "Religion. Dedication. Morbidity. I Am. I Am."

"George," I said. "What protocol am I looking at?"

"This is an automated and whisper-lite delivery stratagem for the 'I Am' and 'Listening' Exercises, combined with the Pain Management and Self-Love protocols, depending on the academic diagnoses and the flexibilities of the students, which are all the same," George said.

"I thought we'd eliminated Non and White mixing, except for a few Qualifieds," I said.

"Carver said at this level it was fine. It gets streamlined again at the lower levels."

"Shouldn't they be ending for the day? It's late."

"They'll get a break in a few hours."

"But what are they watching, and what are they saying?" I moved up toward one of the tables, at which sat approximately thirty students spanning the age ranges of K–12. There seemed an equal distribution of genders, though not races. All of the students had been outfitted with the same ear gear. Their dark and light eyes did not dart toward me as I approached them but fixed onto their computers' large, vivid screens. Upon these monitors flitted images of rockets, bears, clowns, trees, naked women, wasps' nests, corpses, muddy soldiers who looked as if they fought in the Somme, a woman getting her hair pulled and slapped, tulips, teeth crunching down on ice cubes, snowy mountain ranges, and firing squads executing bound and blindfolded victims.

"*This* is a new iteration of 'I Am' and Listening?" I asked, wincing.

"Charm," the students said. I stared at the broad brows of high schoolers and the round, babyish faces of fifth graders, fourth graders—even younger, too. No matter what their age, every single student's lips trembled violently. "Religion. Dedication. Morbidity. I Am. I Am."

George nodded. "Carver redesigned it himself."

"But the last version I saw had more nature scenes and Rewards. And it didn't require fluids. This is—this is—" I stammered. "This is like the Adversative proto that got killed in Committee."

"It works very well, Mrs. Eager," George said, shyly. "I myself was diagnosed as a High Grade Looneytunes and Soft Head Lack of Discipline before I sat through the Advanced Adversative and learned how to behave myself."

I grew very still and looked at him.

"What I learned in Advanced Adversative is that God is a unit of utility that is X plus infinity, and if we assign proper values to human carriers of chaos, then the contagion ratio will dwindle into an appropriate margin and we will all be saved," George went on, in that same, beautiful, bashful voice, his eyes almost transparent, his hair falling away from his radiant forehead. He stopped, frowning, and tapped on his temple with a long, pale finger. "At least I think that's what Carver said."

I backed away from George. I turned around and walked swiftly through the halls and back to the elevator. George moved quickly into the elevator after me. I pressed the Lobby button, and we went sliding down. I hurried through the building's foyer, passed its guards, and moved back out the door.

I stood outside in the gloaming, breathing slowly and trying to shut down irrational thoughts. Lights had turned on from inside the building, and they shone a gold radius out onto the streets. On the road that we'd driven up on, I saw another truck labeled "D/SubD" drive toward the structure higher on the incline. A vehicle with the label "F/W" followed. I stared at a wide, black fan of smoke rising and billowing through the darkening sky. I had been tracking this murky fog ever since I'd arrived at the complex, and I now saw that it came from a farther-off building I could not yet detect from that vantage.

THE WORLD DOESN'T WORK THAT WAY, BUT IT COULD

"Where's that smoke coming from, George?"

"Oh, that's from the building past the SubDs, about two miles up from here. That's Waste," he said. "In Building F/W."

"F/W? I never heard of that before. What is that? It's not a class."

"Yes, it is, ma'am."

"But we end the system at SubDs."

"Carver introduced the new add-ons a while back—F for Failure, and W for Waste."

I squinted at him, beginning to feel ill. "What's 'Waste'?" I asked. "Are you doing sanitation in the same building?"

"There's a sanitation protocol initiated upon the revelation of a judicial announcement of a class-seven-level felony or above, where the unit has been tried as an adult," George explained.

"But what's 'Waste'?" I repeated.

George shrugged and didn't say anything.

My brain would not yet allow the full notion to invade my thoughts, and only the faintest, ludicrous outlines of it flickered through me. But already I could feel my hands trembling. "George, tell me what 'Waste' is."

George stared at the ground, nodding to himself. "I think it's time you were going home now, Mrs. Eager. Carver used to say that our program has too much sophisticated geometrical currency for bureaucrats like you to understand."

I looked at the smoke again and the prisons looming above me.

"Where's Carver?" I said in a softer, tense voice.

"Melinda thinks you're going to get upset at Carver and shut us down, but you shouldn't."

The muscles in my back begin to pulse with pain. "Did he quit?"

George didn't answer.

"Where'd he go?" I said. "I mean, he's *somewhere*—he's not dead."

George looked at me from under his eyelashes.

"He's—he died?"

"Carver said we could all be happy. He said that all it takes to be free is choosing to be. Once that happens, everything else becomes easy. All decisions become simple." George cast his gaze back down. "Carver said a lot of things. He also said I was tiddleywinks and paddywhack who deserved to get my throat slit by the Nons and that he was a fucking monster who was damned."

"What happened to him?"

"Mrs. Eager, after Carver initiated the Wastes' sanitation sequences, he celebrated for a long time with unapproved mind substances, and then he just up and deutilitized himself. But nobody at the Academy knows it except for Melinda and me and just a few others."

"Are you telling me he killed himself?'"

George sniffed and stared off again, in the direction of the lovely grasslands where the A/Bs played. His eyes began to brim with tears.

"He said that he realized he'd gone into the red and that he was going put himself into the black."

* * *

I won't go into all the details of the histrionics and confusions that followed the moments when I finally extracted a clear description of Carver's suicide and my consequent running hither and thither for confirmation. I will say that George refused to allow me to see any other Academy facilities on account of my lack of "sophistication," and I had not insisted. Racing about, I finally found Melinda in a state of semi-catatonia in a barracks that Academy administrators lived in. After I incentivized her, she explained that George had been correct and that Carver had died in the basement of the F/W Building from a self-inflicted gunshot wound to the head. I thereafter lost the energy required for further investigations.

George drove me straight to my hotel. I had a long, hard phone conversation with the Secretary and then lay awake in my bed. I warded off shadowy, echoing, waking nightmares of invisible vampires and bloody-handed murderers, like my son Sheraton suffered from. At around two a.m., I'd gone digging through my duffel bags until I discovered my little plastic baggies of the vitamins and minerals my psychologist had recommended. One purple pill, one blue pill, one white pill, one yellow pill. I took them all but then spent the rest of the night frantically trying to write a coherent report, which I could not finish and abandoned at about five o'clock in the morning.

Three hours later, wearing the same sweatpants and sweatshirt that I'd sweated through all night long and still feeling groggy from my medicine, I'd caught the next flight out of the city. I landed in Dulles and didn't even stop at home. I got my car from the airport lot and went straight to the Agency. The Secretary agreed to see me right away, and thus I quickly found myself standing once again on her eagle rug, at two p.m. the next day.

"Who's running it now?" the Secretary asked, shaking her head.

"His assistant, I think," I said. "A woman, Melinda Gerber."

The Secretary briefly closed her eyes and rubbed them. "Right, that's what you said last night. Yes. I think she came up from the A class. She'd been my contact lately. But I don't know much about her."

"The thing that we have to get in front of here is that Carver merged the school and the prison," I said.

"I told you already, that's not news to me. That was the innovation. It's the efficient consolidation of the for-profits. And it's not just the prisons. They have a juvenile court installed there and a migrant quarantine too. All of it's legal."

"I think, madam," I said slowly, "that there have been excesses."

The Secretary looked at her computer and blew out a breath. "We'll look into it."

I rasped out a cough. "I think there have been—"

"It's sad about Carver," the Secretary said in a brisk tone. "In situations like this, when employees lose colleagues in a work-related tragedy, we often recommend counseling."

I pressed my hands on my exhausted eyes. "Are you going to shut it down?"

"Of course not. But we'll send in inspectors and deal with any violations, and hopefully there won't be any problems with consent decrees." She tapped her nails on the desk. "Though I don't remember the last time I heard of one being issued."

I peered at her, looking for any signs of anxiety or loathing. But I couldn't see any. I nodded.

"Petra, this is just the shock of seeing the sausage factory," the Secretary said. "Most of the time you're parked at a desk. But nothing's changed. We run good programs, and when mistakes get made, we go in and fix them. Like we always have." She cleared her throat. "And, after all, it's your work that helped build these marvelous schools. Carver was the idea man, but you implemented. The mergers, the installation of the judiciary, the licenses for the protocols . . ."

I stared at the eagle on the carpet. "But I didn't know what he was doing."

"Oh, as soon as he asked for Sensitive Class, we all knew, sugar," the Secretary said, tidying some papers on the desk. "Petra, get yourself together. This is the job. This is the work that you signed on for and that you are so good at." She raised her eyes again and watched me carefully for my response.

"Yes," I finally said.

"You're overreacting."

"I see, yes."

"Go home and go to sleep," she said.

For a brief second, I felt my legs start to give and thought I was going to faint from exhaustion, vitamins, and the rest. But I didn't.

"All right," I said.

\* \* \*

Joseph P. Overton came up with the idea of the Overton Window in the mid-1990s, in a series of articles that he wrote at the Mackinac Center, on Mackinac Island, Michigan. The theory draws from public choice economics, which seek to foster maximal liberty within the nourishments offered by the free market and functional democracy. Overton recognized that some of the ideas that grew out of public choice doctrine—like charter schools and vouchers—were too radical for many people to accept before the turn of the century, and so he thought about ways to expand "the window" to open people's receptivity to new ideas, solutions, and principles.

Each of us has an Overton Window, though we usually don't call it that. We feel it opening and closing within our minds, like a physical portal, which can be flung wide open to the universe or slammed shut. Sometimes we call our Overton Window "heartstrings," and sometimes we call it the "still small voice." Or we can call it "conscience" or "common sense" or "grace" or "morality."

What I'm saying, and what I've said before, is that some ideas are just plain repulsive when you first consider them. But the longer you hear blasphemies spoken aloud by your betters and the courts, the more you're able to regard them as possible options that are well within the Window. Still, to truly start seeing these concepts as real solutions, as inevitable conclusions, you might need a visionary to help shepherd you along. You can look to their light for guidance. Carver, in his insanity and his zeal, had once been that light bearer.

I didn't drive home and go to sleep, like the Secretary had counseled. Instead, after I left her office, I spent the rest of that work day laboring furiously in my office, writing intricate lists and drawing graphs as I tried to make sense of Carver's moral math. These calculations did not prevent me from having an attack of the shakes, like the ones I'd weathered back in the late '20s, when the Secretary had asked me to bar the gay and Non kids from the charters. This one was stronger. Eventually, I called my psychologist, and she ordered me a better prescription. I ran to the pharmacist closest to the Agency and got the pills straight off.

By the evening, I felt calmer. I washed myself in the sink in the Agency's women's bathroom, dunking my head under the faucet and splashing my armpits and between my legs. I could smell the stink on me, but I scrubbed hard and washed it away. Finally, around seven p.m. I was all right to go home.

★ ★ ★

I opened our house's front door. I entered our foyer. I proceeded to the dining room. I was a little late for the evening meal. At our table, I saw James, Sheraton, Tina, and Ulrike eating a dinner of broiled chicken, green beans, salad, and potatoes. They all looked up at me with sparkling eyes, excited. Sheraton jumped up from his seat and ran over to hug me.

"Mom!"

"Hey there, hon," James said. He stood up, laughing because I was back home. I could see the funny, frustrated love that he felt for me in the way he waggled his head, like to say, "Well, you're finally back." Ulrike and Tina also clattered up to me, tugging on my sleeves and yelling for my attention. And Sheraton wouldn't let go of me.

"How'd it go?" James asked, taking my bag and pressing his mouth to mine in a quick, dry kiss.

"How'd it go?" I looked down and stroked Sheraton's daisy-bright hair.

"Yeah, your trip. You had that meeting with Carver, right?"

Sheraton still gripped onto my legs and waist, holding me tight, tight, tight. I crouched down and enveloped him in a big bear hug. "Hey you, hey you," I sang to him.

"Hey you," he sang back, whispering it in my ear. "Hey you."

I closed my eyes and buried my face in the crown of his head, which had been so soft and terrifyingly delicate when he'd been an infant. I breathed in all of that purity of him, in and out, and in and out again. And the most beautiful memory flitted through my mind right at that moment. I thought of the day that I gave birth to Sheraton, twelve years before. I saw him red, bloody, screaming, and wriggling, when he'd broken free of the breech and the cord. My firstborn. My first baby. My perfect baby. And that tenderness blossomed inside me and branched out into the love I felt so strongly for all of my beautiful, innocent children and my dear husband.

I may have carved out a window in my soul big enough to fit the devil, but that doesn't mean that I will ever let my family know the filth I'm involved in.

"The trip went fine, sweetheart," I said to James, standing up and nudging the kids back to the table like nothing was wrong. "It was good. Let's eat."✶

# The World Doesn't Work
# That Way, but It Could

"**W**ELL, THAT WAS DARK," Ellen said.

"It was based on *Heart of Darkness*," I said, holding a paperback of Conrad's novella and flapping it at her and Tamar.

"Still, what the hell," Ellen said. Ellen's sixty-five, is divorced from her wife, has blond hair and blue eyes, and wears a lot of necklaces. She's a white, Jewish woman who used to be a pharmacist but then retired and now is a volunteer tutor, like me. She looked at Tamar and then back at me. "A little intense for kids, don't you think?"

"Was it?" I asked Tamar. "You guys read *Hunger Games* and books about vampires."

"It was fine," Tamar said. "And I'm not a kid anymore."

"You know all that crap's not going to happen, right?" Ellen asked me.

"No," I said. "Not today." My name's Sandra, and I'm fifty-one. I have black-silver hair and brown eyes and wear big Land's End dresses and Allbirds without socks. I'm a single, bisexual, Latina law professor/fiction writer/tutor and was all fucked up because for the past week I'd been researching Betsy DeVos, overcrowded immigrant camps in Clint, Texas, the prison industrial complex, and the manifesto of the El Paso shooter all at the same time. Actually, I don't know if it was research exactly. It was more just staring blankly at the news and feeling like I was having a heart attack.

"I liked it," Tamar said. Tamar's eighteen years old and black. Her mother and stepfather kicked her out of her house for being queer two years ago. She has enormous brown eyes and a small silver piercing in her nose. She wears clothes like jeans and Nike T-shirts. She listens to dissonant music on some kind of new iPod contraption that involves having little white pipes stick out of your ears and seems *Star Trek* to me. She wants to be a veterinarian after graduating from a four-year and the UC Davis vet program. She reads a lot, though, and her comments on the books we study together are always deep and thoughtful, and so secretly I'm hoping that she'll become a writer.

Still, I started feeling freaked out because maybe I shouldn't have told her the story I'd feverishly written on my computer last night, because she was too young and living in a shelter. "Did you really think it was good?"

Tamar shrugged. "I mean, sort of. Sure. Yeah."

"I was inspired by your assignment," I said.

"You're such a weirdo," Tamar said, laughing.

"I know," I said.

Ellen, Tamar, and I sat in the group house's dining-room area, which doubled as tutorial spaces. This was on Vermont Street, in LA. Ellen and I worked as tutors for the Los Angeles Children's Network (LACN), an LGBTQIA youth homeless shelter in South LA. The group home was an old Craftsman decorated with soft, ancient sofas and easy chairs. In the TV room, toward the front of the house, there was a big TV, where about five kids right now were watching *Castle*. The show's theme song drifted over to us: *Ta deee ta dooo ta deeee*. The kids had covered the walls of every single room in the house with homemade self-portraits (collage; splashy watercolors) and colorful posters announcing that we were in a "safe space" and "queer is love." A big table, covered with a daisy-patterned plastic tablecloth, occupied the center of the dining room. We'd cluttered the table with paper, pencils, and an old Penguin binding of Conrad's famous story, because Tamar had to write a paper on the book for her City College English class. Actually, the paper was due last week, but she had to get an extension because she'd been working overtime at HealthGreen, which is a health-food restaurant here in LA that is insufficiently supportive of its employees' educational needs. Tamar was eighteen, but LACN still lets you live in the shelter up to the age of nineteen.

"How's your meditation practice?" Ellen asked me. She was waiting for Sasha, her three o'clock, and hanging out while we supposedly worked on Tamar's paper.

"Really good," I said, in a voice that said, *Are you joking?*

"You can't give up," Ellen said, cracking her neck and sighing.

"I'm just on hiatus," I said, in a voice that said, *I'm sick of meditating, and I'm never going to do it again.*

"I'm not just talking about the meditation," she said. "It's not Kristallnacht; it's still a democracy here."

"What about what went down in Clint? What about what just happened in El Paso?"

Ellen pointed her chin at Tamar. "It's bad, but people like you, me, and her are going to fix it."

"How?" I asked. "How?"

"I don't know, vote Biden in 2020."

"Biden smells women's hair," I said.

"I'm just saying, don't throw in the towel."

I rubbed my face. "Everything just feels very *Heart of Darknessy* right now."

Tamar picked up the novel from the table and flipped through it. "Actually, I think this book is sort of racist," she said.

"Oh, yeah," I said. I'd heard people say that before, and I knew they were probably right, but I never understood what they were talking about. I thought *Heart of Darkness* was a classic and pure genius.

"I haven't read it," Ellen said.

"What?" I said. "It's *Heart of Darkness*."

"I tutor math," Ellen said. "But I saw *Apocalypse Now*."

"You should read it, but it's really full of white supremacy," Tamar said. "Maybe it was racist to even assign it for our class."

"Do you really not like it?" I asked, feeling hurt.

"No, I liked it," Tamar said.

"Why is it racist?" I asked. I grabbed a pencil and prepared to take notes. Maybe we'd come up with the thesis for her paper.

"Well, the black people in the story never get to talk except for once, when that guy tells Marlowe that Kurtz is dead, but Conrad doesn't even let him say it normal but like he's a slave on a plantation. 'Mistah Kurtz he dead.'"

I wrote that down on a piece of paper.

"And the chick who's Kurtz's girlfriend never gets to talk either, and she's just running around looking exotic. And then she gets shot while she's standing out on the beach with her arms wide open while they all point their guns at her, when what she'd really be doing is hauling ass out of there."

I wrote that down too.

"I mean, it's sort of like your story," Tamar said. "Everybody in it who gets to talk is white and the POCs are just totally enslaved and controlled."

I wrote that down as well, but not for her paper but more for my own literary purposes, like an edit.

"Point taken," I said.

"How would you write it?" Ellen asked.

"Well, for Sandra's story, I would write it from the point of the view of one of the SubD kids," Tamar said. "And I'd show how the testing schemes of the white supremacists were all super biased and that my SubD hero was actually incredibly intelligent and that if he'd just taken a different test, he would have scored in the ninety-ninth percentile."

I didn't say anything. I was just writing it all down.

"And then I'd have this kid who's really in the ninety-ninth percentile, I'd call him Malcom, and make him a black gay kid," she went on. "Malcom would fall in love with another kid called Lance, and then the white supremacists would find out, and they'd punish the boys by separating them. They'd move Lance to the F building, so that maybe Lance was going to get killed and made into Waste."

"What's Lance?" I asked.

"What do you mean, 'What's Lance?'" Tamar said.

"Like, is he black?"

"Oh, I don't know, maybe he's Asian. He can be Asian or black. Or Latinx. Or white. The important thing is that they're in love, but Lance is captured, and so Malcolm knows that he is going to have to save Lance, because he loves Lance so much. So Malcom starts leading a rebellion in the SubD building."

"How?" I asked.

Tamar had two braids on each side of her head, and she pulled on one, thinking. "Well, one of the things that the white-supremacist tests would not have picked up on was that Malcolm is a computer genius. And because he is a genius, he secretly re-programs the 'I Am' computer protocol thing so that instead of seeing scary mind-control pictures on their computers, the kids start seeing messages that say things like, 'You Are Not Alone' and 'You Are Loved' and 'Meet Me in the Basement Tonight So That We Can Plan a Rebellion and Be Free.'"

"And then what?" Ellen asked.

"And then the kids read the messages, and one by one they take the needles out of their arms and rip the little rubber thought-control caps off their heads. And then later that night they all meet up in the basement and plan their rebellion."

Ellen and I sat there and just listened.

"And then the kids race through the SubD building yelling and crying and screaming with happiness because they have finally stopped listening to the terrible computer that was telling them to hate themselves and to obey. And the guy George and that lady Melinda run away because they are outnumbered. And then the guards get scared, because now Melinda and George aren't there to tell them what to do. Either that or the guards take off their jumpsuits and start running around with the kids too. And so then Malcolm and everybody in the SubD building run out to the Failure/Waste building, still screaming and crying and yelling with freedom and happiness. And the guards in the Failure/Waste building get scared like in the SubD building and run away or join in. And then Malcolm runs through the jails breaking them open—"

"With what?" I asked. "What does he use to break the jails open?"

"He uses his computer smarts and finds a control box in the building that controls all of the locks. And he reprograms it, and then all of the jails open up. So then all of the kids who were Failures and Waste rush out and hug each other and grab each other's hands and run outside to where the trees and the fresh air is. And now they're just kids and not F/Ws."

"And then what happens?" Ellen asked.

"Malcom continues running through the jail cells until he finally finds Lance. He finds Lance in the last jail cell. Lance is extremely terrified and really thin from starvation and torture and is shivering in a corner. And Malcom comes in and say, 'Lance, Lance, I came to get you out. You're safe now. You're with me.' And Lance looks up at Malcolm and is barely able to believe his eyes because he has suffered so much in the prison. Lance has forgotten what it means to be free and have feelings and to have hope. But when Malcolm wraps his arms around Lance, then Lance suddenly remembers that he is human and a good person. And he knows that Malcom loves him and that being able to love somebody is the most important thing in the world, and so he's going to be okay."

At this point I was pressing my balled up fists into my eyes and Ellen was sniffling.

"And then do they kill all the white supremacists and start a new society?" I managed to ask.

"No," Tamar said. "Malcolm and the other kids decide to love the white supremacists instead."

"What?" Ellen rasped out. "Why?"

"Because if we love them hard enough, then someday they'll have to love us back," Tamar said.

"Oh, Tamar," I said.

"I think it's a better ending," she said.

"But the world doesn't work that way," I said.

"I know, but it could," Tamar said.

Ellen and I were still just sitting there with tears brimming in our eyes and me stuffing my fists into my face to calm down.

"Yeah, maybe it could," I finally said.

From the TV room, we could hear the kids watching their TV show. The theme song continued playing: *Ta deee ta dooo ta deeee.* *Heart of Darkness* still sat on the table in front of us. The paperback had a terrifying cover, showing a picture of a shirtless white man crawling on all fours on the ground. I looked back up at Tamar and smiled at her and picked a piece of lint off her sleeve.

"See what I mean?" Ellen said, gesturing at her.

I rubbed my face furiously and worried that if I answered, I'd start crying in a strangely and overreactively cathartic way. So I just looked down at my notes, which were illegible.

Tamar gazed at us for a moment. She shook her head and laughed gently.

"You guys," she said. ⋆

# Additional Sources

*Miss USA 2015*
Katie Reilly, "Miss USA Contestant: Donald Trump Walked in on Naked Women in Dressing Room," *Time*, October 12, 2016, https://time.com /4528075/donald-trump-miss-usa-naked/ ("'He just came strolling right in. There was no second to put a robe on or any sort of clothing or anything. Some girls were topless. Other girls were naked,' Tasha Dixon, former Miss Arizona, told CBS Los Angeles on Tuesday. Dixon competed in the 2001 Miss USA pageant when she was 18.").

*The Prisoner's Dilemma*
Barry Lank, "On the Market: $1.7 Million Angeleno Heights Victorian; $390,000 Boyle Heights Starter Home; $729,000 Glassell Park Bungalow," *Eastsider*, February 7, 2019, https://www.theeastsiderla.com/real _estate/on-the-market-million-angeleno-heights-victorian-boyle -heights-starter/article_oof19594-b34e-5247-ad10-6b7e5070e36c.html ("Boyle Heights: 3-bedroom ranch home. First time back on the market since it was built in 1966. $390,000.").

Defend Boyle Heights, "About Self-Help Graphics Accountability Session and Beyond," Alianza Contra Artwashing, July 2, 2016, http:// alianzacontraartwashing.org/en/coalition-statements/dbh-about-the -self-help-graphics-accountability-session-and-beyond/ ("All new art galleries must immediately leave Boyle Heights and . . . those buildings should be utilized by our community members the ways we best see fit, which may be converting them into emergency housing, shelters or centers for job training.").

Alexander Nazaryan, "The 'Artwashing' of America: The Battle for the Soul of Los Angeles against Gentrification," *Newsweek*, May 21, 2017,

https://www.newsweek.com/2017/06/02/los-angeles-gentrification
-california-developers-art-galleries-la-art-scene-608558.html ("*Hop-
scotch Los Angeles* and their art, their performers, their supporters, their
capital, are not welcomed in Boyle Heights,' [BHAAAD affiliate] Serve the
People Los Angeles wrote after that day's confrontation in a blog post
studded with quotations from Mao Zedong. That was the last time *Hop-
scotch* came to Boyle Heights.").

A. W. Tucker, "The Mathematics of Tucker: A Sampler," *Two-Year College Mathematics Journal* 14, no. 3 (June 1983): 228–232, https://www.jstor
.org/stable/3027092?seq=1#page_scan_tab_contents ("Clearly, for each
man the pure strategy 'confess' dominates the pure strategy 'not confess.'
Hence, there is a unique equilibrium point given by the two pure strategies 'confess.' In contrast with this non-cooperative solution one sees
that both men would profit if they could form a coalition binding each
other to 'not confess.' The game becomes zero-sum three-person by in-
troducing the State as a third player." [228]).

*After Maria*
Yxta Maya Murray, "'FEMA Has Been a Nightmare': Epistemic Injustice
in Puerto Rico," *Willamette Law Review* 55 (2019): 321–393.

*Acid Reign*
Every character in this story is fictional except for Senator Joni Ernst,
Donald Trump, and the Administrator, who is based on Scott Pruitt. The
scene in which Pruitt appears never happened; it is part of the fiction.
However, the cites that follow refer to the documented background facts
on which this story was based.

"Chlorpyrifos; Order Denying PANNA and NRDC's Petition to Revoke
Tolerances," 82 FR 16581-01, April 5, 2017 ("EPA has concluded that, despite several years of study, the science addressing neurodevelopmental
effects remains unresolved and that further evaluation of the science
during the remaining time for completion of registration review is war-
ranted to achieve greater certainty as to whether the potential exists for
adverse neurodevelopmental effects to occur from current human exposures to chlorpyrifos. EPA has therefore concluded that it will not complete the human health portion of the registration review or any
associated tolerance revocation of chlorpyrifos without first attempting
to come to a clearer scientific resolution on those issues.").

This is the history of the proposed revocation as per the April 5, 2017, order, as relayed in "Chlorpyrifos; Order Denying PANNA and NRDC's Petition to Revoke Tolerances," 82 FR 16581-01:

On June 30, 2015, EPA informed the court that it intended to propose by April 15, 2016, the revocation of all chlorpyrifos tolerances in the absence of pesticide label mitigation that ensures that exposures will be safe. On August 10, 2015, the court rejected EPA's time line and issued a mandamus order directing EPA to "issue either a proposed or final revocation rule or a full and final response to the administrative Petition by October 31, 2015."

On October 30, 2015, EPA issued a proposed rule to revoke all chlorpyrifos tolerances which it published in the Federal Register on November 6, 2015 (80 FR 69080). On December 10, 2015, the Ninth Circuit issued a further order requiring EPA to complete any final rule (or petition denial) and fully respond to the Petition by December 30, 2016. On June 30, 2016, EPA sought a 6-month extension to that deadline in order to allow EPA to fully consider the most recent views of the FIFRA SAP with respect to chlorpyrifos toxicology. The FIFRA SAP report was finalized and made available for EPA consideration on July 20, 2016. (Ref. 2) On August 12, 2016, the court rejected EPA's request for a 6-month extension and ordered EPA to complete its final action by March 31, 2017 (effectively granting EPA a three-month extension). On November 17, 2016, EPA published a notice of data availability (NODA) seeking public comment on both EPA's revised risk and water assessments and reopening the comment period on the proposal to revoke all chlorpyrifos (81 FR 81049). The comment period for the NODA closed on January 17, 2017.

Hannah Gold, "Scott Pruitt Twice Proposed Anti-Abortion Legislation Granting Men 'Property Rights' over Fetuses," *Jezebel*, May 24, 2018, https://theslot.jezebel.com/scott-pruitt-twice-proposed-anti-abortion -legislation-g-1826314010.

Randy Krehbiel, "State AG Scott Pruitt Is 'Head Bully' on Transgender Bathroom Issue, LGBT Advocate Says," *Tulsa World*, May 27, 2016, https:// www.tulsaworld.com/news/local/government-and-politics/state-ag -scott-pruitt-is-head-bully-on-transgender-bathroom/article_43785b0d -9caa-5530-b650-96d433ca8b77.html ("Pruitt, on the state's behalf, joined 10 other states on Wednesday in filing a lawsuit to block implementation of Obama administration guidance on school policy regarding transgender students' use of restrooms, locker rooms and other facilities typically separated by gender.").

Samantha Page, "Trump's Pick for EPA Admits Acting on Behalf of Oil and Gas Interests as State Attorney General," *ThinkProgress*, January 18, 2017, https://thinkprogress.org/pruitt-presents-fundamental-conflict-of -interest-between-epa-and-oil-companies-cf83f394fdc5/ ("In 2014, he wrote a letter to the EPA on state letterhead that was later found to have been written by Devon Energy. The letter opposed the agency's Mercury Air Toxics Standard.").

"Senator Merkley Asks Scott Pruitt about Asthma & Air Quality," CSPAN, January 18, 2017, https://www.c-span.org/video/?c4648588/senator -merkley-asks-scott-pruitt-asthma-air-quality ("Senator, let me say to you with respect to the program when you look at to the nonattainment, we have in this country is precisely around 40%. Increasing attainment is [an] important role of the EPA and we should take those marginal and moderate areas that are nonattainment and work with local officials and counties through monitoring and assistance to help move the nonattainment to attainment.").

Gregory Wallace, "EPA Paid $1,560 for 12 Fountain Pens, Emails Show," CNN, June 1, 2018 ("A close aide to Scott Pruitt last year ordered a set of 12 fountain pens that cost the Environmental Protection Agency $1,560, according to agency documents. Each $130 silver pen bore the agency's seal and Administrator Pruitt's signature, according to the documents, which were obtained by the Sierra Club through a Freedom of Information Act request. 'Yes, please order,' an aide wrote.").

NRDC, "The Case for Firing Scott Pruitt," 2018, https://www.nrdc.org /case-firing-scott-pruitt ("In order to shield his secretive actions from scrutiny, Pruitt has reportedly banned some agency staff from bringing cell phones to meetings with him or from taking notes.").

Brendan McDermid, "Scott Pruitt's Staff Asked for a Bulletproof Vehicle and $70,000 in Bulletproof Furniture for His Office—The Request Was Denied," *Business Insider*, April 7, 2018 ("A request for a $100,000-per-month private jet membership, a bulletproof vehicle, and $70,000 for furniture that included a bulletproof desk for an armed security guard was made.").

EPA, "EPA Revised Chlorpyrifos Assessment Shows Risk to Workers," January 5, 2015, https://archive.epa.gov/epa/newsreleases/epa-revised -chlorpyrifos-assessment-shows-risk-workers.html ("This assessment shows some risks to workers who mix, load and apply chlorpyrifos pesticide products.").

National Pesticide Information Center, "Chlorpyrifos General Fact Sheet," http://npic.orst.edu/factsheets/chlorpgen.html, accessed on January 25, 2020 ("Some people have suffered delayed nervous system damage if they were exposed to very large amounts of chlorpyrifos. This is very rare, and scientists and doctors do not understand it very well.").

Julien Josephen, "Cancer: New Chlorpyrifos Link?," *Environmental Health Perspectives* 113, no. 3 (March 2005): A158, https://www.ncbi.nlm .nih.gov/pmc/articles/PMC1253789/ ("About 3.8% of the applicators developed malignant lung neoplasms.").

*Abundance*
Eman A. Emam, "Gas Flaring: An Overview," *Petroleum & Coal* 57, no. 5 (2015): 534, http://large.stanford.edu/courses/2016/ph240/miller1/docs /emam.pdf ("Gas flaring is one of the most challenging energy and environmental problems facing the world today. Environmental consequences associated with gas flaring have a considerable impact on local populations, often resulting in severe health issues.").

*The Perfect Palomino*
Tara Law, "Here Are the Details of the Abortion Legislation in Alabama, Georgia, Louisiana and Elsewhere," *Time*, July 2, 2019, https:// time.com/5591166/state-abortion-laws-explained/ (detailing "heartbeat" abortion bans in Alabama, Louisiana, Mississippi, Missouri, and Ohio, which do not contain exceptions for rape and incest).

*Option 3*
Jeff Sessions, "Zero-Tolerance for Offenses under 8 U.S.C. § 1325(a)," Office of the Attorney General, April 6, 2018, https://www.justice.gov /opa/press-release/file/1049751/download ("Accordingly, I direct each United States Attorney's Office along the Southwest Border—to the extent practicable, and in consultation with DHS—to adopt immediately a zero-tolerance policy for all offenses referred for prosecution under section 1325(a). This zero-tolerance policy shall supersede any existing

policies. If adopting such a policy requires additional resources, each office shall identify and request such additional resources.").

Jesse Franzblau, "Newly Released Memo Reveals Secretary of Homeland Security Signed Off on Family Separation Policy," Open the Government, September 24, 2018, https://www.openthegovernment.org /newly-released-memo-reveals-secretary-of-homeland-security-signed -off-on-family-separation-policy/ ("The memo states that DHS could 'permissibly direct the separation of parents or legal guardians and minors held in immigration detention so that the parent or legal guardian can be prosecuted.' It outlines three options for implementing 'zero tolerance,' the policy of increased prosecution of immigration violations. Of these, it recommends 'Option 3,' referring for prosecution all adults crossing the border without authorization, 'including those presenting with a family unit,' as the 'most effective.'").

*Ms. L. v. U.S. Immigration & Customs Enf't ("ICE")*, 310 F. Supp. 3d 1133, 1145–46 (S.D. Cal. 2018), *modified*, 330 F.R.D. 284 (S.D. Cal. 2019) ("A practice of this sort implemented in this way is likely to be 'so egregious, so outrageous, that it may fairly be said to shock the contemporary conscience,' *Lewis*, 523 U.S. at 847 n.8, 118 S.Ct. 1708, interferes with rights 'implicit in the concept of ordered liberty[,]' *Rochin v. Cal.*, 342 U.S. 165, 169, 72 S.Ct. 205, 96 L.Ed. 183 (1952) (quoting *Palko v. State of Conn.*, 302 U.S. 319, 325, 58 S.Ct. 149, 82 L.Ed. 288 (1937)), and is so 'brutal' and 'offensive' that it [does] not comport with traditional ideas of fair play and decency." *Breithaupt v. Abram*, 352 U.S. 432, 435, 77 S.Ct. 408, 1 L.Ed.2d 448 (1957).).

Trafficking Victims Protection and Reauthorization Act, 8 U.S.C.A. § 1232 (b)(3) (West): ("Except in the case of exceptional circumstances, any department or agency of the Federal Government that has an unaccompanied alien child in custody shall transfer the custody of such child to the Secretary of Health and Human Services not later than 72 hours after determining that such child is an unaccompanied alien child.")

*Mrs. L.*, 310 F. Supp. 3d at 1138 n.3 ("The TVPRA provides that 'the care and custody of all unaccompanied alien children, including responsibility for their detention, where appropriate, shall be the responsibility of HHS and its sub-agency, ORR. 8 U.S.C. § 1232(b)(1).'").

Second Amended Class Action Complaint and Petition for a Writ of Habeas Corpus in *J.E.C.M. v. Lloyd*, Case No.1:18-cv-903-lmb, Eastern District Court of Virginia, filed 8/16/18, at page 18, para. 46, https://www.justice4all.org/wp-content/uploads/2018/11/jecm-Second-Am-Compl.pdf:

> Beginning when a child comes into orr custody, the agency's online guide provides that orr may place him or her in one of three levels of care based on an assessment of the level of security risk and harm to self or others that the child poses: (i) "shelter care" is the least restrictive custodial setting; (ii) "staff secure" is the intermediate level; and (iii) "secure" care is the most restrictive level. Secure facilities are like juvenile jails; there are only three such facilities in use nationwide, one in California and two in Virginia: svjc in Staunton where b.g.s.s. is detained, and nova in Alexandria, where j.e.c.m. was detained. Staff-secure facilities, while not using locked pods or cells, are still very restrictive in that children's movement inside the unit is controlled; children are not permitted to leave the facility except to attend court; outdoor recreation is limited to one hour a day in a fenced in area; and there is a higher staff-to-child ratio than in shelter units. Shelter-level placements, while less restrictive than staff-secure or secure custody, are nonetheless much more restrictive than a home environment. Children are not permitted to move between rooms or up and down the stairs without staff permission; external doors are locked; children are deprived of human touch and even prevented from hugging a sibling, and time outdoors is limited.

David V. Aguilar, Chief, U.S. Border Patrol, "Memorandum/Hold Rooms and Short Term Custody," June 28, 2008, graphs 6.8–6.11, https://www.openthegovernment.org/wp-content/uploads/other-files/cbp%20cbp-2018-070727_Redacted.pdf ("Meals. Detainees will be provided snacks and juice every four hours. . . . Potable drinking water will be available to detainees. . . . Restrooms will be available to detainees. Detainees using the restrooms will have access to toilet items; such as soap, toilet paper, and sanitary napkins. Families with small children will also have access to diapers and wipes. . . . Bedding. Detainees requiring bedding will be given clean bedding.").

*Zero Tolerance*

8 U.S.C.A. § 1325 (a) (West) ("Any alien who (1) enters or attempts to enter the United States at any time or place other than as designated by immigration officers, or (2) eludes examination or inspection by immigration officers, or (3) attempts to enter or obtains entry to the United States by a willfully false or misleading representation or the willful concealment of a material fact, shall, for the first commission of any such offense, be fined under Title 18 or imprisoned not more than 6 months, or both, and, for a subsequent commission of any such offense, be fined under Title 18, or imprisoned not more than 2 years, or both.").

Jeff Sessions, "Zero-Tolerance for Offenses under 8 U.S.C. § 1325(a)," Office of the Attorney General, April 6, 2018, https://www.justice.gov/opa/press-release/file/1049751/download.

Julia Preston, "Detention Center Presented as Deterrent to Border Crossings," *New York Times*, December 15, 2014, https://www.nytimes.com/2014/12/16/us/homeland-security-chief-opens-largest-immigration-detention-center-in-us.html ("The 50-acre center in Dilley, 85 miles northeast of Laredo, will hold up to 2,400 migrants who have illegally crossed the border and is especially designed to hold women and their children.... About 480 women and children will be housed here while a much larger, permanent facility is built next door, officials said.").

Catherine Powers, "I Spent 5 Days at a Family Detention Center. I'm Still Haunted by What I Saw," *HuffPost*, August 23, 2018, https://www.huffpost.com/entry/family-detention-center-border_n_5b7c2673e4b0a5b1febf3abf ("The women I worked with at the South Texas Family Residential Center in Dilley had been separated from their children for up to two and a half months because of a policy instituted by the Trump administration in April 2018, under which families were targeted for detention and separation in an attempt to dissuade others from embarking on similar journeys.... Most [of the women] had been raped, tormented, threatened or beaten (and in many cases, all of the above) in their countries (predominantly Honduras and Guatemala).").

Emma Platoff, "Report: Toddler Died after Contracting Infection at ICE Family Detention Facility," *Texas Tribune*, August 27, 2018, https://www.texastribune.org/2018/08/27/toddler-died-ICE-custody-vice-news

-dilley/ ("Yazmin Juárez told the news outlet in a story published Monday evening that she and her daughter, Mariee, crossed the border from Guatemala in March and were soon sent to an ICE family detention center in Dilley. There, according to the story, 18-month-old Mariee developed an infection and respiratory symptoms that ultimately led to her death. She died of viral pneumonitis six weeks after being released from the facility, VICE reported. She would have turned two this month.").

Cf. Alice Sperri, "At Largest Ice Detention Center in the Country, Guards Called Attempted Suicides 'Failures,'" *Intercept*, October 11, 2018, https://theintercept.com/2018/10/11/adelanto-ice-detention-center -abuse/ ("'I've seen a few attempted suicides using the braided sheets by the vents and then the guards laugh at them and call them "suicide failures" once they're back from medical,' one detainee told inspectors.").

Human Rights First, "Credible Fear: A Screening Mechanism in Expedited Removal," February 2018, https://www.humanrightsfirst.org/sites /default/files/Credible_Fear_Feb_2018.pdf ("The number of positive credible fear decisions fell sharply after the lesson plan was issued—from 78 percent in February 2017 down to a low of 68 percent in June 2017. The pass rates until September 2017, the latest date for which we have data, remained lower than their respective 2016 rates.").

Toni Briscoe, "Chicago Shelter, Sessions Sued after 2 Brazilian Boys Separated from Parents at Border Transferred Here," *Chicago Tribune*, June 20, 2019, https://www.chicagotribune.com/news/ct-met-heartland -alliance-children-shelter-20180621-story.html ("The Heartland Alliance confirmed this week that some of the children separated from their parents are staying at its Chicago shelters.").

Cf. David Cortez, "I Asked Latinos Why They Joined Immigration Law Enforcement. Now I'm Urging Them to Leave," *USA Today*, July 3, 2019, https://www.usatoday.com/story/opinion/voices/2019/07/03/latino -border-patrol-ice-agents-immigration-column/1619511001/ ("Latinos make up more than 50% of Border Patrol agents and 24% of ICE agents, the most recent publicly available numbers I found. I wanted to understand what possesses Latinos to work for agencies that round up or deport neighbors and family members from the very communities they call home. How do Latinos do this to their own people, I asked. Is it self-hatred? A denial of ethnic identity? Or do they think that being party to the state's exclusionary machinery cements, in a way, their own individual claims to belonging as Americans—to whiteness? In one interview after another over the span of 13 months, the answer became clear: It's not any of these. For Latino agents, it's about the money.").

Josh Chafetz and David E. Pozen, "How Constitutional Norms Break Down," *UCLA Law Review* 65 (2018): 1435 ("Norm destruction occurs when a norm is flouted or repudiated and, in consequence, ceases to exist, at least for a while. . . . Norm decomposition occurs when a norm is interpreted or applied in ways that are held out as compliant but that, over time, substantially alter or reduce whatever regulative force the norm previously possessed.").

Jennifer Nou, "Civil Servant Disobedience," *Chicago-Kent Law Review* 94 (2019): 352–53 ("Civil servants have historically held a strong sense of 'role perception,' backed by powerful norms regarding appropriate institutional behavior. These norms have included respect for politically appointed superiors and the need to channel dissent through appropriate internal channels. One defining characteristic of the Trump presidency, however, has been its willingness to undermine long held norms coupled with its open hostility to the civil service.").

Affording Congress an Opportunity to Address Family Separation Immigration, Section (1), issued on June 20, 2018, available at https://go.ksbar.org/2MzAEcN ("It is also the policy of this Administration to maintain family unity, including by detaining alien families together where appropriate and consistent with law and available resources. It is unfortunate that Congress's failure to act and court orders have put the Administration in the position of separating alien families to effectively enforce the law.").

*Walmart*
Philip Bump, "Trump Keeps Framing the El Paso Shooting as His Side against His Opponents'," *Washington Post*, August 7, 2019, https://www.washingtonpost.com/politics/2019/08/07/trump-keeps-framing-el-paso-shooting-his-side-against-his-opponents/ ("'I am concerned about the rise of any group of hate,' Trump replied. 'I don't like it, any group of hate, whether it's white supremacy, whether it's any other kind of supremacy, whether it's antifa, whether it's any group of hate, I am very concerned about it, and I'll do something about it.'").

*The Overton Window*
Miranda Green, "Watchdog Faults EPA Response to Lead Paint Hazards," *The Hill*, September 9, 2019, https://thehill.com/policy/energy-environment/460558-watchdog-finds-epa-not-taking-measurable-action-on-lead-based-paint ("The Environmental Protection Agency (EPA) is not effectively using a rule meant to protect against exposure to lead-based paint, an agency watchdog found. The EPA's Office of the Inspector General found, in a report released Monday, that the agency's Lead Action Plan, which is meant to curb children's exposure to lead, lacked measurable outcomes.").

Timothy McClaughlin, "The Weird, Dark History of 8chan," *Wired*, August 6, 2019, https://www.wired.com/story/the-weird-dark-history-8chan/ ("The El Paso shooter posted an anti-immigration manifesto on 8chan minutes before he opened fire on people in a WalMart not far from the US-Mexico border.").

*The World Doesn't Work That Way, but It Could*
"250 Children Living under Inhumane Conditions at Texas Border Facility, Doctors and Attorneys Say," *CBS News*, June 21, 2019, https://www.cbsnews.com/news/children-at-border-facility-children-living-inhumane-conditions-texas-border-facility-doctors-attorneys-say/ ("Doctors and attorneys say hundreds of young people are living under inhumane conditions at a border control station in Clint, Texas. They say they found about 250 infants, children and teens locked up for weeks without adequate food, water and sanitation.").

# Acknowledgments

The author thanks and remembers Fred MacMurray, Thelma Diaz Quinn, Maggie MacMurray, Maria Adastik, Walter Adastik, Clark Whitehorn, Sara Hendricksen, Lisa Teasley, Medaya Ocher, Tom Lutz, Boris Dralyuk, the Ucross Foundation, Ellie Duke, Sacha Idell, David Wanczyk, Professor Barbara Babcock, Brad Morrow, Pam Madsen, Anne Austin Pearce, Nikki A. Greene, Cara Tomlinson, Ashley Robinson, Mika Taylor, Leah Reid, Carolyn Monastra, Mark Ritchie, Taylor Ho Bynum, Cyndi Reed, Tracy Y. Kikut, Sharon Dynak, Donna Mines, Cindy Brooks, Carly Fraysier, Gordy, Mike Latham, William Belcher, Mel Smith, Shelly Stoner, Allen Smith, Kel Harris, Marty Jelly, Loyola Law School, Colin Goward, Marina Castañeda, Liz Luk, Chris Jarvis, Elizabeth Baldwin, Ryan Botev, Professor Victor Gold, Professor Deborah Weissman, Professor Kathleen Kim, Professor David Leonard, Susan Leonard, Professor Justin Levitt, Dean Michael Waterstone, Professor Lauren Willis, the Los Angeles Youth Network/Youth Emerging Stronger, Maceo Montoya, Patricia Santana, Babs Brown, and my dearest Andrew Brown.

The author would like to thank the journals that published some of these stories before they were assembled into this collection. "After Maria" was published in *Conjunctions: Earth Elegies* 30 (Fall 2019); "Paradise" appeared in *The Southern Review* (Summer 2020); "Miss USA 2015" appeared in *New Ohio Review* (Spring 2020); "Abundance" appeared in *Contra Viento* (Fall 2019); "The Prisoner's Dilemma" was featured in the *Los Angeles Review of Books* (September 2016) under the title "Zillow Listing of 1329 E 3rd St, Los Angeles, CA 90033"; and "Draft of a Letter of Recommendation to the Honorable Alex Kozinski, Which I Guess I'm Not Going to Send Now" appeared in the *Michigan Journal of Gender & Law* (2018).

# About the Author

YXTA MAYA MURRAY is an art critic, author, and law professor at Loyola Law School in Los Angeles. She has won a Whiting Writer's Award and an Art Writer's Grant. She was a finalist for the ASME Fiction Award in 2019. She is the author of *Locas, What It Takes to Get to Vegas*, among other books, and her work has also been published in *Artforum, Aperture, Ploughshares, Conjunction,* the *Georgia Review, Guernica,* the *Los Angeles Review of Books*, and other magazines.